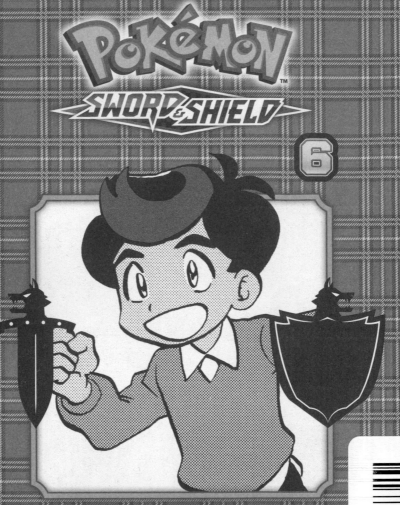

POKÉMON

SWORD & SHIELD

6

STORY

Hidenori Kusaka

ART

Satoshi Yamamoto

D0067439

Henry
SWORD

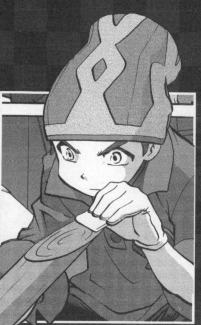

HENRY IS AN ARTISAN WHO UNDERSTANDS POKÉMON GEAR. HE IS THE DESCENDANT OF A RENOWNED SWORDSMITH AND USES FAMILY SECRETS TO ENHANCE THE GEAR HE COMES ACROSS.

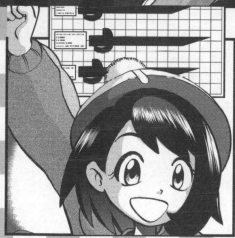

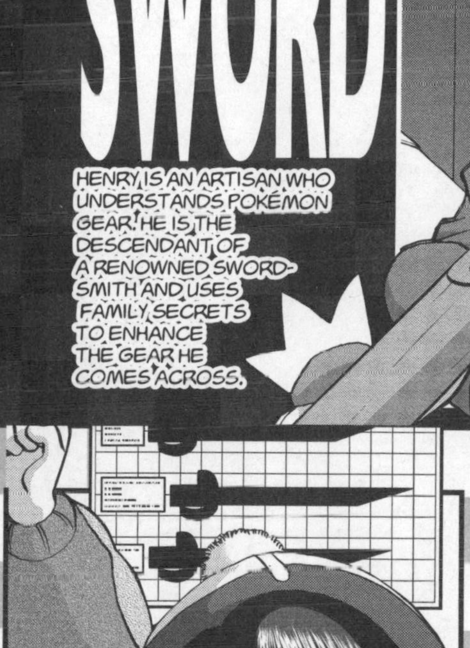

Casey
SHIELD

CASEY IS AN ACE COMPUTER HACKER WHO CAN CRACK ANY CODE AND GUESS ANY PASSWORD. SHE'S PROFESSOR MAGNOLIA'S ASSISTANT AND CHIPS IN AS THE TEAM'S DATA ANALYST.

The Story So Far

UPON ARRIVING IN THE GALAR REGION, MARVIN SEES A DYNAMAXED POKÉMON AND FALLS OFF A CLIFF! HE IS SAVED BY HENRY SWORD AND CASEY SHIELD AND JOINS THEM ON THEIR JOURNEY TO COMPLETE THEIR GYM CHALLENGE AND DISCOVER THE SECRET OF DYNAMAXING WITH PROFESSOR MAGNOLIA. HENRY AND HIS FRIENDS THEN GET THE OPPORTUNITY TO VISIT THE HAMMERLOCKE VAULT, WHERE THEY LEARN ABOUT THE FOUNDING OF THE GALAR REGION FROM A TAPESTRY.

Marvin

A ROOKIE TRAINER WHO RECENTLY MOVED TO GALAR. HE'S EXCITED TO LEARN EVERYTHING HE CAN ABOUT POKÉMON!

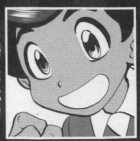

Professor Magnolia

A FAMED RESEARCHER WHO STUDIES DYNAMAXING, THE GIGANTIFICATION OF POKÉMON. SHE IS A GENTLE SOUL WHO IS FOND OF DRINKING TEA.

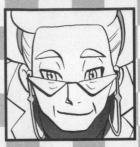

Leon

LEON IS THE BEST TRAINER IN GALAR. HE'S THE UNDEFEATED CHAMPION!

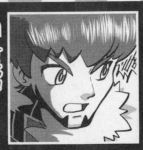

Sonia

PROFESSOR MAGNOLIA'S GRANDDAUGHTER AND LEON'S CHILDHOOD FRIEND. SHE'S HELPING THE PROFESSOR INVESTIGATE THE GALAR REGION!

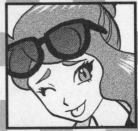

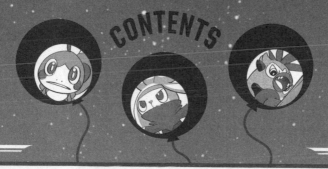

CONTENTS

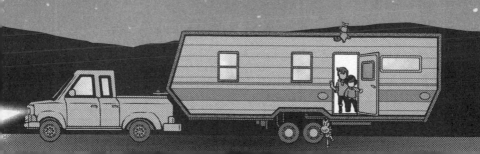

Adventure 17 Stealth!! Infiltrate the Energy Plant

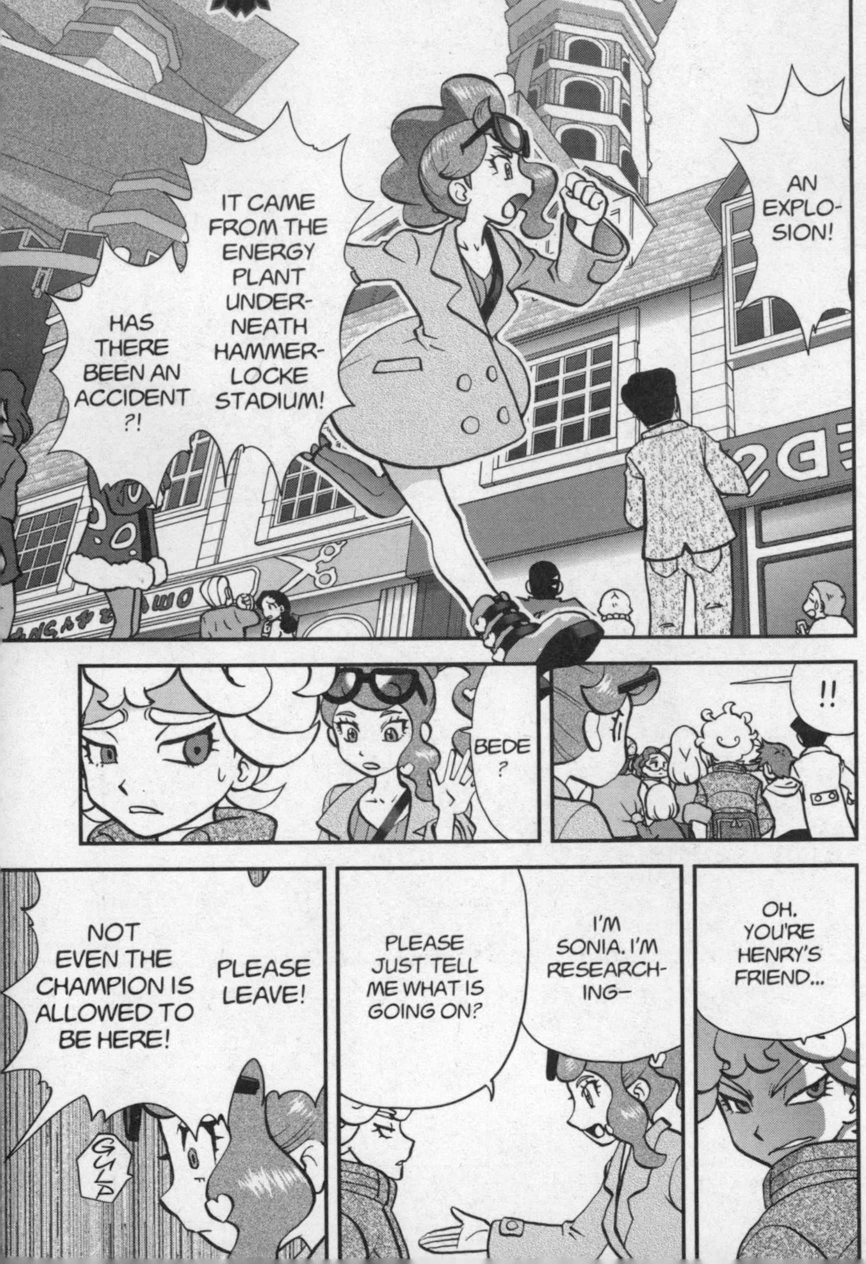
AN EXPLOSION!
IT CAME FROM THE ENERGY PLANT UNDERNEATH HAMMERLOCKE STADIUM!
HAS THERE BEEN AN ACCIDENT?!
!!
BEDE?
OH. YOU'RE HENRY'S FRIEND...
I'M SONIA. I'M RESEARCHING—
PLEASE JUST TELL ME WHAT IS GOING ON?
PLEASE LEAVE!
NOT EVEN THE CHAMPION IS ALLOWED TO BE HERE!
GULP

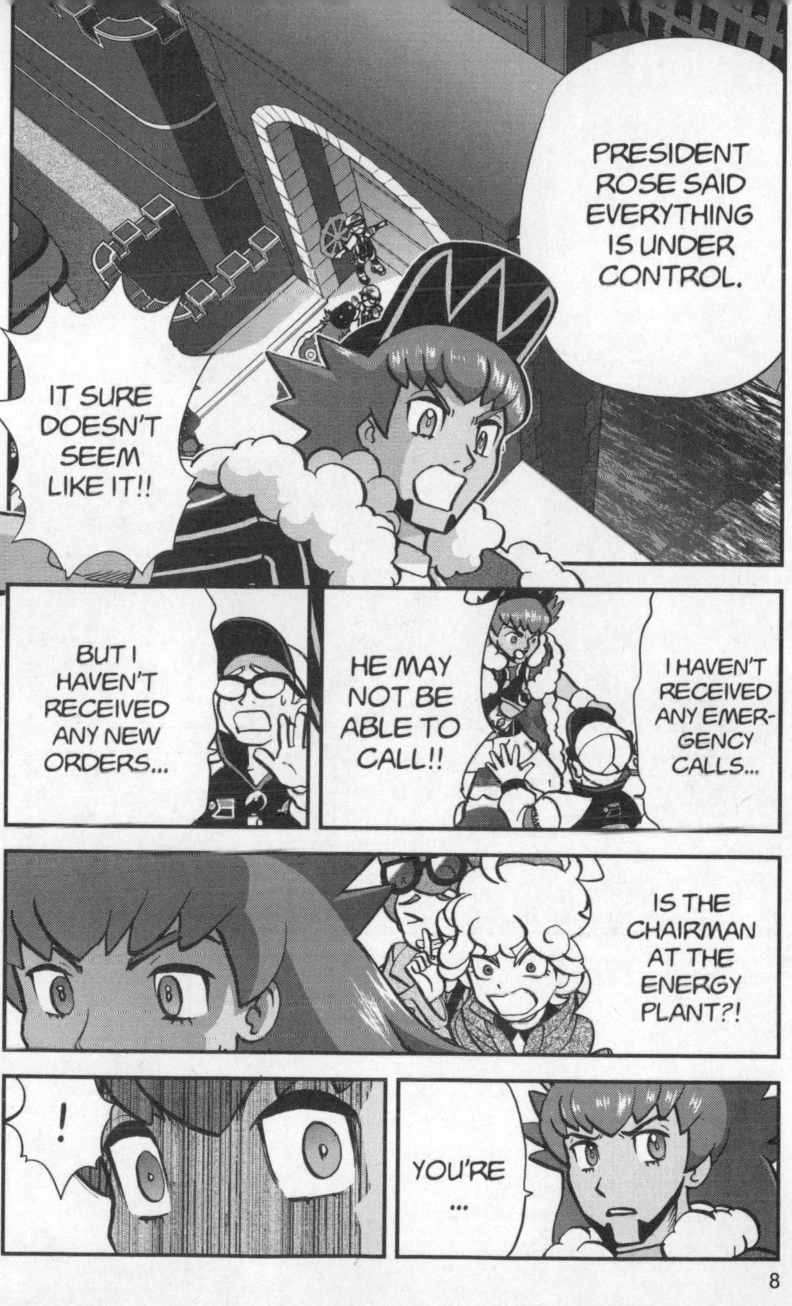
PRESIDENT ROSE SAID EVERYTHING IS UNDER CONTROL.
IT SURE DOESN'T SEEM LIKE IT!!
I HAVEN'T RECEIVED ANY EMER-GENCY CALLS...
HE MAY NOT BE ABLE TO CALL!!
BUT I HAVEN'T RECEIVED ANY NEW ORDERS...
IS THE CHAIRMAN AT THE ENERGY PLANT?!
YOU'RE ...
!

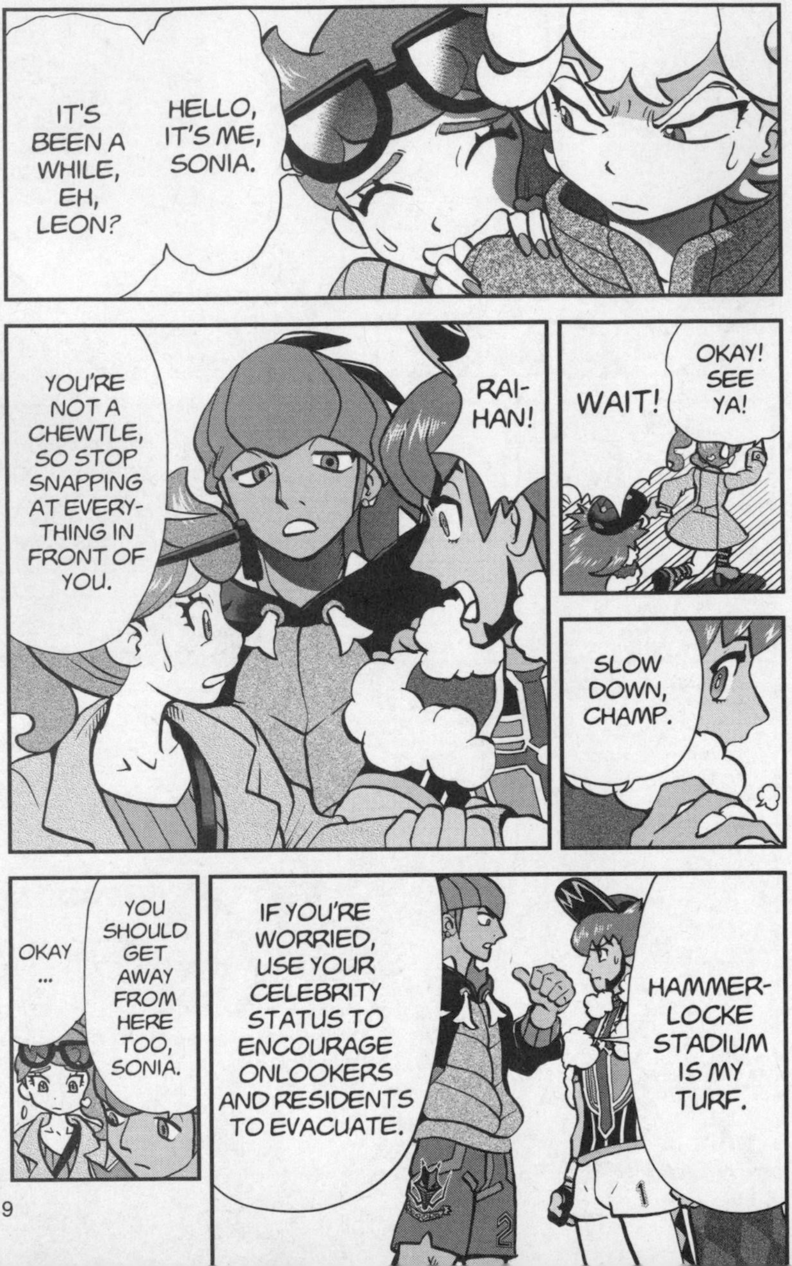
HELLO, IT'S ME, SONIA.
IT'S BEEN A WHILE, EH, LEON?
OKAY! SEE YA!
WAIT!
SLOW DOWN, CHAMP.
RAI-HAN!
YOU'RE NOT A CHEWTLE, SO STOP SNAPPING AT EVERY-THING IN FRONT OF YOU.
HAMMER-LOCKE STADIUM IS MY TURF.
IF YOU'RE WORRIED, USE YOUR CELEBRITY STATUS TO ENCOURAGE ONLOOKERS AND RESIDENTS TO EVACUATE.
YOU SHOULD GET AWAY FROM HERE TOO, SONIA.
OKAY ...

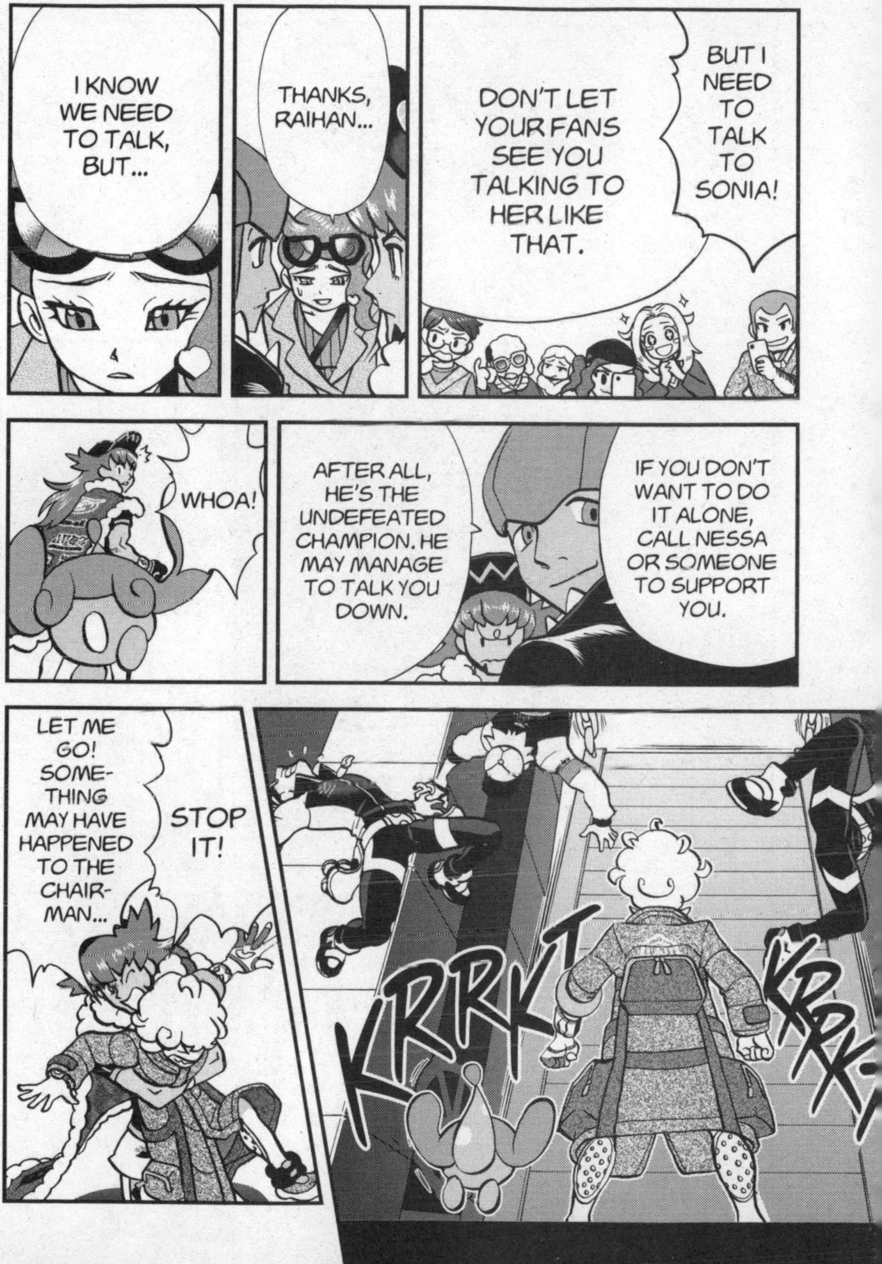
BUT I NEED TO TALK TO SONIA!
DON'T LET YOUR FANS SEE YOU TALKING TO HER LIKE THAT.
THANKS, RAIHAN...
I KNOW WE NEED TO TALK, BUT...
IF YOU DON'T WANT TO DO IT ALONE, CALL NESSA OR SOMEONE TO SUPPORT YOU.
AFTER ALL, HE'S THE UNDEFEATED CHAMPION. HE MAY MANAGE TO TALK YOU DOWN.
WHOA!
KRRK-
KRRKT
STOP IT!
LET ME GO! SOME-THING MAY HAVE HAPPENED TO THE CHAIR-MAN...

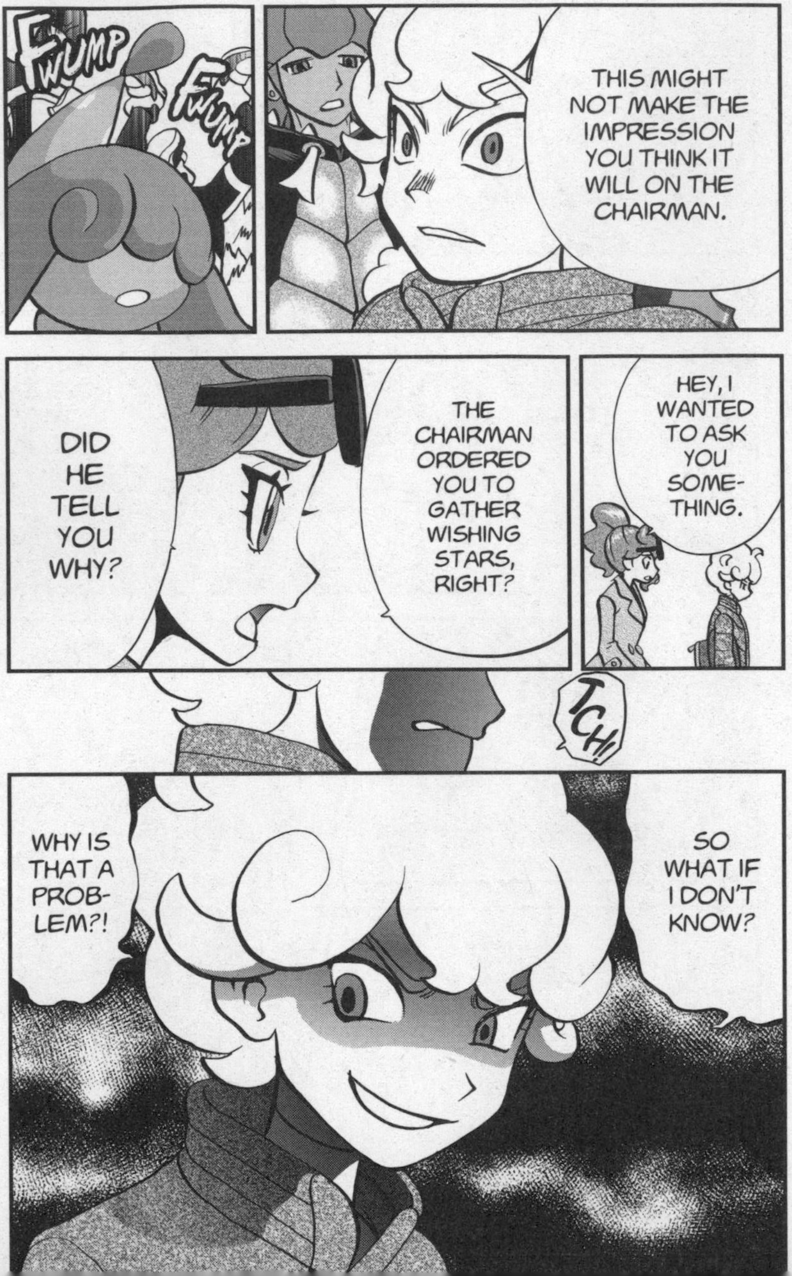
THIS MIGHT NOT MAKE THE IMPRESSION YOU THINK IT WILL ON THE CHAIRMAN.
FWUMP
FWUMP
HEY, I WANTED TO ASK YOU SOME-THING.
THE CHAIRMAN ORDERED YOU TO GATHER WISHING STARS, RIGHT?
DID HE TELL YOU WHY?
TCH!!
SO WHAT IF I DON'T KNOW?
WHY IS THAT A PROB-LEM?!

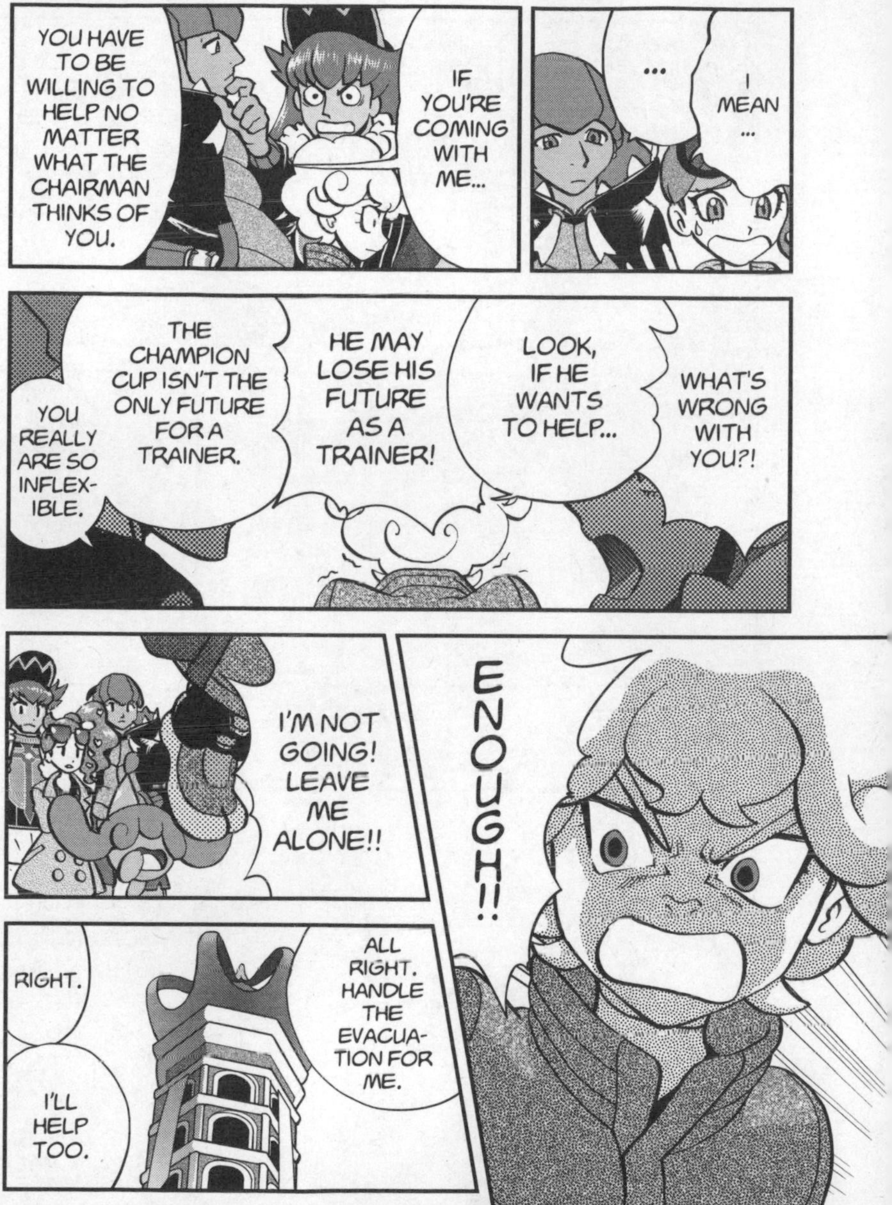
...
I MEAN ...
IF YOU'RE COMING WITH ME...
YOU HAVE TO BE WILLING TO HELP NO MATTER WHAT THE CHAIRMAN THINKS OF YOU.
WHAT'S WRONG WITH YOU?!
LOOK, IF HE WANTS TO HELP...
HE MAY LOSE HIS FUTURE AS A TRAINER!
THE CHAMPION CUP ISN'T THE ONLY FUTURE FOR A TRAINER.
YOU REALLY ARE SO INFLEX-IBLE.
ENOUGH!!
I'M NOT GOING! LEAVE ME ALONE!!
ALL RIGHT. HANDLE THE EVACUA-TION FOR ME.
RIGHT.
I'LL HELP TOO.

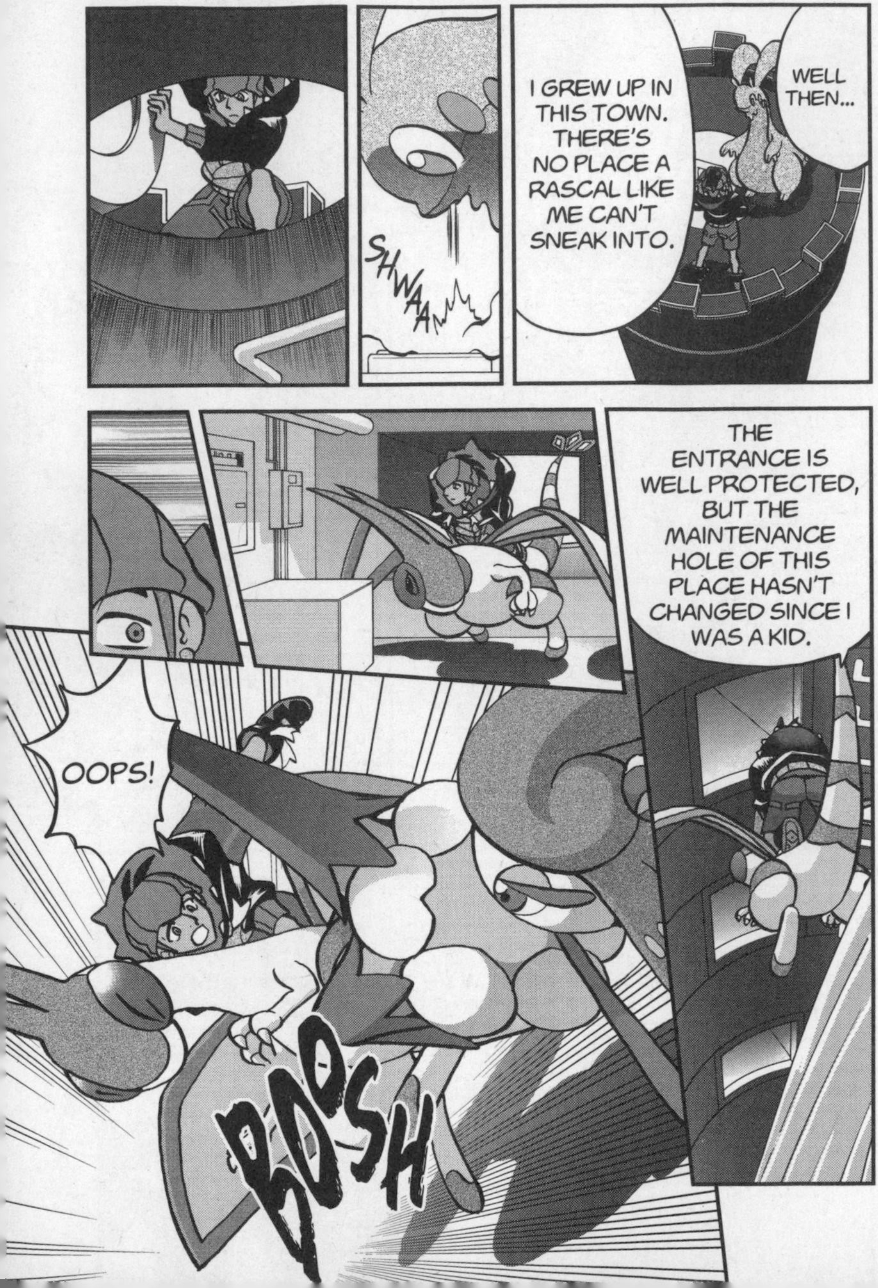
WELL THEN...
I GREW UP IN THIS TOWN. THERE'S NO PLACE A RASCAL LIKE ME CAN'T SNEAK INTO.
SHWAAA
THE ENTRANCE IS WELL PROTECTED, BUT THE MAINTENANCE HOLE OF THIS PLACE HASN'T CHANGED SINCE I WAS A KID.
OOPS!
BOOSH

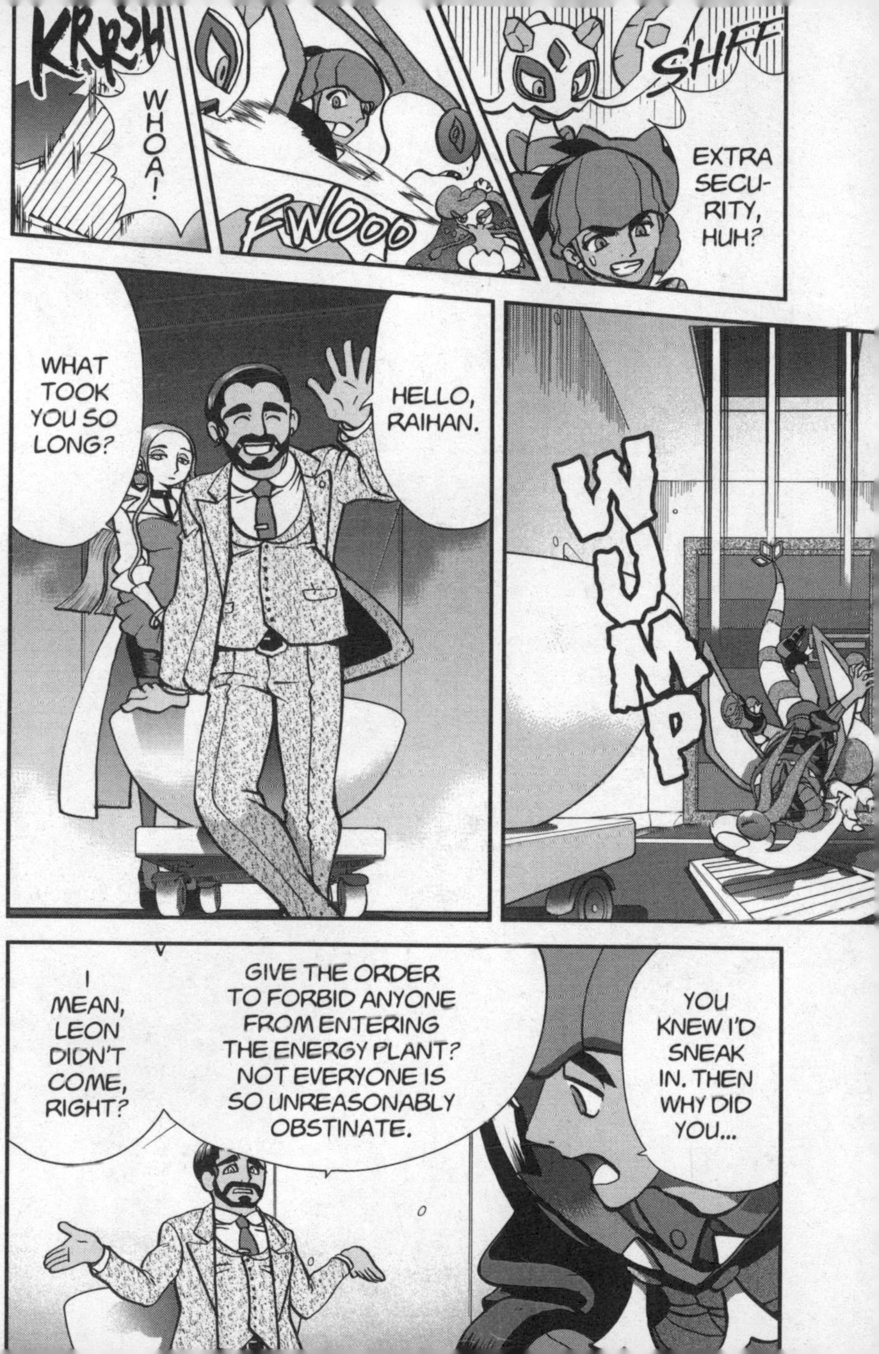
SHFF
EXTRA SECU-RITY, HUH?
FWOOO
KRRSH
WHOA!
WUMP
HELLO, RAIHAN.
WHAT TOOK YOU SO LONG?
YOU KNEW I'D SNEAK IN. THEN WHY DID YOU...
GIVE THE ORDER TO FORBID ANYONE FROM ENTERING THE ENERGY PLANT? NOT EVERYONE IS SO UNREASONABLY OBSTINATE.
I MEAN, LEON DIDN'T COME, RIGHT?

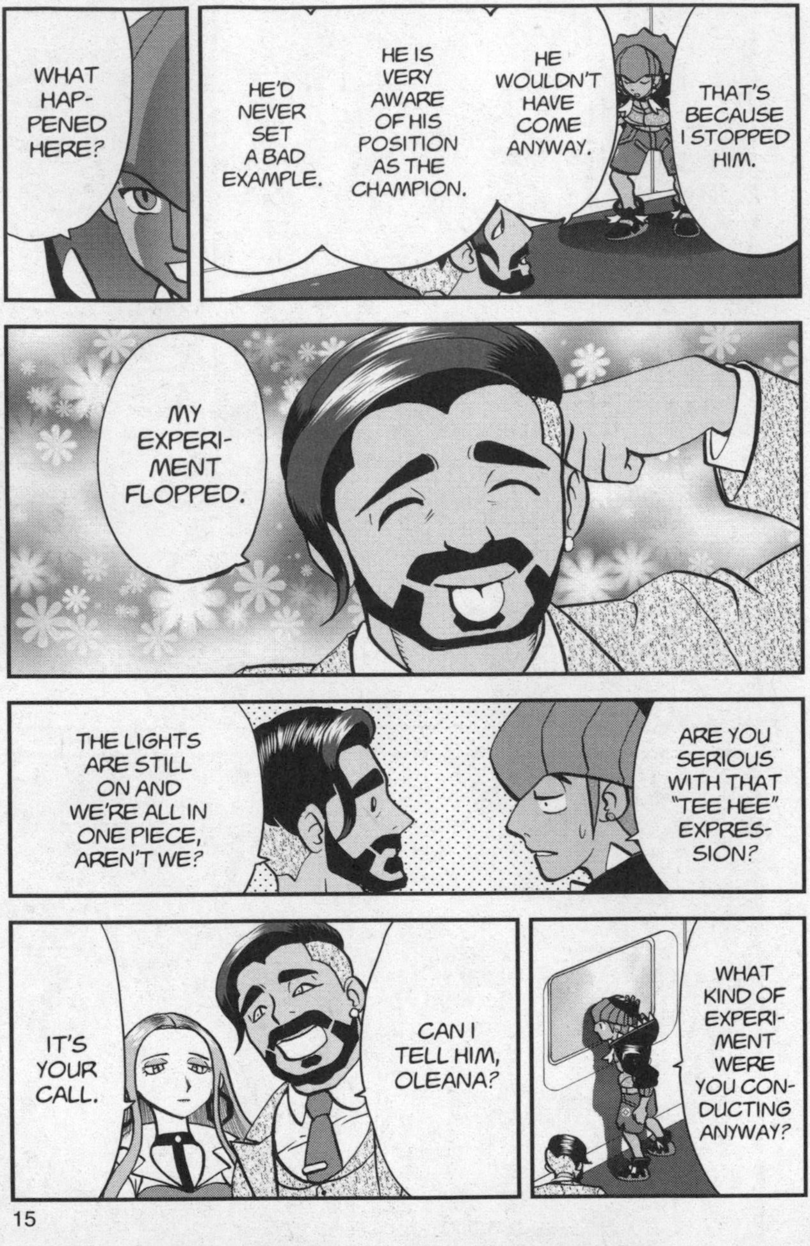
THAT'S BECAUSE I STOPPED HIM.
HE WOULDN'T HAVE COME ANYWAY.
HE IS VERY AWARE OF HIS POSITION AS THE CHAMPION.
HE'D NEVER SET A BAD EXAMPLE.
WHAT HAPPENED HERE?
MY EXPERIMENT FLOPPED.
ARE YOU SERIOUS WITH THAT "TEE HEE" EXPRESSION?
THE LIGHTS ARE STILL ON AND WE'RE ALL IN ONE PIECE, AREN'T WE?
WHAT KIND OF EXPERIMENT WERE YOU CONDUCTING ANYWAY?
CAN I TELL HIM, OLEANA?
IT'S YOUR CALL.

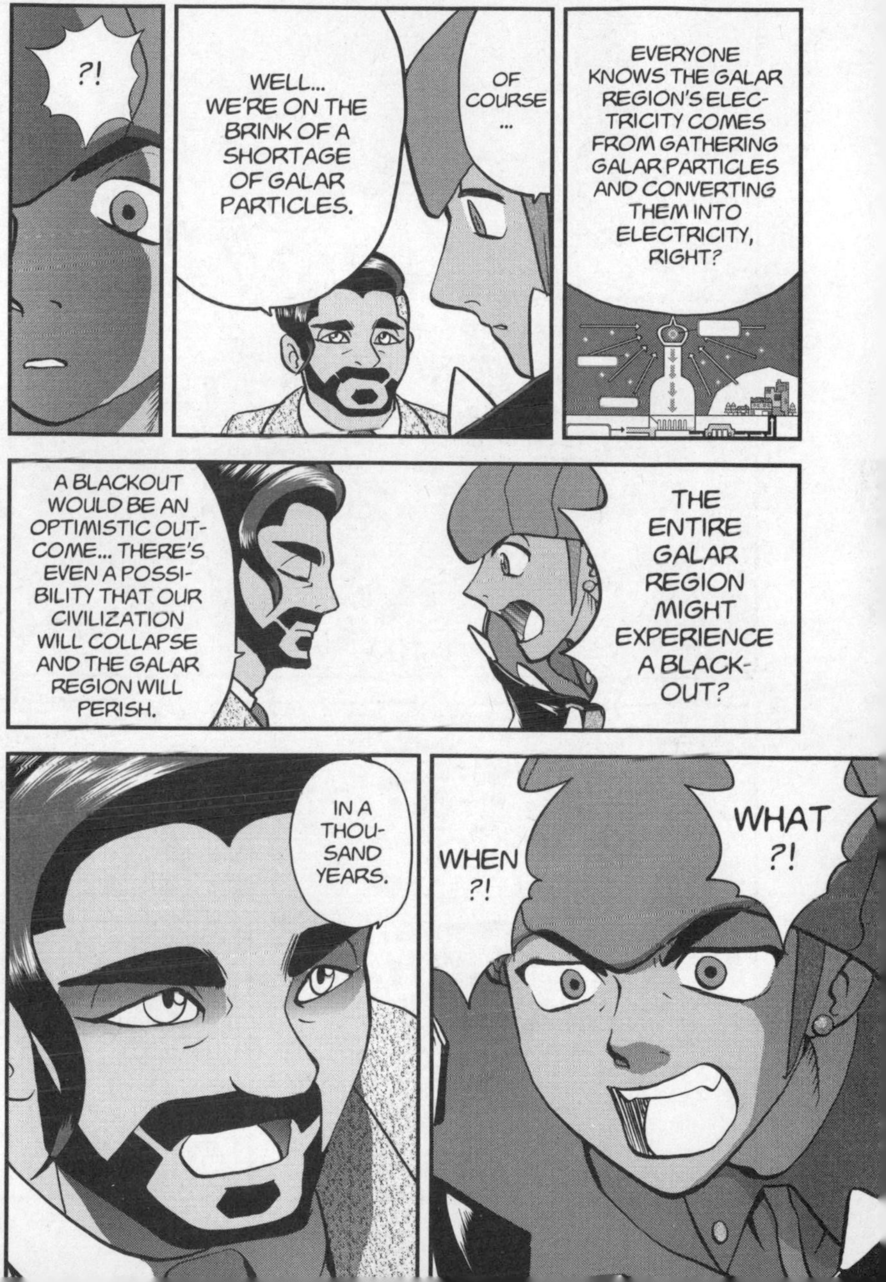
EVERYONE KNOWS THE GALAR REGION'S ELEC-TRICITY COMES FROM GATHERING GALAR PARTICLES AND CONVERTING THEM INTO ELECTRICITY, RIGHT?
OF COURSE...
WELL... WE'RE ON THE BRINK OF A SHORTAGE OF GALAR PARTICLES.
?!
THE ENTIRE GALAR REGION MIGHT EXPERIENCE A BLACK-OUT?
A BLACKOUT WOULD BE AN OPTIMISTIC OUT-COME... THERE'S EVEN A POSSI-BILITY THAT OUR CIVILIZATION WILL COLLAPSE AND THE GALAR REGION WILL PERISH.
WHAT ?!
WHEN ?!
IN A THOU-SAND YEARS.

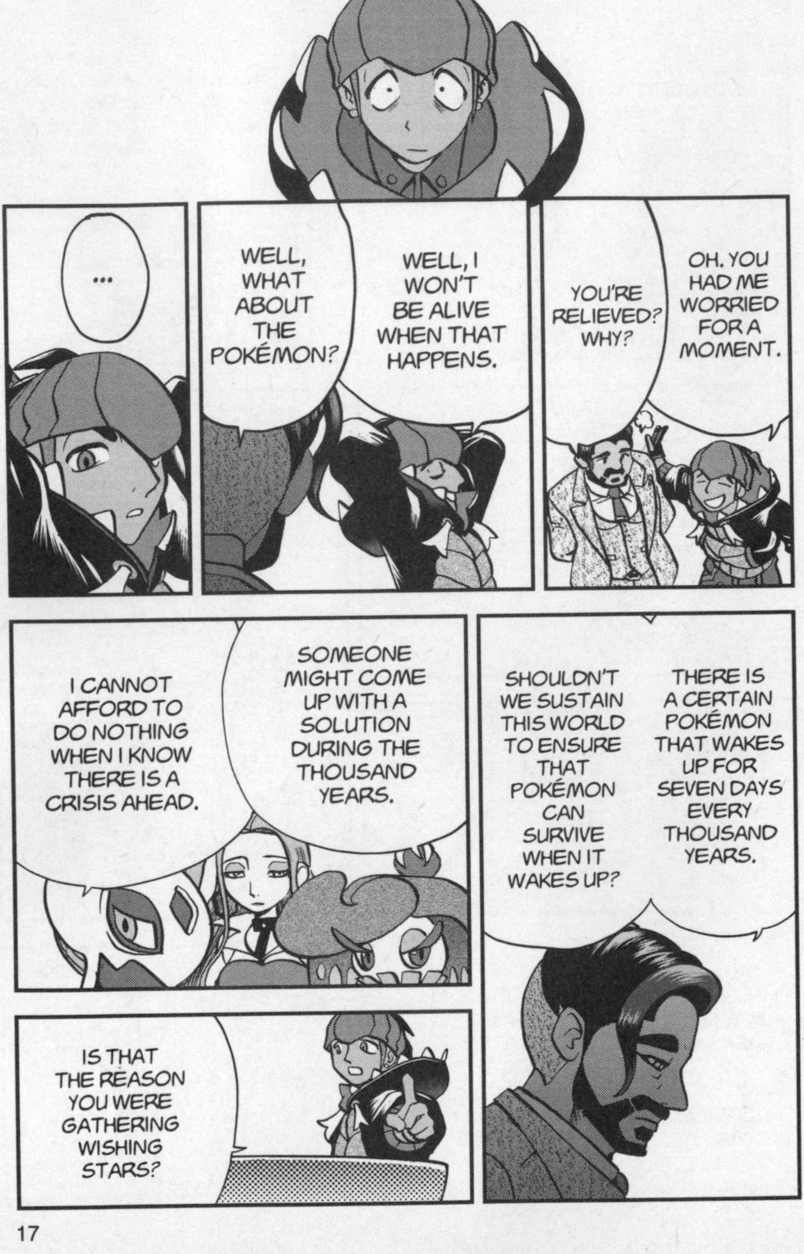
OH. YOU HAD ME WORRIED FOR A MOMENT.
YOU'RE RELIEVED? WHY?
WELL, I WON'T BE ALIVE WHEN THAT HAPPENS.
WELL, WHAT ABOUT THE POKÉMON?
...
THERE IS A CERTAIN POKÉMON THAT WAKES UP FOR SEVEN DAYS EVERY THOUSAND YEARS.
SHOULDN'T WE SUSTAIN THIS WORLD TO ENSURE THAT POKÉMON CAN SURVIVE WHEN IT WAKES UP?
SOMEONE MIGHT COME UP WITH A SOLUTION DURING THE THOUSAND YEARS.
I CANNOT AFFORD TO DO NOTHING WHEN I KNOW THERE IS A CRISIS AHEAD.
IS THAT THE REASON YOU WERE GATHERING WISHING STARS?

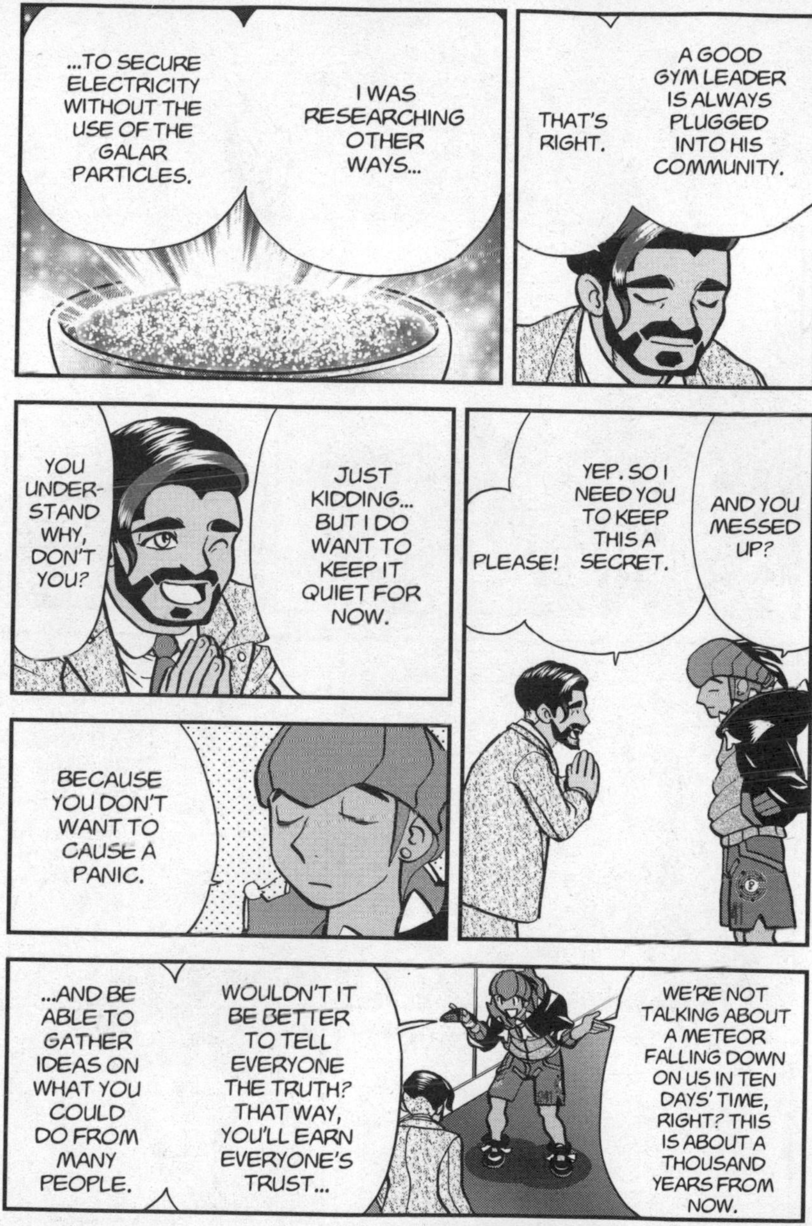
A GOOD GYM LEADER IS ALWAYS PLUGGED INTO HIS COMMUNITY.
THAT'S RIGHT.
I WAS RESEARCHING OTHER WAYS...
...TO SECURE ELECTRICITY WITHOUT THE USE OF THE GALAR PARTICLES.
AND YOU MESSED UP?
YEP. SO I NEED YOU TO KEEP THIS A SECRET.
PLEASE!
JUST KIDDING... BUT I DO WANT TO KEEP IT QUIET FOR NOW.
YOU UNDER-STAND WHY, DON'T YOU?
BECAUSE YOU DON'T WANT TO CAUSE A PANIC.
WE'RE NOT TALKING ABOUT A METEOR FALLING DOWN ON US IN TEN DAYS' TIME, RIGHT? THIS IS ABOUT A THOUSAND YEARS FROM NOW.
WOULDN'T IT BE BETTER TO TELL EVERYONE THE TRUTH? THAT WAY, YOU'LL EARN EVERYONE'S TRUST...
...AND BE ABLE TO GATHER IDEAS ON WHAT YOU COULD DO FROM MANY PEOPLE.

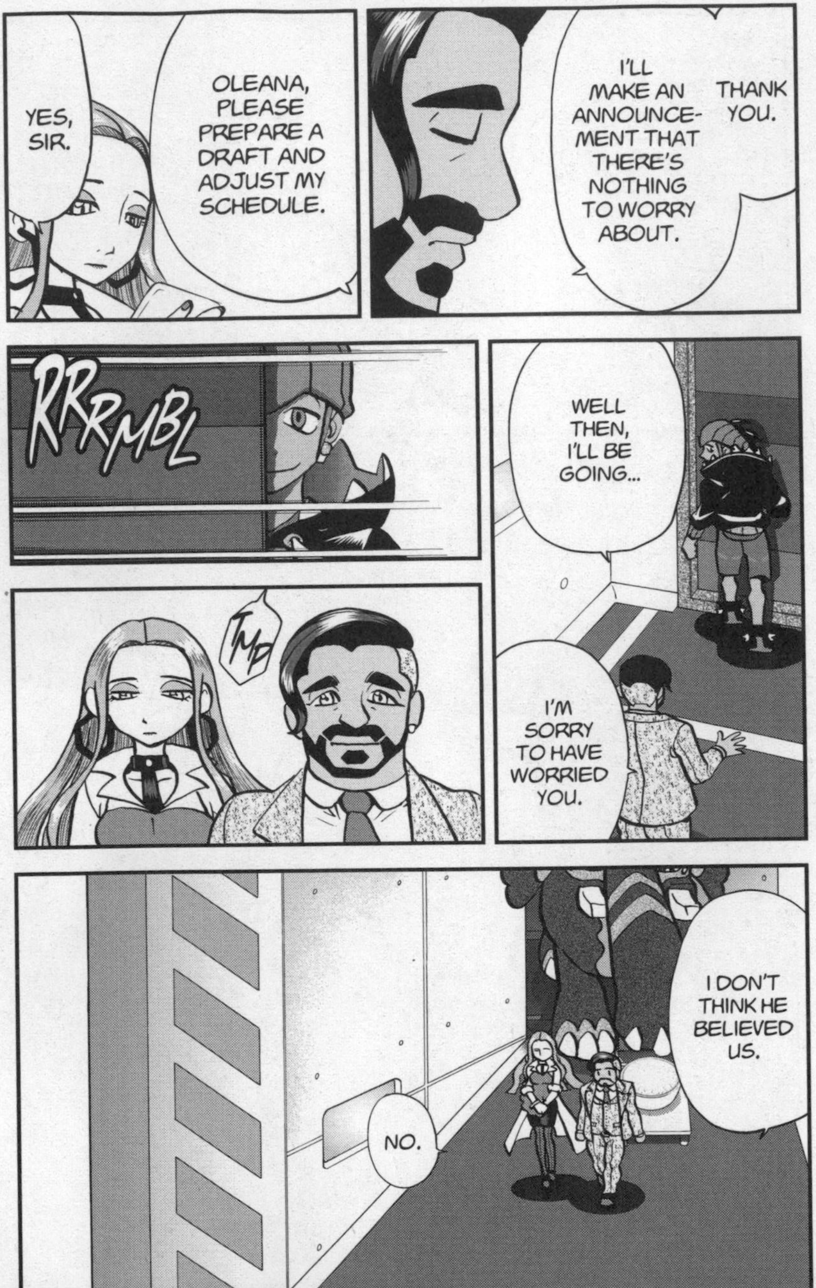
THANK YOU.
I'LL MAKE AN ANNOUNCEMENT THAT THERE'S NOTHING TO WORRY ABOUT.
OLEANA, PLEASE PREPARE A DRAFT AND ADJUST MY SCHEDULE.
YES, SIR.
WELL THEN, I'LL BE GOING...
I'M SORRY TO HAVE WORRIED YOU.
RRRMBL
TMP
I DON'T THINK HE BELIEVED US.
NO.

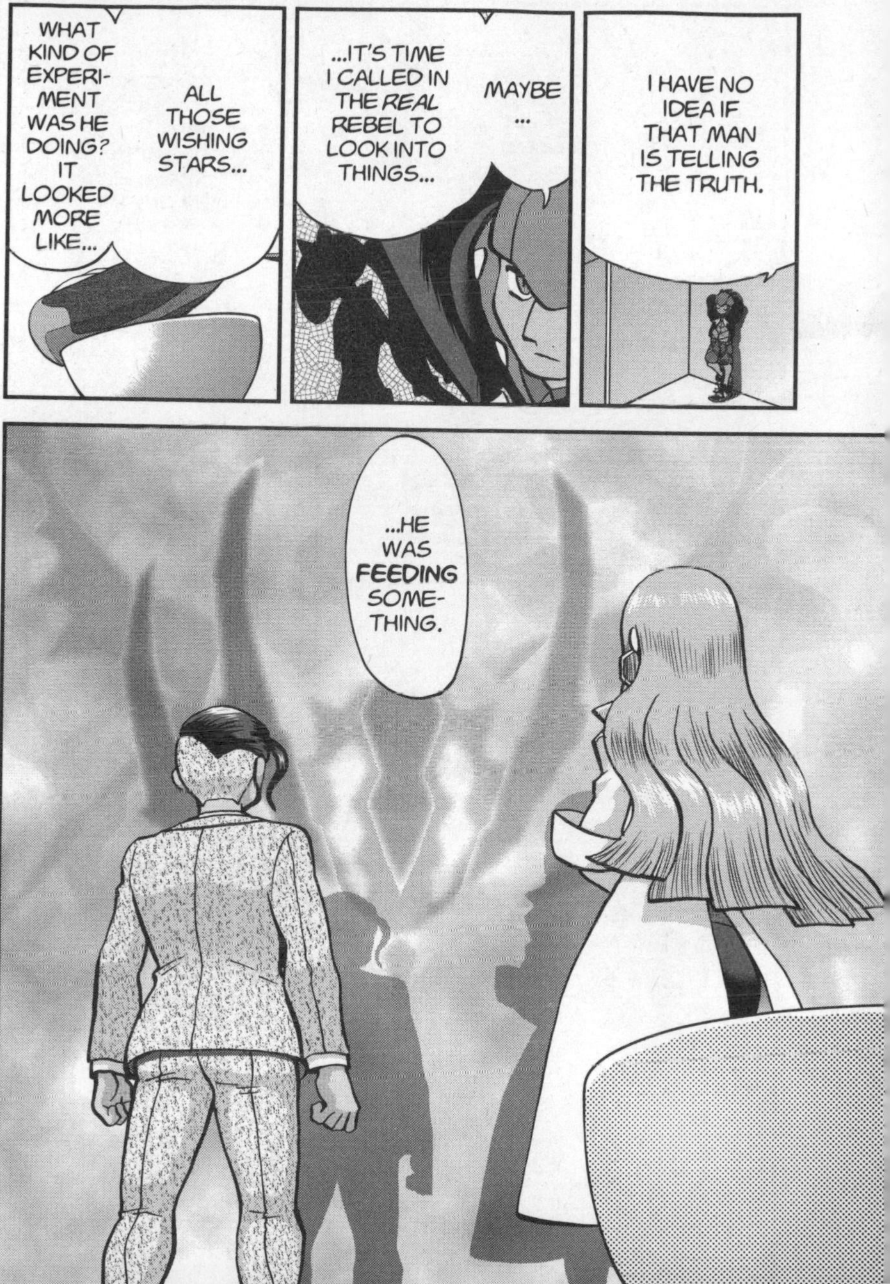
I HAVE NO IDEA IF THAT MAN IS TELLING THE TRUTH.
MAYBE ...
...IT'S TIME I CALLED IN THE *REAL* REBEL TO LOOK INTO THINGS...
ALL THOSE WISHING STARS...
WHAT KIND OF EXPERIMENT WAS HE DOING? IT LOOKED MORE LIKE...
...HE WAS **FEEDING** SOMETHING.

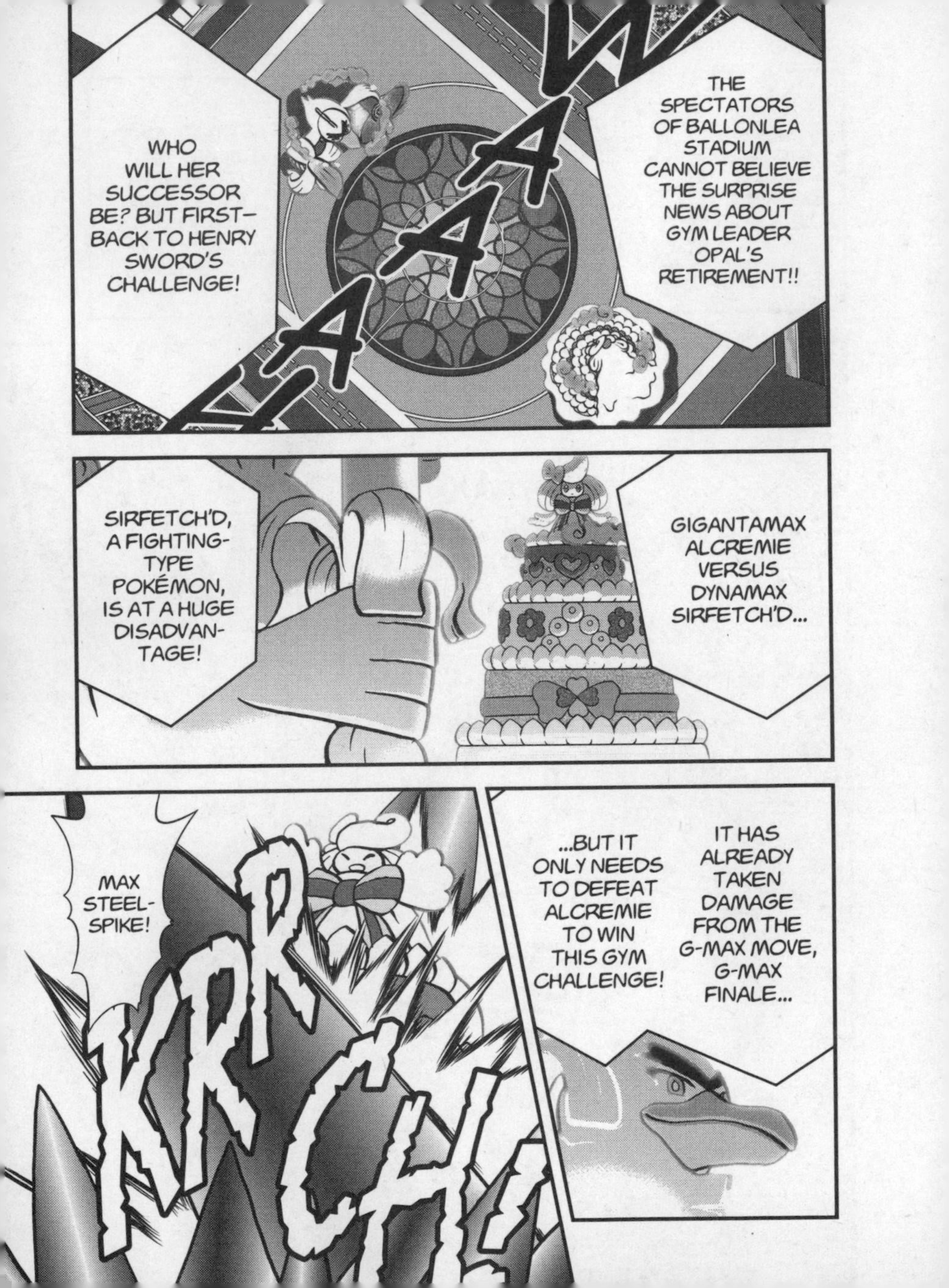

THE SPECTATORS OF BALLONLEA STADIUM CANNOT BELIEVE THE SURPRISE NEWS ABOUT GYM LEADER OPAL'S RETIREMENT!!
WAAAA
WHO WILL HER SUCCESSOR BE? BUT FIRST—BACK TO HENRY SWORD'S CHALLENGE!
GIGANTAMAX ALCREMIE VERSUS DYNAMAX SIRFETCH'D...
SIRFETCH'D, A FIGHTING-TYPE POKÉMON, IS AT A HUGE DISADVANTAGE!
IT HAS ALREADY TAKEN DAMAGE FROM THE G-MAX MOVE, G-MAX FINALE...
...BUT IT ONLY NEEDS TO DEFEAT ALCREMIE TO WIN THIS GYM CHALLENGE!
MAX STEEL-SPIKE!
KR CH

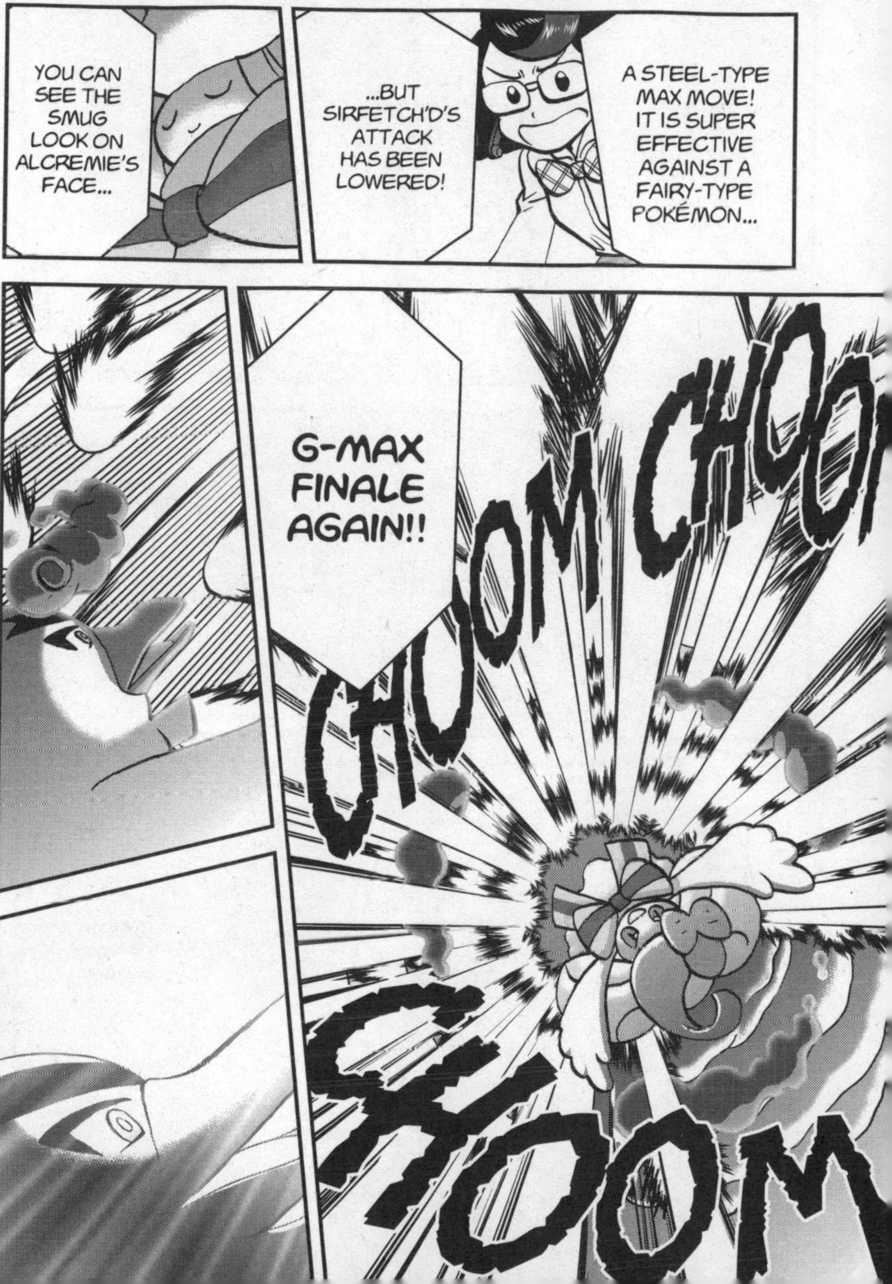
A STEEL-TYPE MAX MOVE! IT IS SUPER EFFECTIVE AGAINST A FAIRY-TYPE POKÉMON...
...BUT SIRFETCH'D'S ATTACK HAS BEEN LOWERED!
YOU CAN SEE THE SMUG LOOK ON ALCREMIE'S FACE...
G-MAX FINALE AGAIN!!
CHOOM CHOO
CHOOM

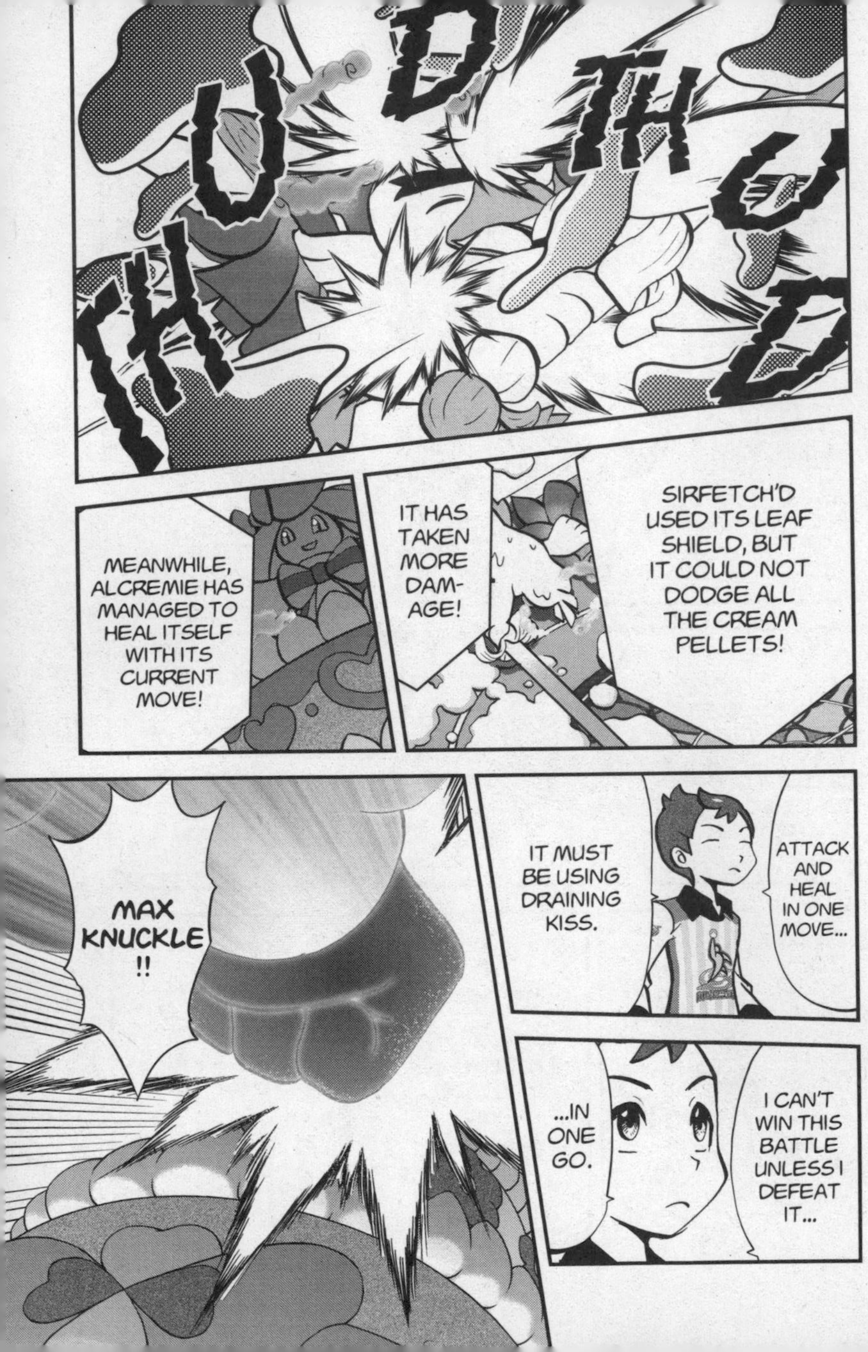
THUD
THUD
SIRFETCH'D USED ITS LEAF SHIELD, BUT IT COULD NOT DODGE ALL THE CREAM PELLETS!
IT HAS TAKEN MORE DAM-AGE!
MEANWHILE, ALCREMIE HAS MANAGED TO HEAL ITSELF WITH ITS CURRENT MOVE!
ATTACK AND HEAL IN ONE MOVE...
IT MUST BE USING DRAINING KISS.
I CAN'T WIN THIS BATTLE UNLESS I DEFEAT IT...
...IN ONE GO.
MAX KNUCKLE!!

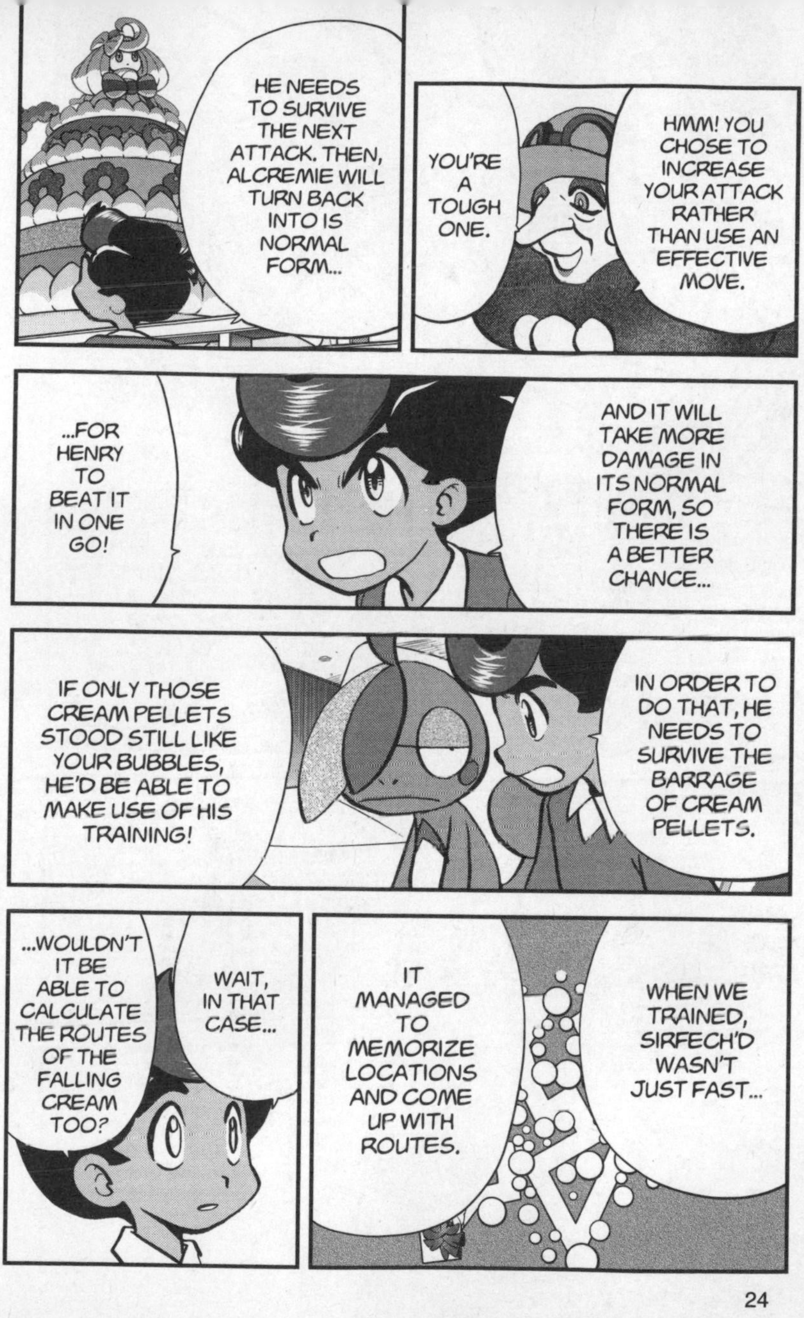
HMM! YOU CHOSE TO INCREASE YOUR ATTACK RATHER THAN USE AN EFFECTIVE MOVE.
YOU'RE A TOUGH ONE.
HE NEEDS TO SURVIVE THE NEXT ATTACK. THEN, ALCREMIE WILL TURN BACK INTO IS NORMAL FORM...
AND IT WILL TAKE MORE DAMAGE IN ITS NORMAL FORM, SO THERE IS A BETTER CHANCE...
...FOR HENRY TO BEAT IT IN ONE GO!
IN ORDER TO DO THAT, HE NEEDS TO SURVIVE THE BARRAGE OF CREAM PELLETS.
IF ONLY THOSE CREAM PELLETS STOOD STILL LIKE YOUR BUBBLES, HE'D BE ABLE TO MAKE USE OF HIS TRAINING!
WHEN WE TRAINED, SIRFECH'D WASN'T JUST FAST...
IT MANAGED TO MEMORIZE LOCATIONS AND COME UP WITH ROUTES.
WAIT, IN THAT CASE...
...WOULDN'T IT BE ABLE TO CALCULATE THE ROUTES OF THE FALLING CREAM TOO?

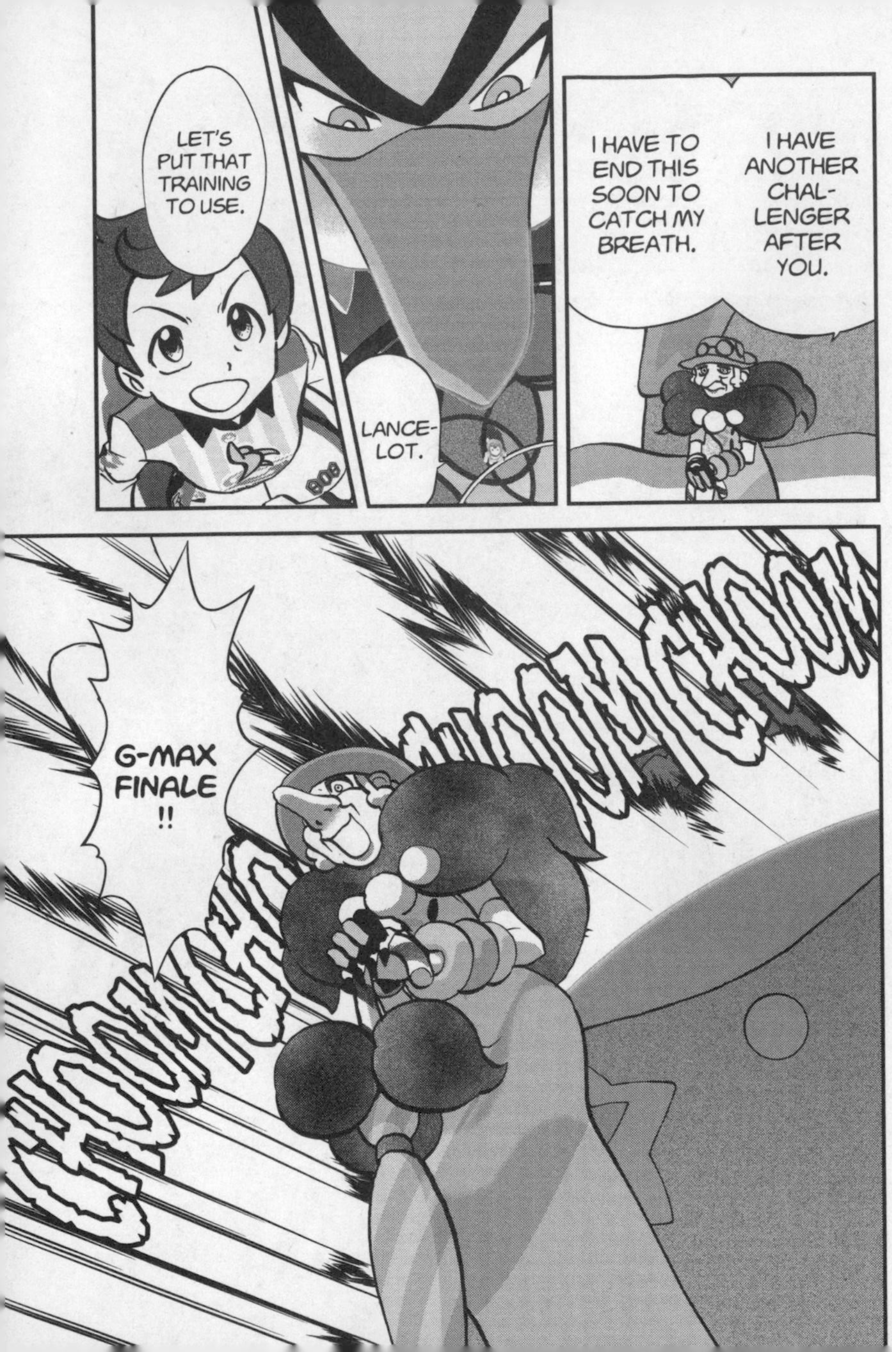

I HAVE ANOTHER CHAL-LENGER AFTER YOU.
I HAVE TO END THIS SOON TO CATCH MY BREATH.
LANCE-LOT.
LET'S PUT THAT TRAINING TO USE.
G-MAX FINALE !!
CHOOMCHOOMCHOOMCHOOM

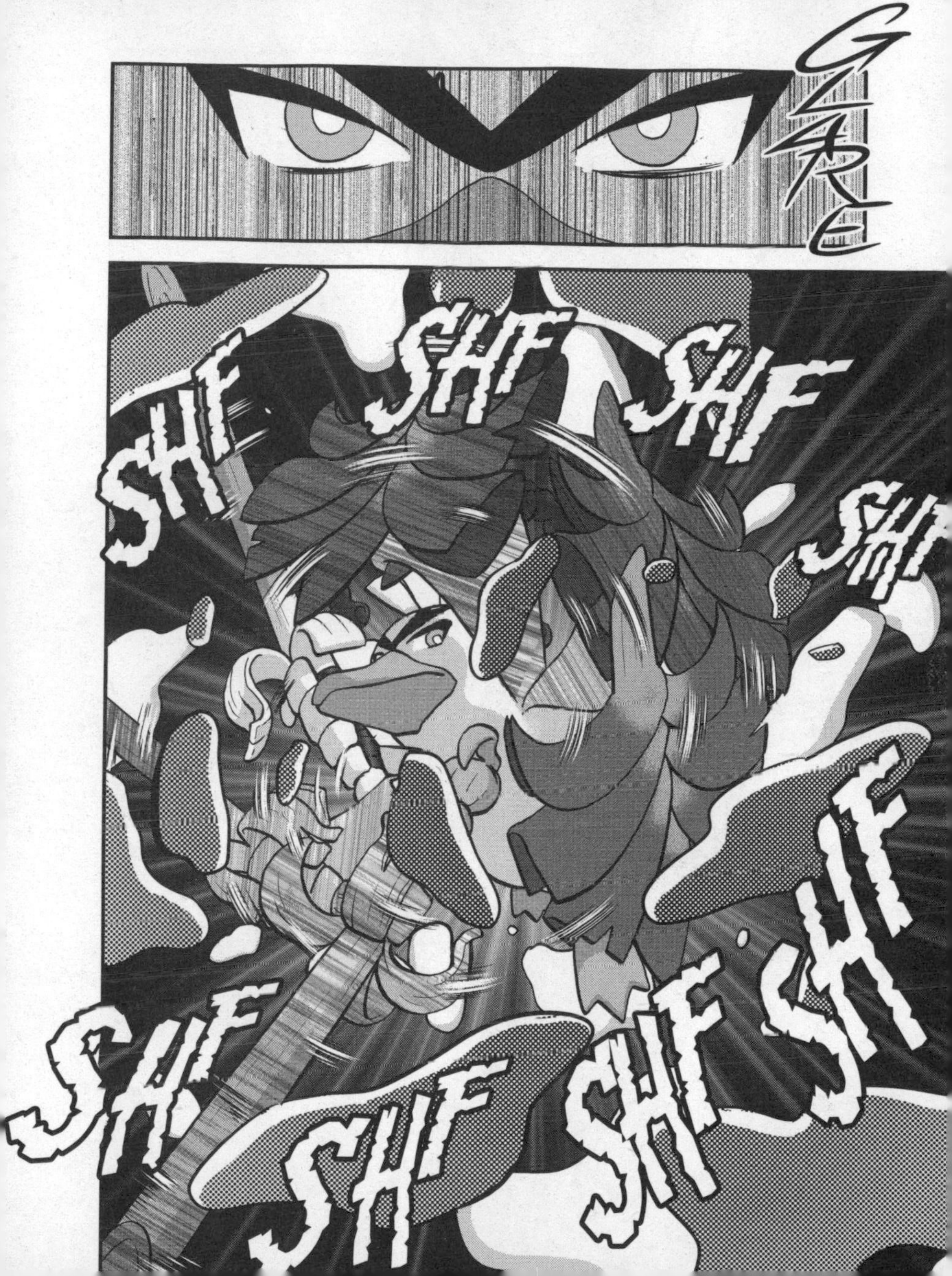
GLARE
SHF
SHF
SHF
SHF
SHF
SHF
SHF
SHF

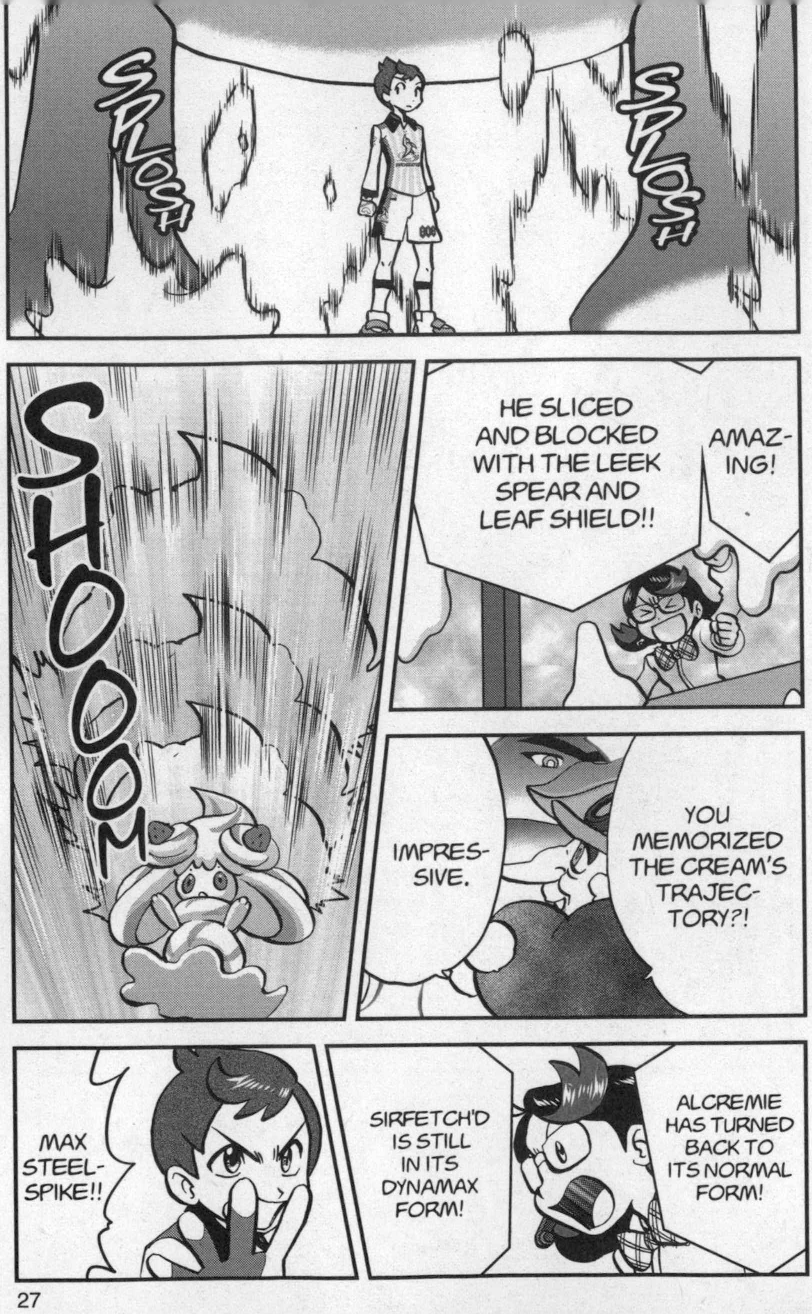
SPLOSH
SPLOSH
AMAZ-ING!
HE SLICED AND BLOCKED WITH THE LEEK SPEAR AND LEAF SHIELD!!
YOU MEMORIZED THE CREAM'S TRAJEC-TORY?!
IMPRES-SIVE.
SHOOOOM
ALCREMIE HAS TURNED BACK TO ITS NORMAL FORM!
SIRFETCH'D IS STILL IN ITS DYNAMAX FORM!
MAX STEEL-SPIKE!!

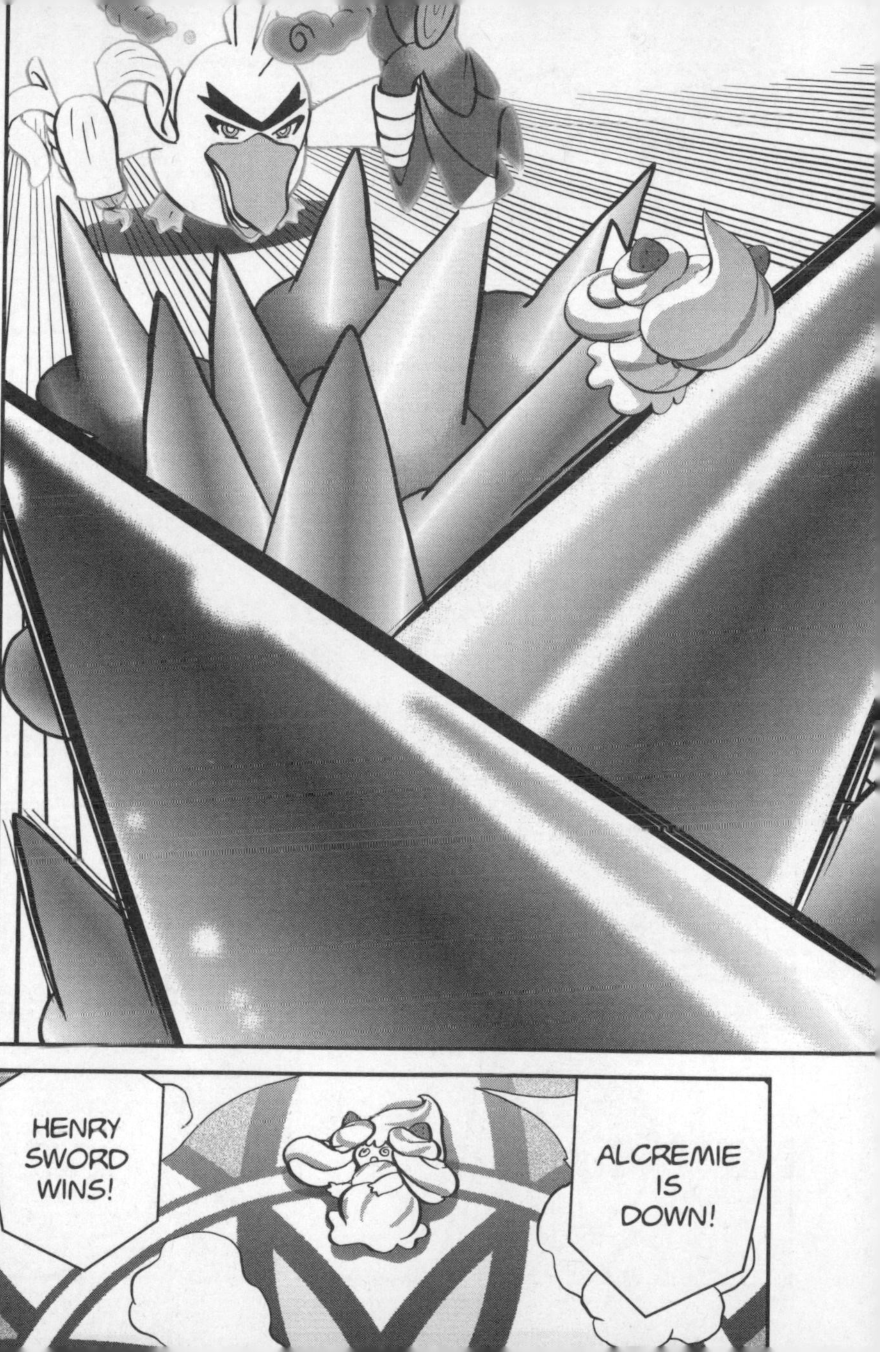
ALCREMIE IS DOWN!
HENRY SWORD WINS!

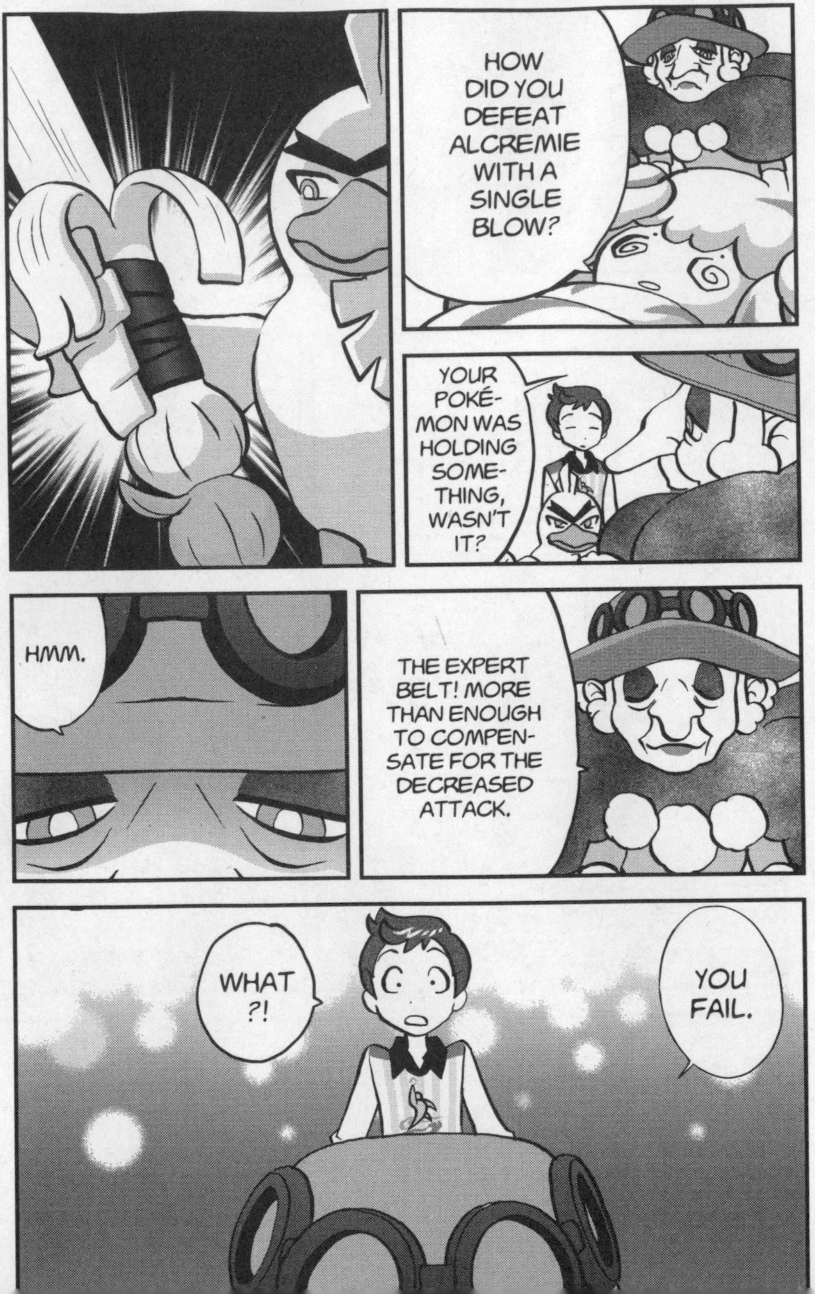
HOW DID YOU DEFEAT ALCREMIE WITH A SINGLE BLOW?
YOUR POKÉ-MON WAS HOLDING SOME-THING, WASN'T IT?
THE EXPERT BELT! MORE THAN ENOUGH TO COMPEN-SATE FOR THE DECREASED ATTACK.
HMM.
YOU FAIL.
WHAT?!

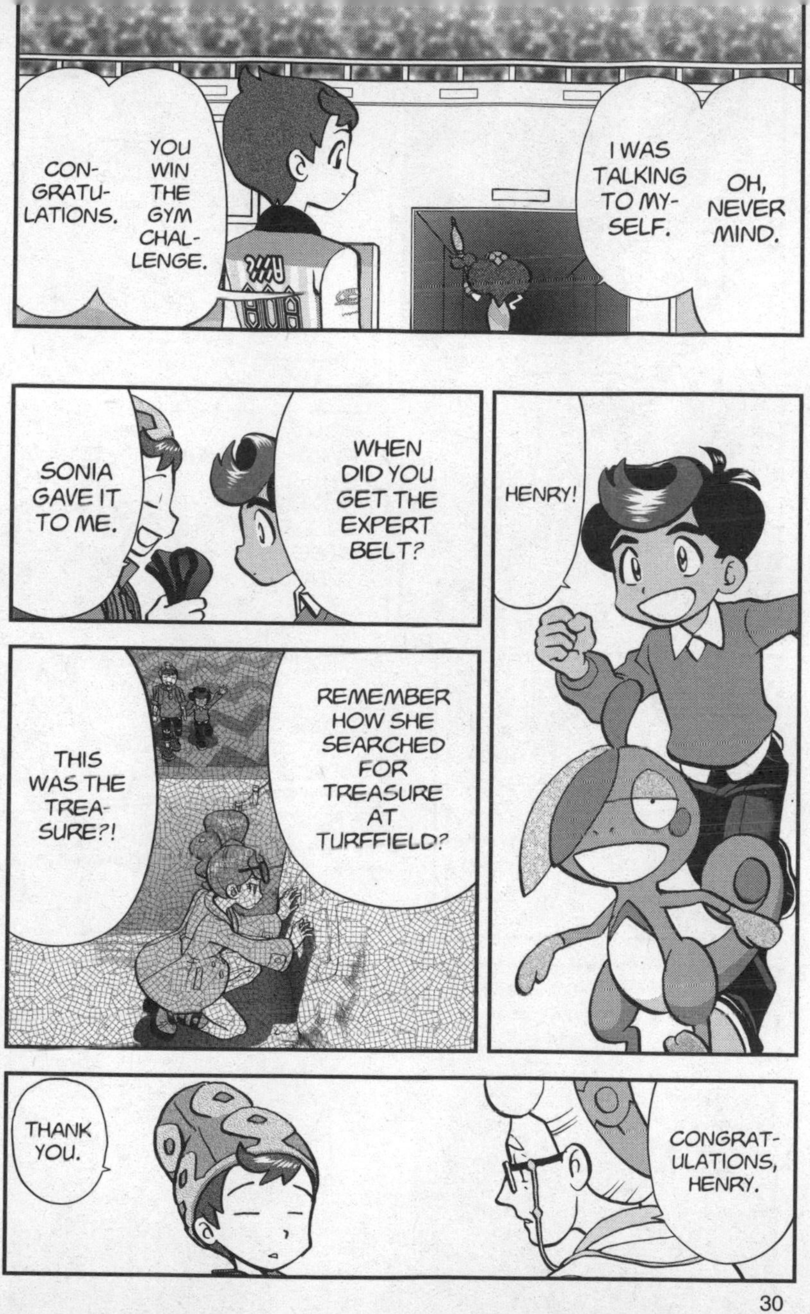
YOU WIN THE GYM CHALLENGE.
CON-GRATU-LATIONS.
OH, NEVER MIND.
I WAS TALKING TO MY-SELF.
HENRY!
WHEN DID YOU GET THE EXPERT BELT?
SONIA GAVE IT TO ME.
REMEMBER HOW SHE SEARCHED FOR TREASURE AT TURFFIELD?
THIS WAS THE TREA-SURE?!
CONGRAT-ULATIONS, HENRY.
THANK YOU.

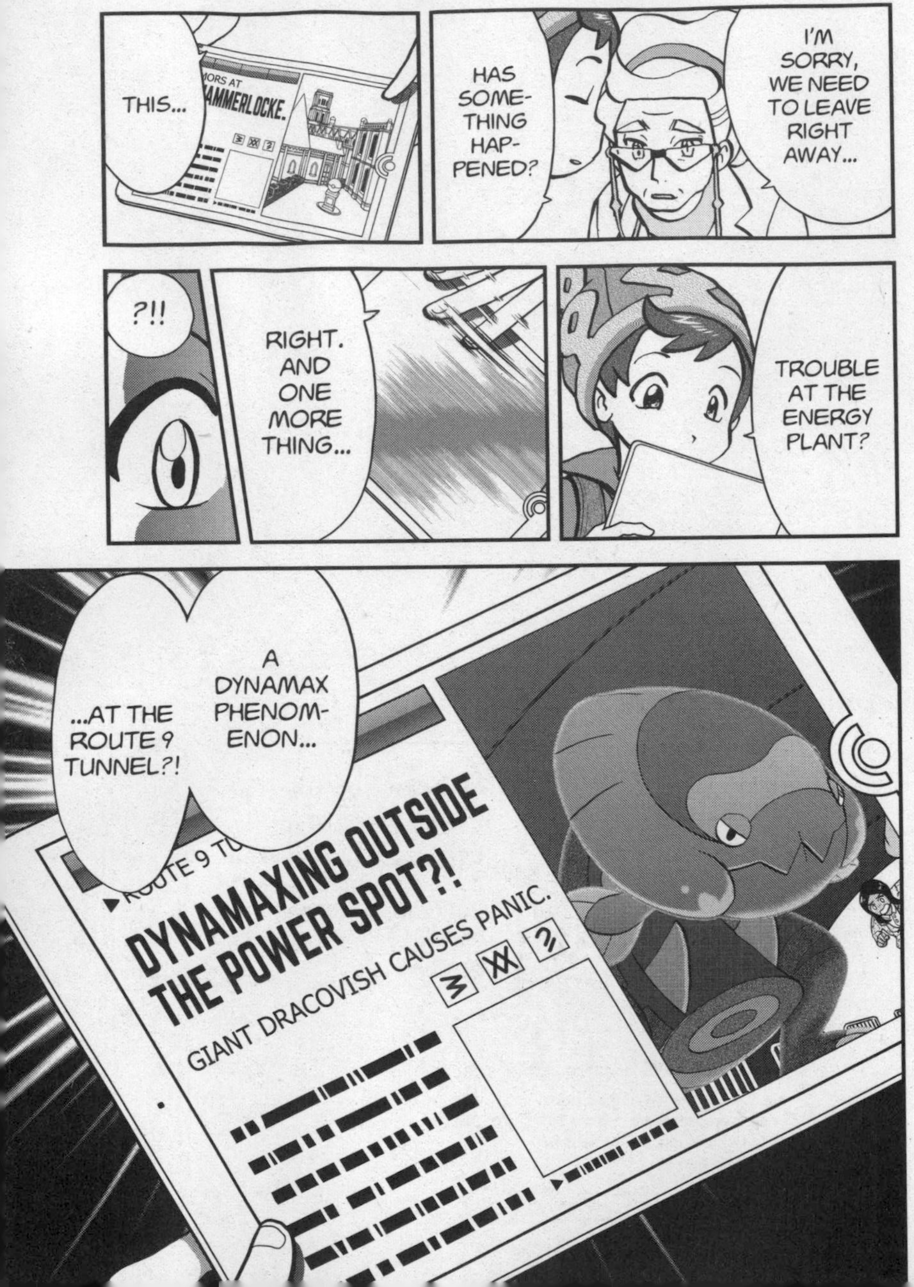
I'M SORRY, WE NEED TO LEAVE RIGHT AWAY...
HAS SOME-THING HAP-PENED?
THIS...
TROUBLE AT THE ENERGY PLANT?
RIGHT. AND ONE MORE THING...
?!!
A DYNAMAX PHENOM-ENON...
...AT THE ROUTE 9 TUNNEL?!
DYNAMAXING OUTSIDE THE POWER SPOT?!
GIANT DRACOVISH CAUSES PANIC.

THE SECRETS OF DYNAMAX, PART 14

HOMP!
▲ Once the barrier appears, you must take your time to break through it. There is no need to panic!

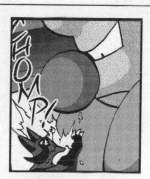

Mysterious Barrier

During a Max Raid Battle, the Dynamaxed Pokémon inside the Pokémon Den will protect itself with a barrier!

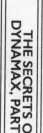

Adventure 18 Chomp!! It's Dracovish

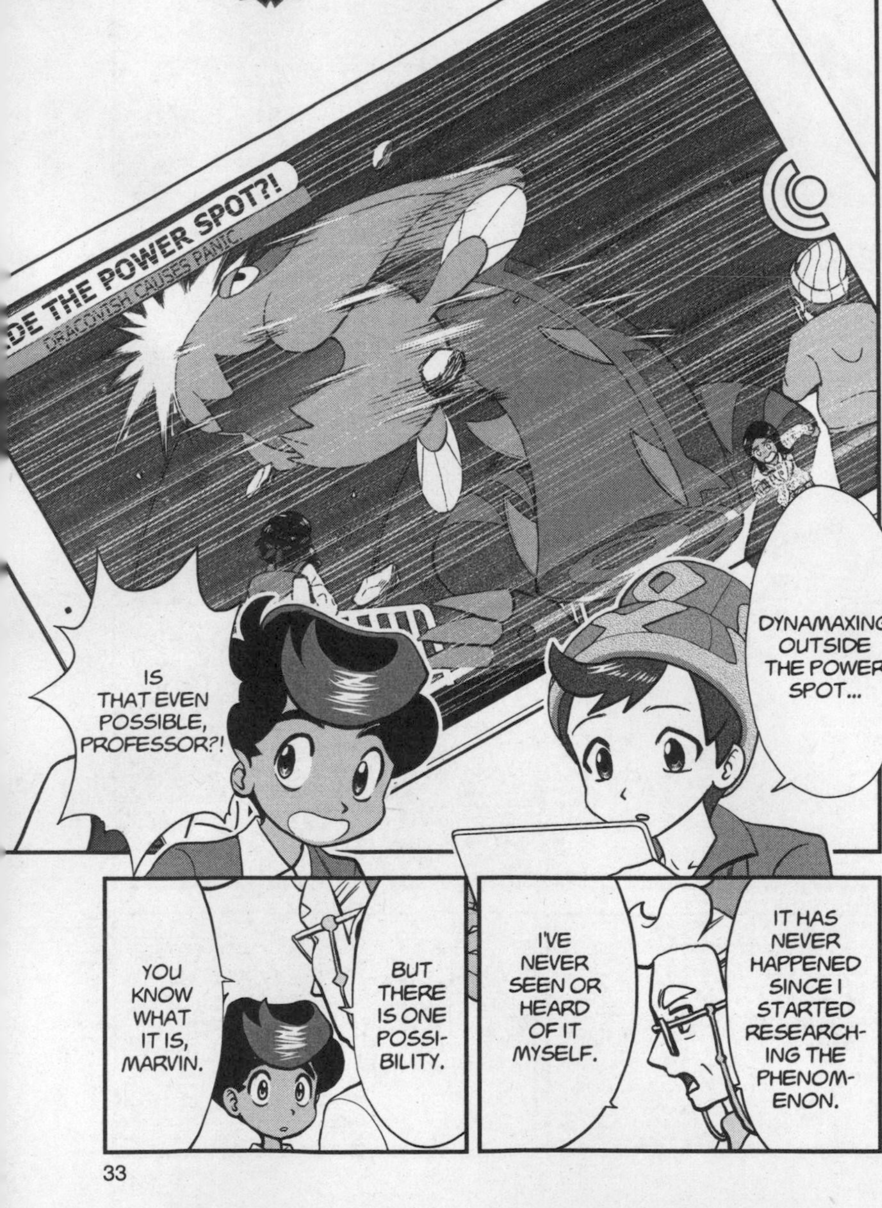
DE THE POWER SPOT?!
DRACOVISH CAUSES PANIC.
DYNAMAXING OUTSIDE THE POWER SPOT...
IS THAT EVEN POSSIBLE, PROFESSOR?!
IT HAS NEVER HAPPENED SINCE I STARTED RESEARCHING THE PHENOMENON.
I'VE NEVER SEEN OR HEARD OF IT MYSELF.
BUT THERE IS ONE POSSIBILITY.
YOU KNOW WHAT IT IS, MARVIN.

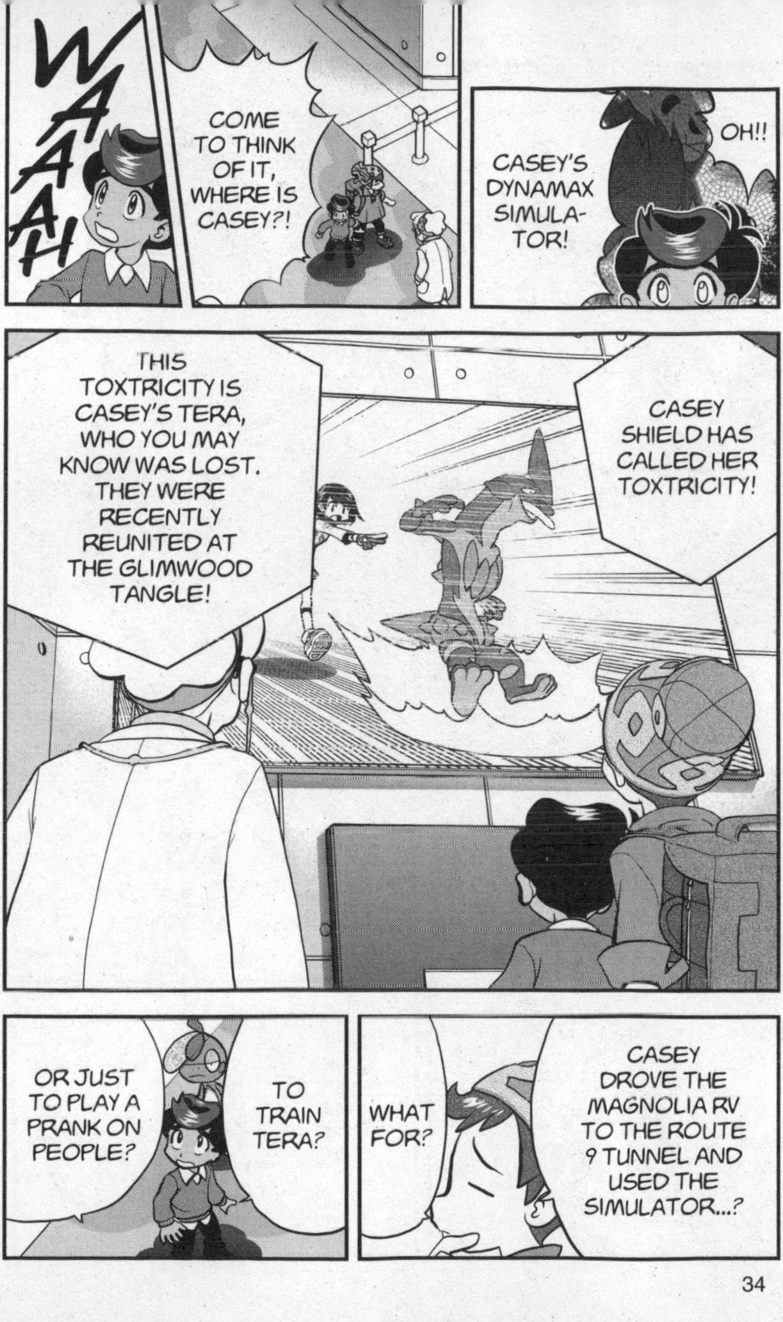
OH!!
CASEY'S DYNAMAX SIMULATOR!
COME TO THINK OF IT, WHERE IS CASEY?!
WAAAH
CASEY SHIELD HAS CALLED HER TOXTRICITY!
THIS TOXTRICITY IS CASEY'S TERA, WHO YOU MAY KNOW WAS LOST. THEY WERE RECENTLY REUNITED AT THE GLIMWOOD TANGLE!
CASEY DROVE THE MAGNOLIA RV TO THE ROUTE 9 TUNNEL AND USED THE SIMULATOR...?
WHAT FOR?
TO TRAIN TERA?
OR JUST TO PLAY A PRANK ON PEOPLE?

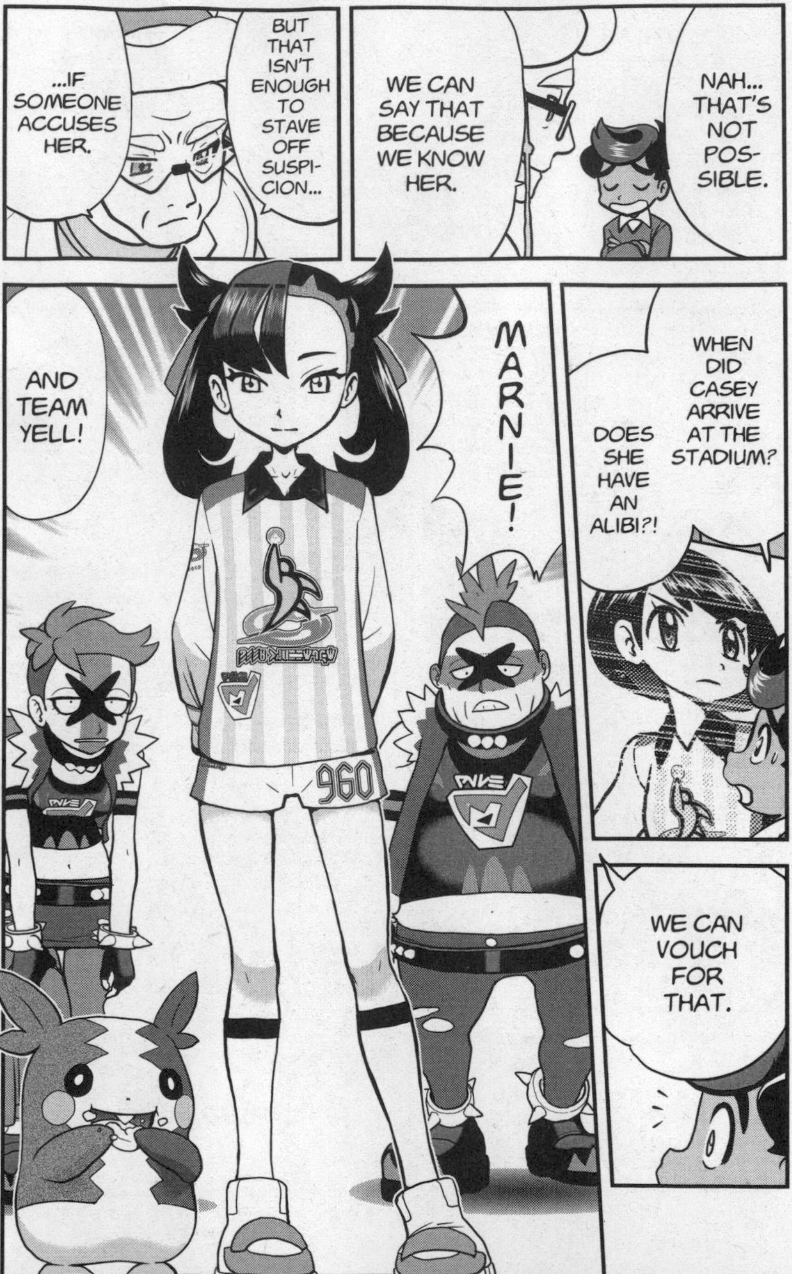
NAH... THAT'S NOT POS-SIBLE.
WE CAN SAY THAT BECAUSE WE KNOW HER.
BUT THAT ISN'T ENOUGH TO STAVE OFF SUSPI-CION...
...IF SOMEONE ACCUSES HER.
WHEN DID CASEY ARRIVE AT THE STADIUM?
DOES SHE HAVE AN ALIBI?!
WE CAN VOUCH FOR THAT.
MARNIE!
AND TEAM YELL!
960

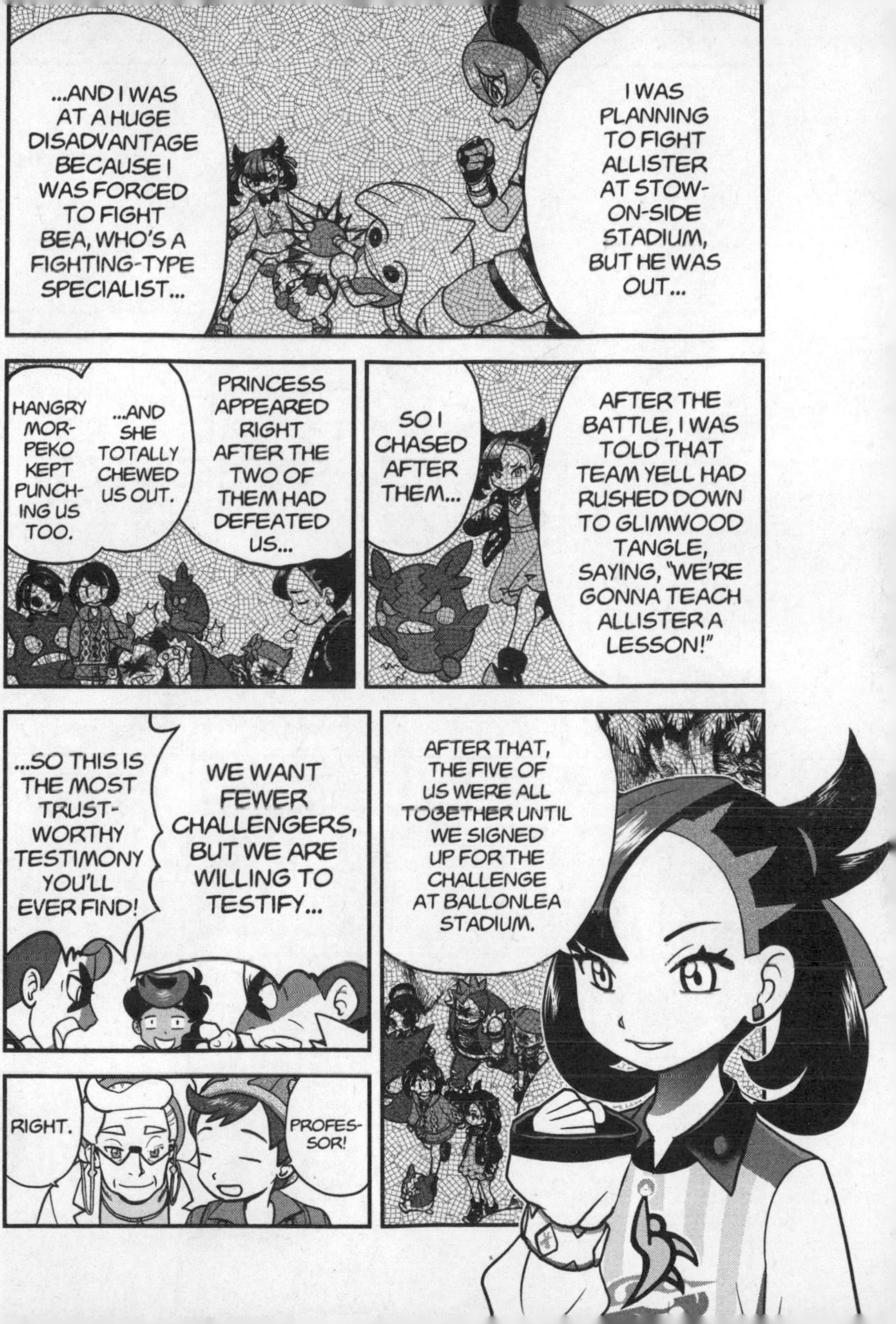

I WAS PLANNING TO FIGHT ALLISTER AT STOW-ON-SIDE STADIUM, BUT HE WAS OUT...
...AND I WAS AT A HUGE DISADVANTAGE BECAUSE I WAS FORCED TO FIGHT BEA, WHO'S A FIGHTING-TYPE SPECIALIST...
AFTER THE BATTLE, I WAS TOLD THAT TEAM YELL HAD RUSHED DOWN TO GLIMWOOD TANGLE, SAYING, "WE'RE GONNA TEACH ALLISTER A LESSON!"
SO I CHASED AFTER THEM...
PRINCESS APPEARED RIGHT AFTER THE TWO OF THEM HAD DEFEATED US...
...AND SHE TOTALLY CHEWED US OUT.
HANGRY MOR-PEKO KEPT PUNCH-ING US TOO.
AFTER THAT, THE FIVE OF US WERE ALL TOGETHER UNTIL WE SIGNED UP FOR THE CHALLENGE AT BALLONLEA STADIUM.
WE WANT FEWER CHALLENGERS, BUT WE ARE WILLING TO TESTIFY...
...SO THIS IS THE MOST TRUST-WORTHY TESTIMONY YOU'LL EVER FIND!
PROFES-SOR!
RIGHT.

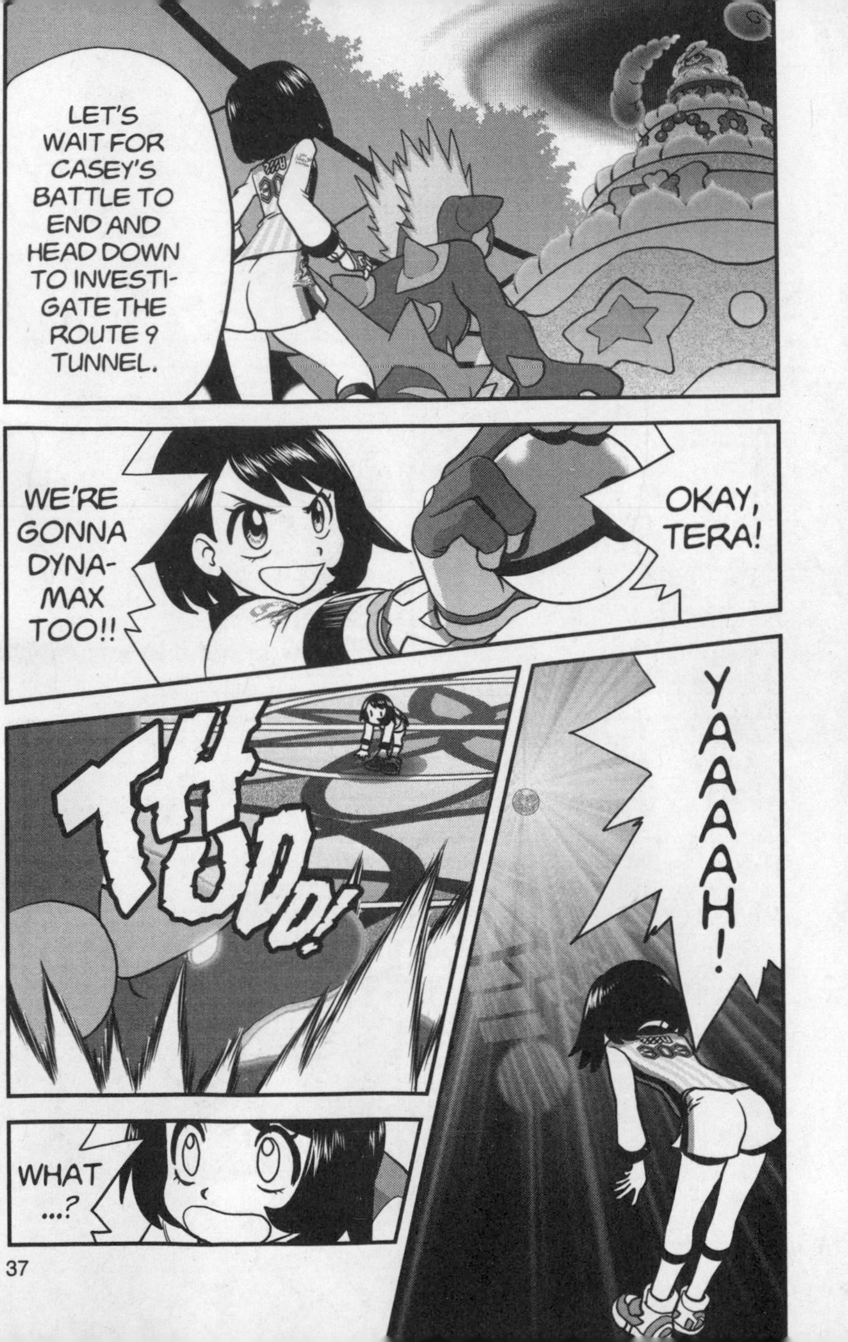
LET'S WAIT FOR CASEY'S BATTLE TO END AND HEAD DOWN TO INVESTI-GATE THE ROUTE 9 TUNNEL.
OKAY, TERA!
WE'RE GONNA DYNA-MAX TOO!!
YAAAAAH!
THOOD!
WHAT ...?

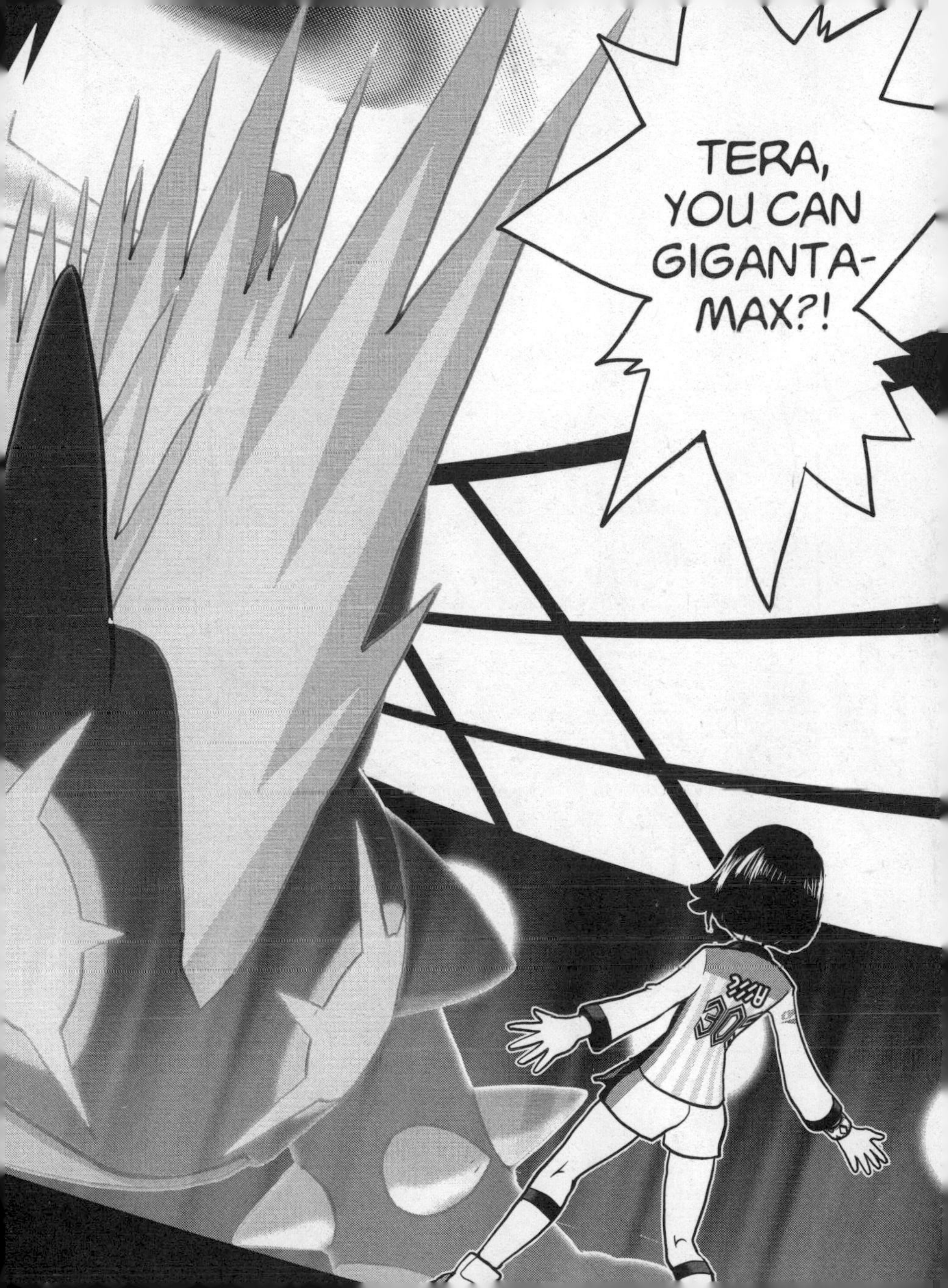
TERA, YOU CAN GIGANTA-MAX?!

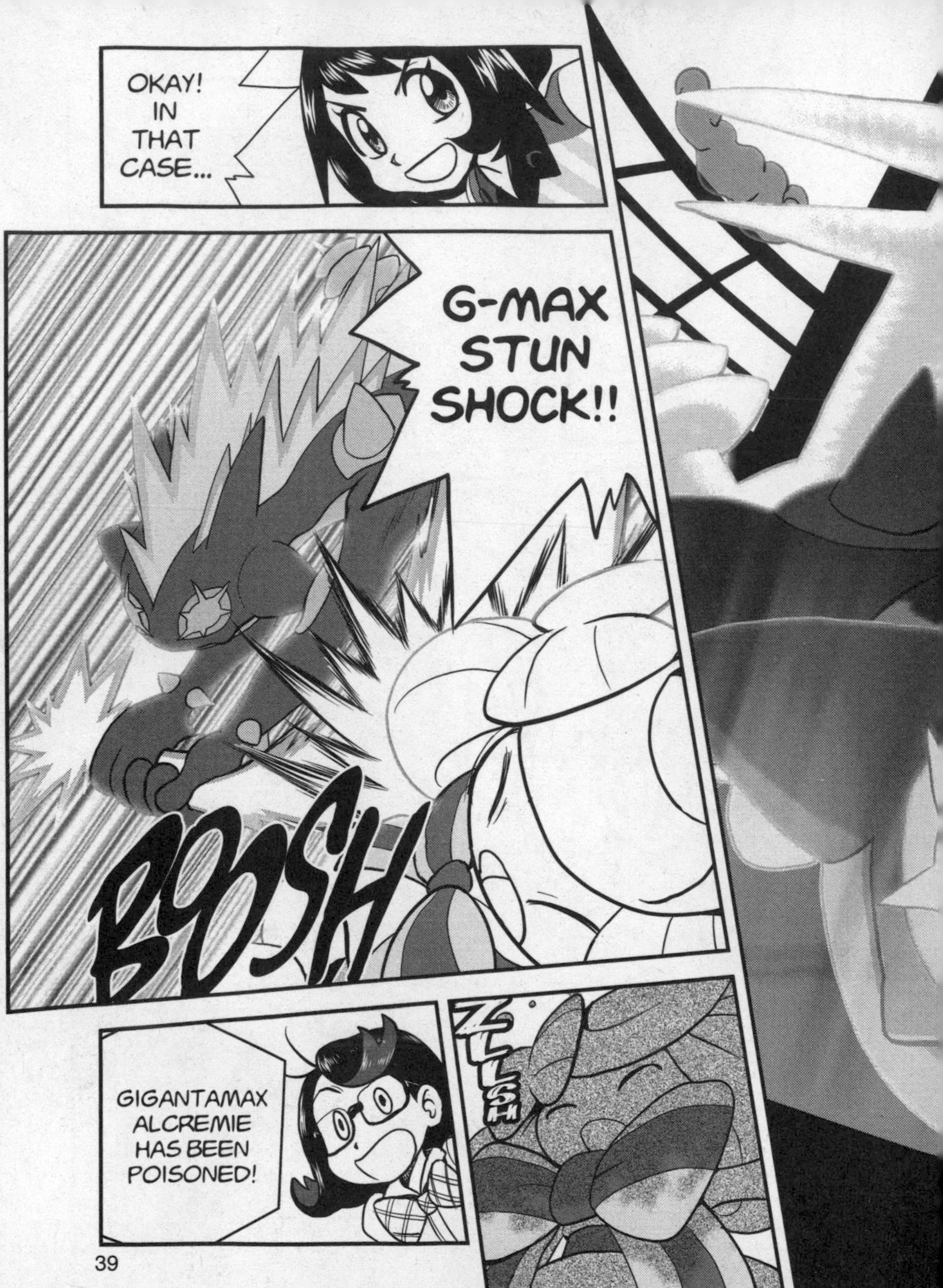
OKAY! IN THAT CASE...
G-MAX STUN SHOCK!!
BOOSH
ZLLSH
GIGANTAMAX ALCREMIE HAS BEEN POISONED!

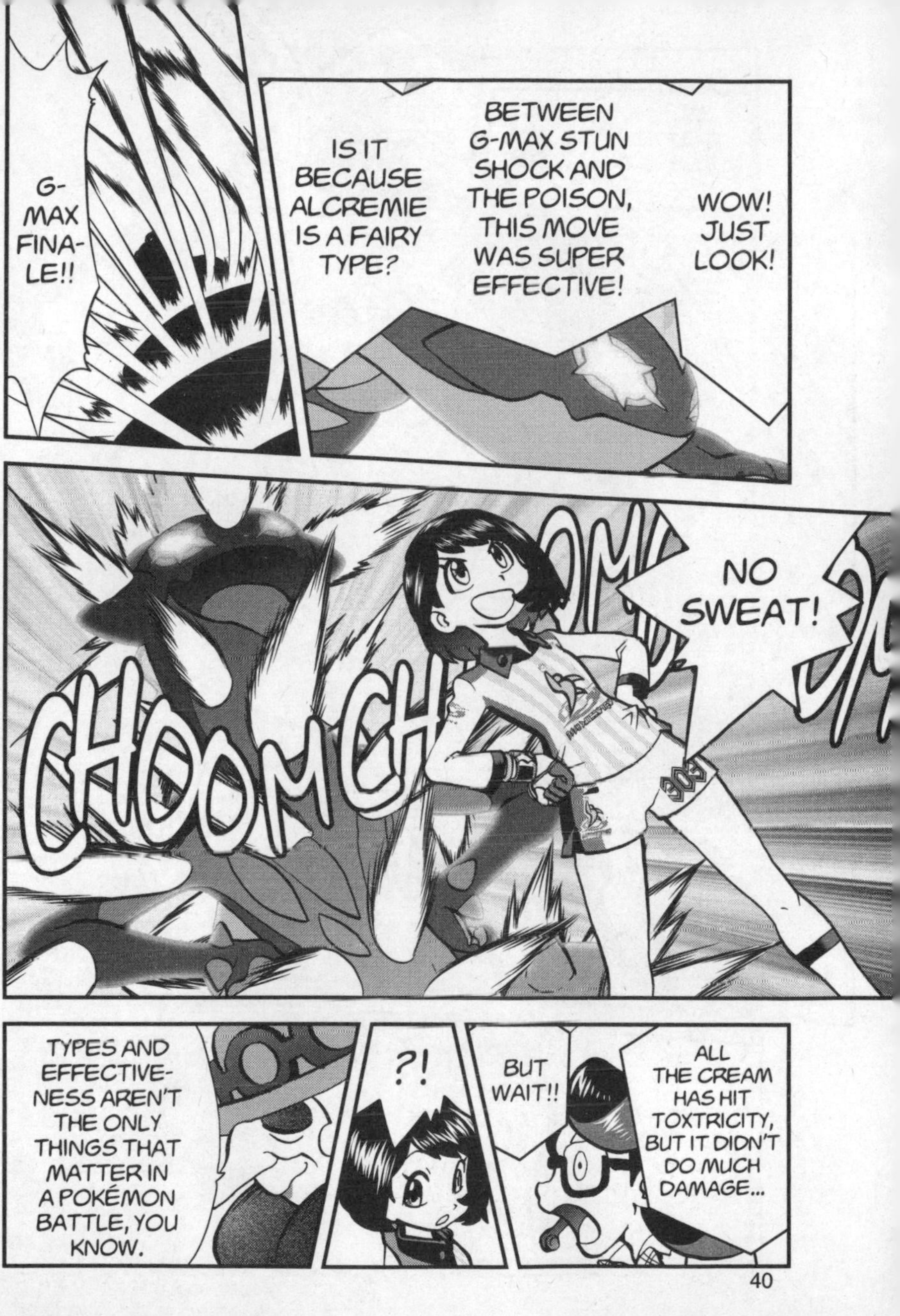
WOW! JUST LOOK!
BETWEEN G-MAX STUN SHOCK AND THE POISON, THIS MOVE WAS SUPER EFFECTIVE!
IS IT BECAUSE ALCREMIE IS A FAIRY TYPE?
G-MAX FINALE!!
NO SWEAT!
CHOOM CH
ALL THE CREAM HAS HIT TOXTRICITY, BUT IT DIDN'T DO MUCH DAMAGE...
BUT WAIT!!
?!
TYPES AND EFFECTIVENESS AREN'T THE ONLY THINGS THAT MATTER IN A POKÉMON BATTLE, YOU KNOW.

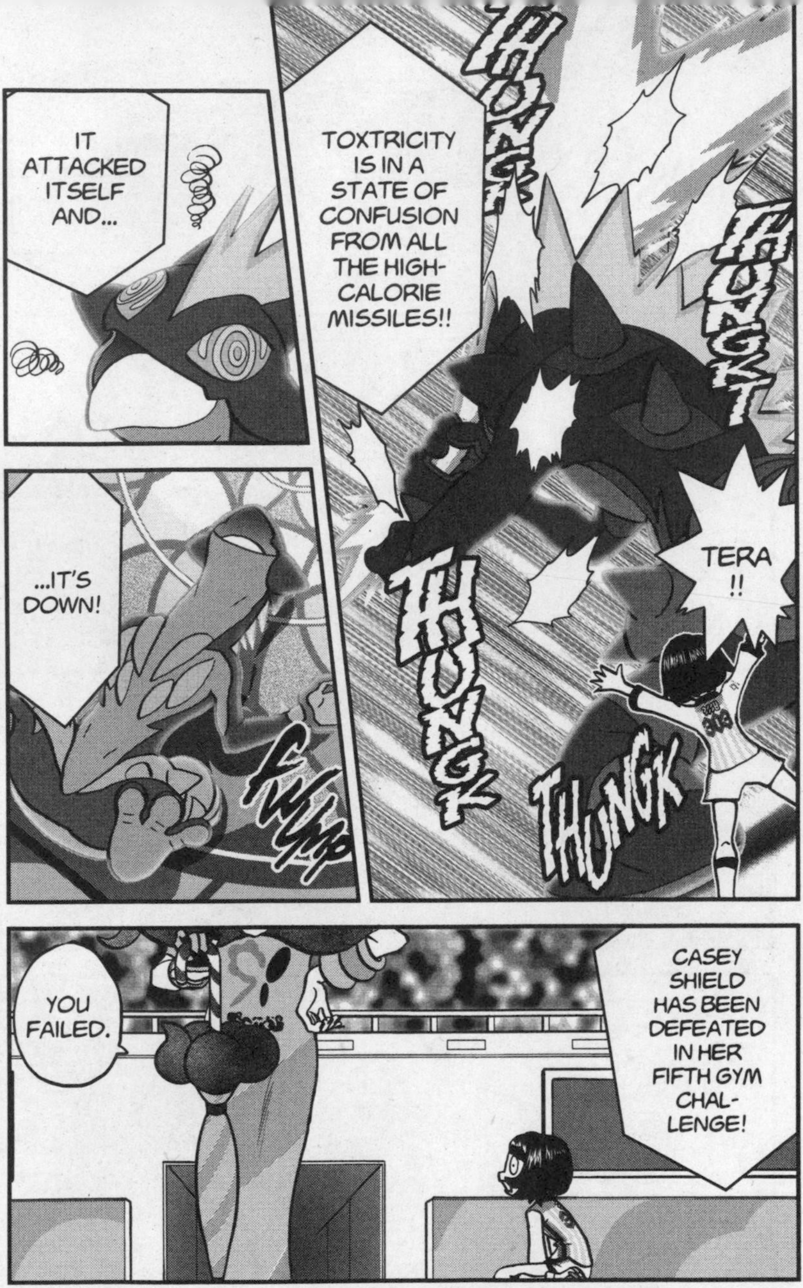
TOXTRICITY IS IN A STATE OF CONFUSION FROM ALL THE HIGH-CALORIE MISSILES!!
THUNGK
TERA !!
THUNGK
THUNGK
IT ATTACKED ITSELF AND...
...IT'S DOWN!
CASEY SHIELD HAS BEEN DEFEATED IN HER FIFTH GYM CHAL-LENGE!
YOU FAILED.

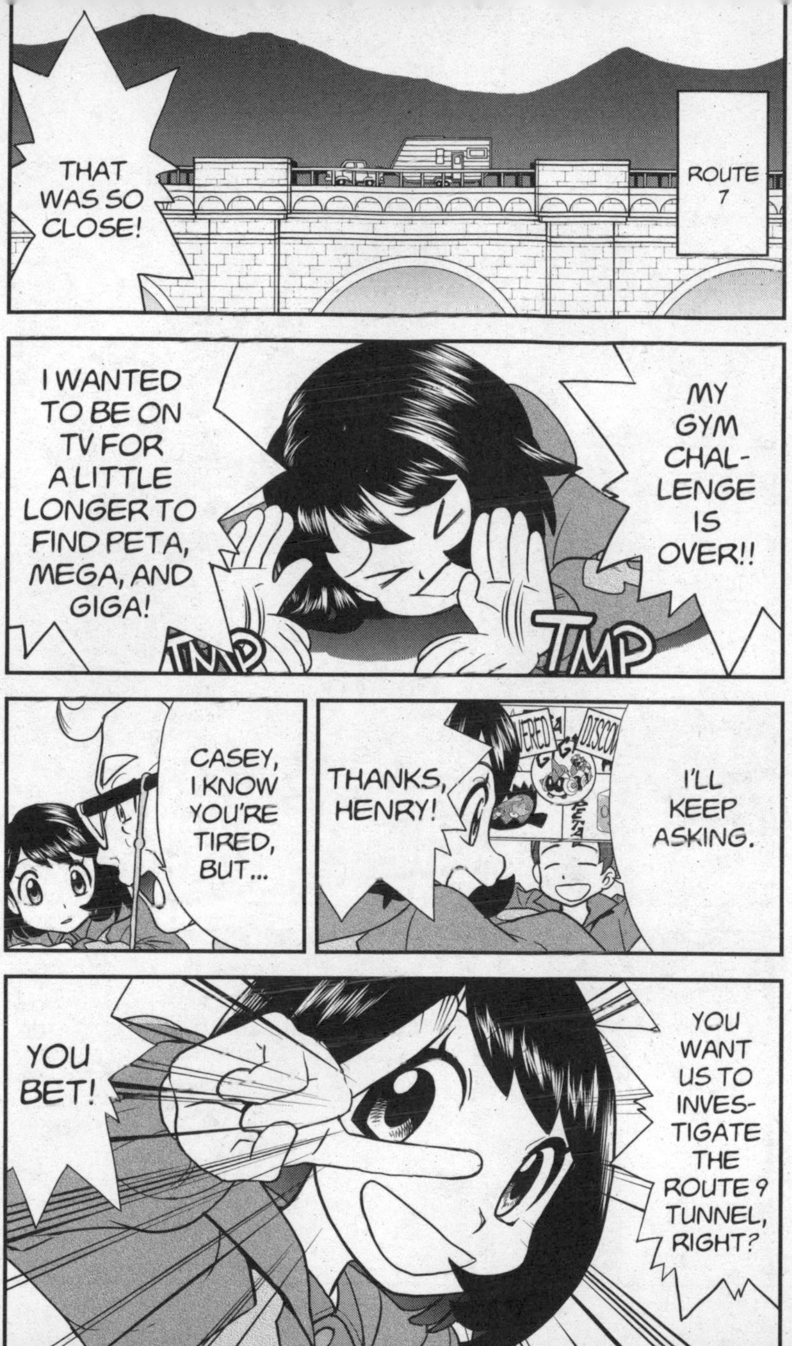
ROUTE 7
THAT WAS SO CLOSE!
MY GYM CHAL-LENGE IS OVER!!
I WANTED TO BE ON TV FOR A LITTLE LONGER TO FIND PETA, MEGA, AND GIGA!
TMP
TMP
I'LL KEEP ASKING.
THANKS, HENRY!
CASEY, I KNOW YOU'RE TIRED, BUT...
YOU WANT US TO INVES-TIGATE THE ROUTE 9 TUNNEL, RIGHT?
YOU BET!

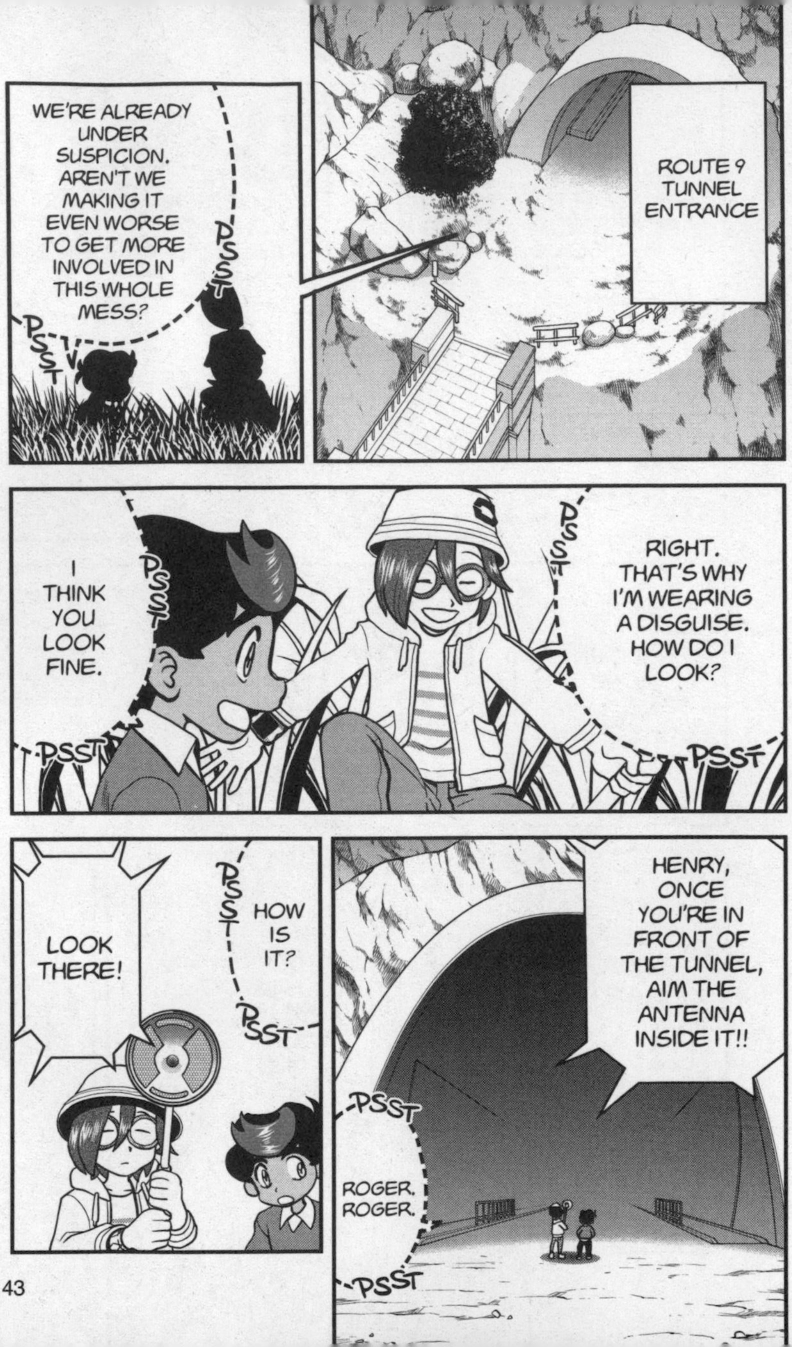
ROUTE 9 TUNNEL ENTRANCE
WE'RE ALREADY UNDER SUSPICION. AREN'T WE MAKING IT EVEN WORSE TO GET MORE INVOLVED IN THIS WHOLE MESS?
PSST
PSST
RIGHT. THAT'S WHY I'M WEARING A DISGUISE. HOW DO I LOOK?
PSST
PSST
I THINK YOU LOOK FINE.
PSST
PSST
HENRY, ONCE YOU'RE IN FRONT OF THE TUNNEL, AIM THE ANTENNA INSIDE IT!!
PSST
ROGER. ROGER.
PSST
PSST
HOW IS IT?
PSST
LOOK THERE!

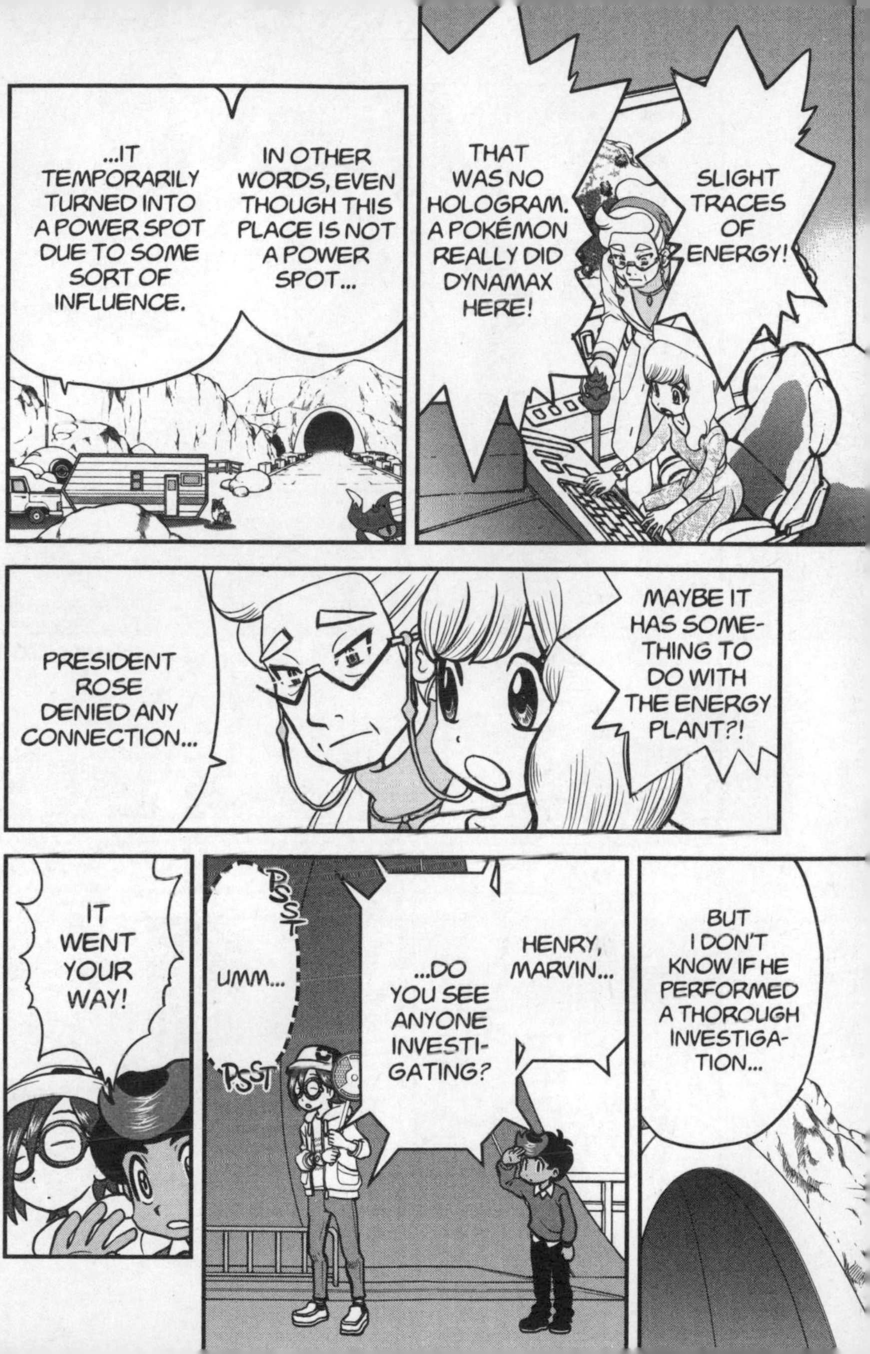
SLIGHT TRACES OF ENERGY!
THAT WAS NO HOLOGRAM. A POKÉMON REALLY DID DYNAMAX HERE!
IN OTHER WORDS, EVEN THOUGH THIS PLACE IS NOT A POWER SPOT...
...IT TEMPORARILY TURNED INTO A POWER SPOT DUE TO SOME SORT OF INFLUENCE.
MAYBE IT HAS SOME-THING TO DO WITH THE ENERGY PLANT?!
PRESIDENT ROSE DENIED ANY CONNECTION...
BUT I DON'T KNOW IF HE PERFORMED A THOROUGH INVESTIGA-TION...
HENRY, MARVIN...
...DO YOU SEE ANYONE INVESTI-GATING?
PSST
UMM...
PSST
IT WENT YOUR WAY!

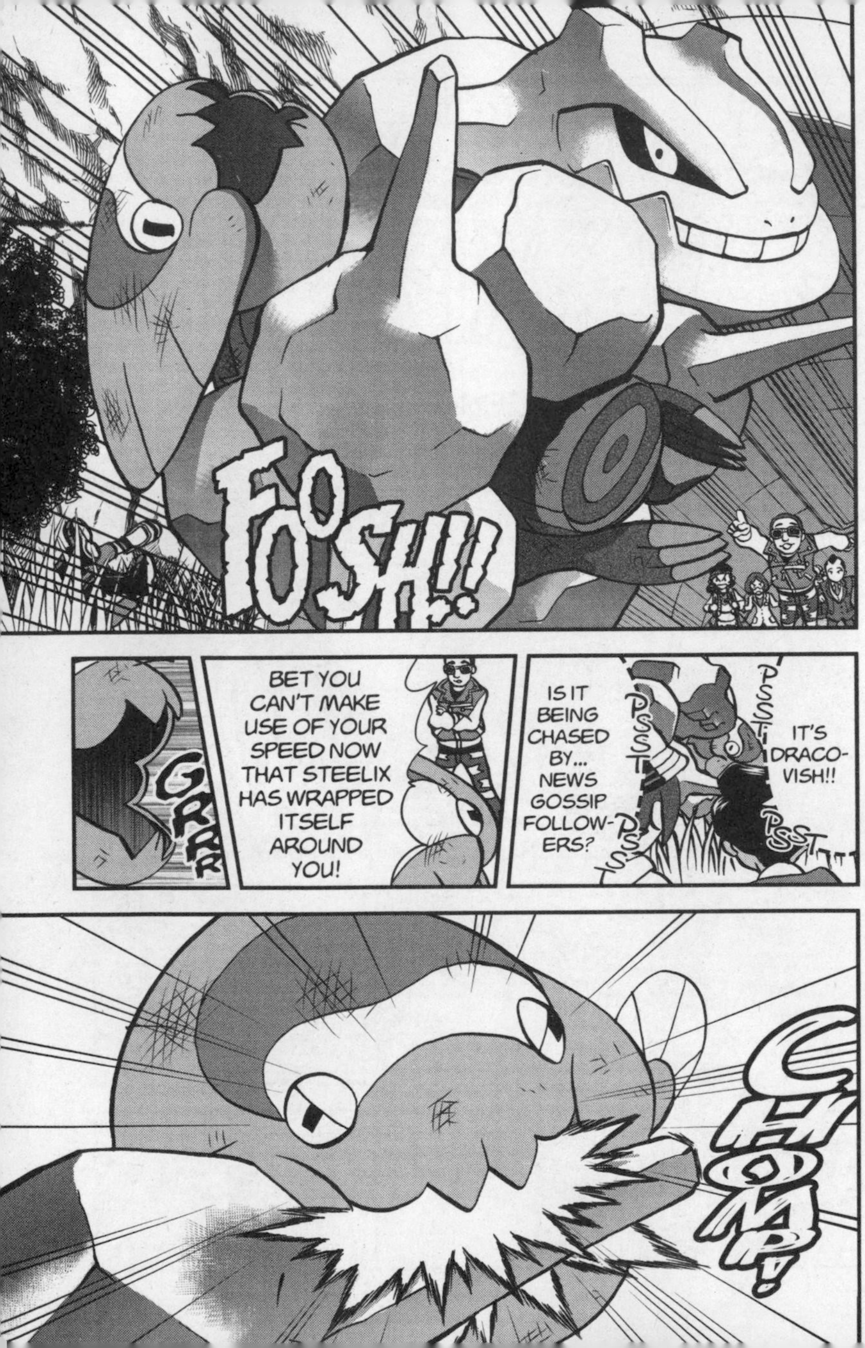
FOOSH!!
PSST PSST
IT'S DRACO-VISH!!
IS IT BEING CHASED BY... NEWS GOSSIP FOLLOW-ERS?
PSST PSST
BET YOU CAN'T MAKE USE OF YOUR SPEED NOW THAT STEELIX HAS WRAPPED ITSELF AROUND YOU!
GRRR
CHOMP!

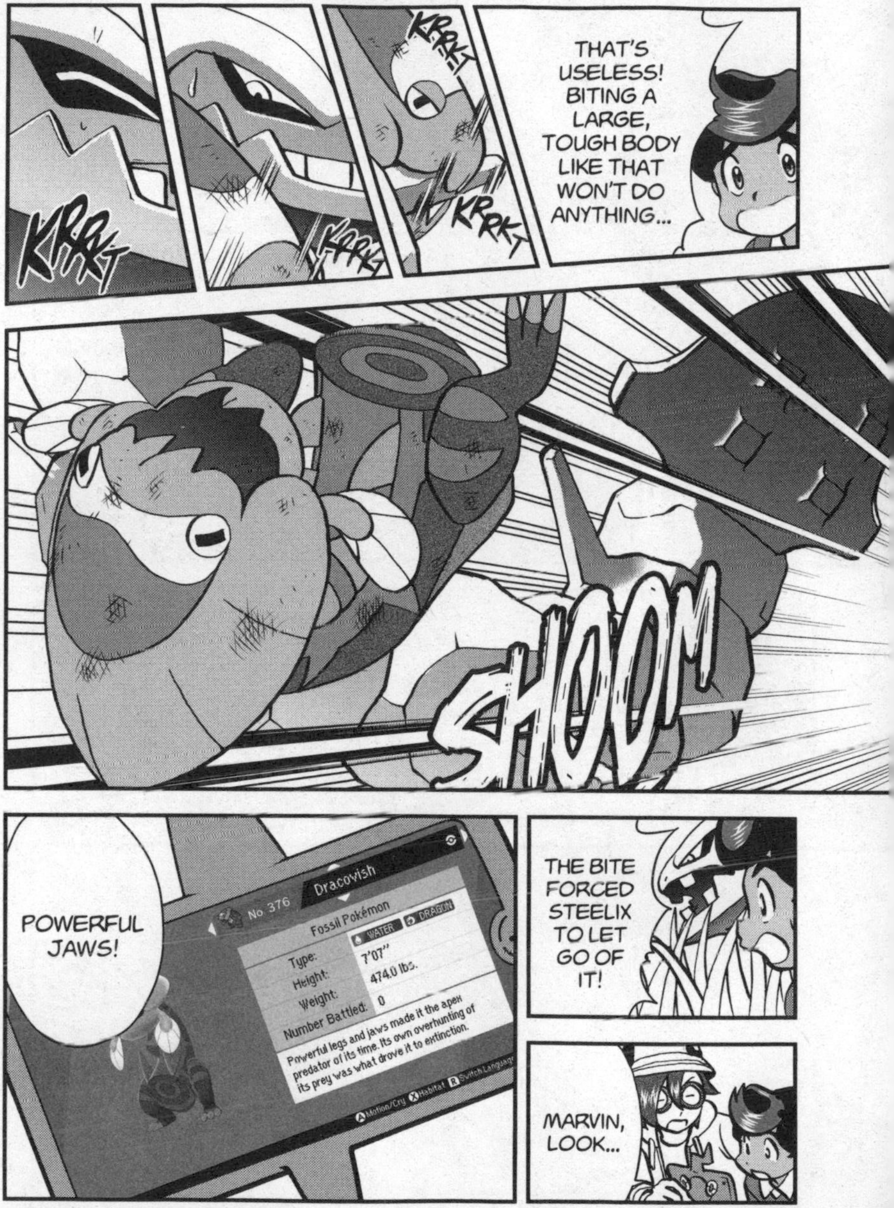
THAT'S USELESS! BITING A LARGE, TOUGH BODY LIKE THAT WON'T DO ANYTHING...
KRRKT
KRRKT
KRRKT
KRRRKT
SHOOM
THE BITE FORCED STEELIX TO LET GO OF IT!
MARVIN, LOOK...
POWERFUL JAWS!
Dracovish
No. 376
Fossil Pokémon
WATER
DRAGON
Type:
Height: 7'07"
Weight: 474.0 lbs.
Number Battled: 0
Powerful legs and jaws made it the apex predator of its time. Its own overhunting of its prey was what drove it to extinction.
Motion/Cry
Habitat
Switch Language

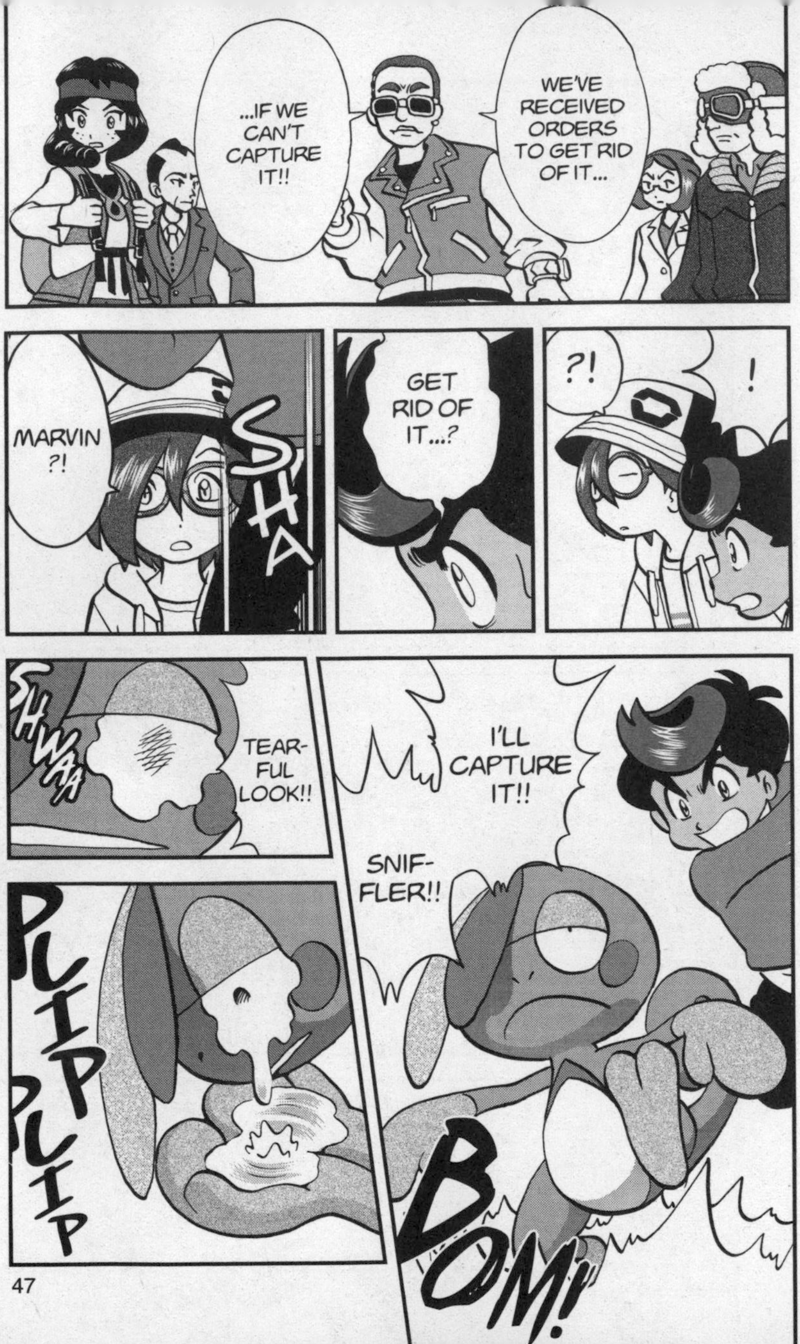
WE'VE RECEIVED ORDERS TO GET RID OF IT...
...IF WE CAN'T CAPTURE IT!!
!
?!
GET RID OF IT...?
SHA
MARVIN ?!
I'LL CAPTURE IT!!
SNIF-FLER!!
BOM!
SHWAA
TEAR-FUL LOOK!!
PLIP PLIP

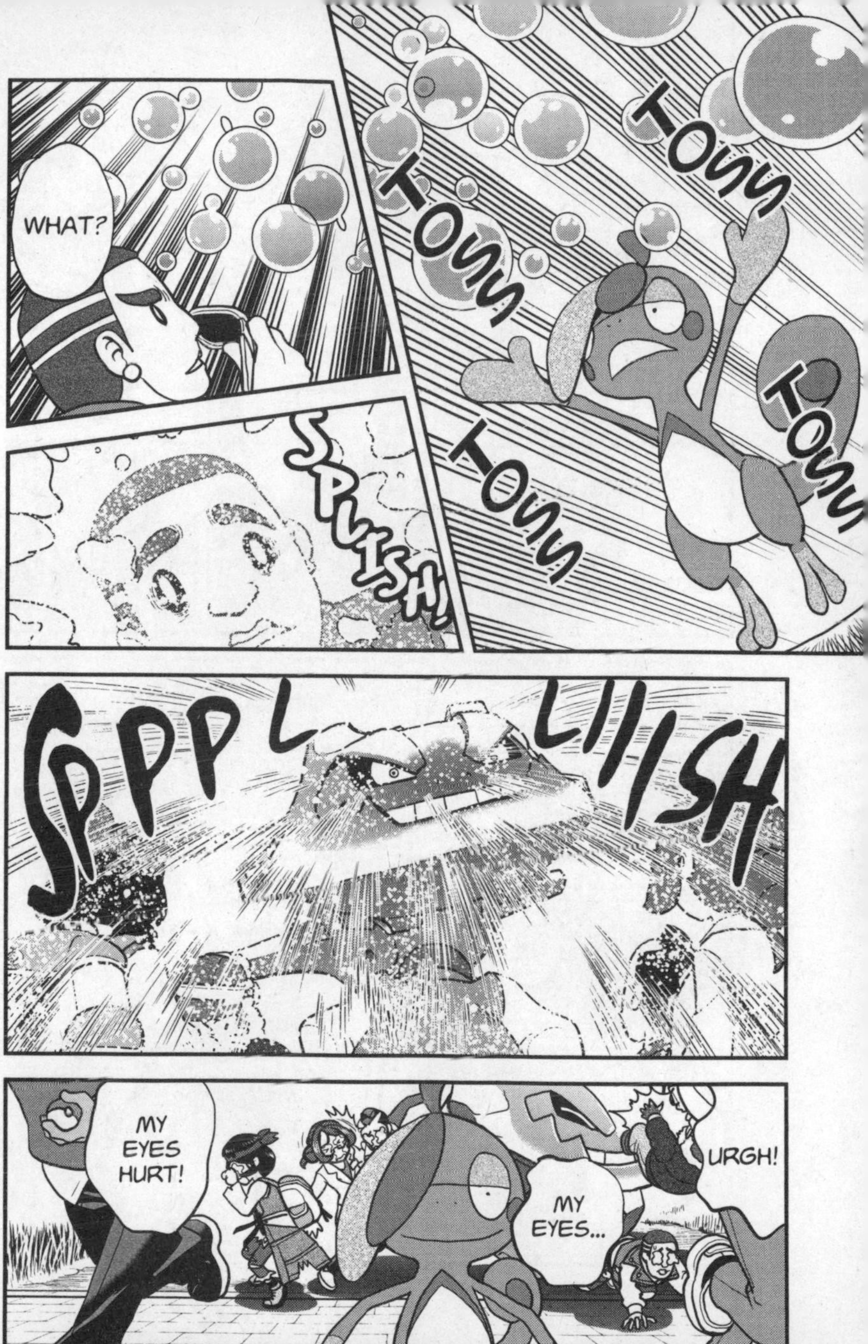
WHAT?
SPLISH!
SPPLIIISH
URGH!
MY EYES...
MY EYES HURT!

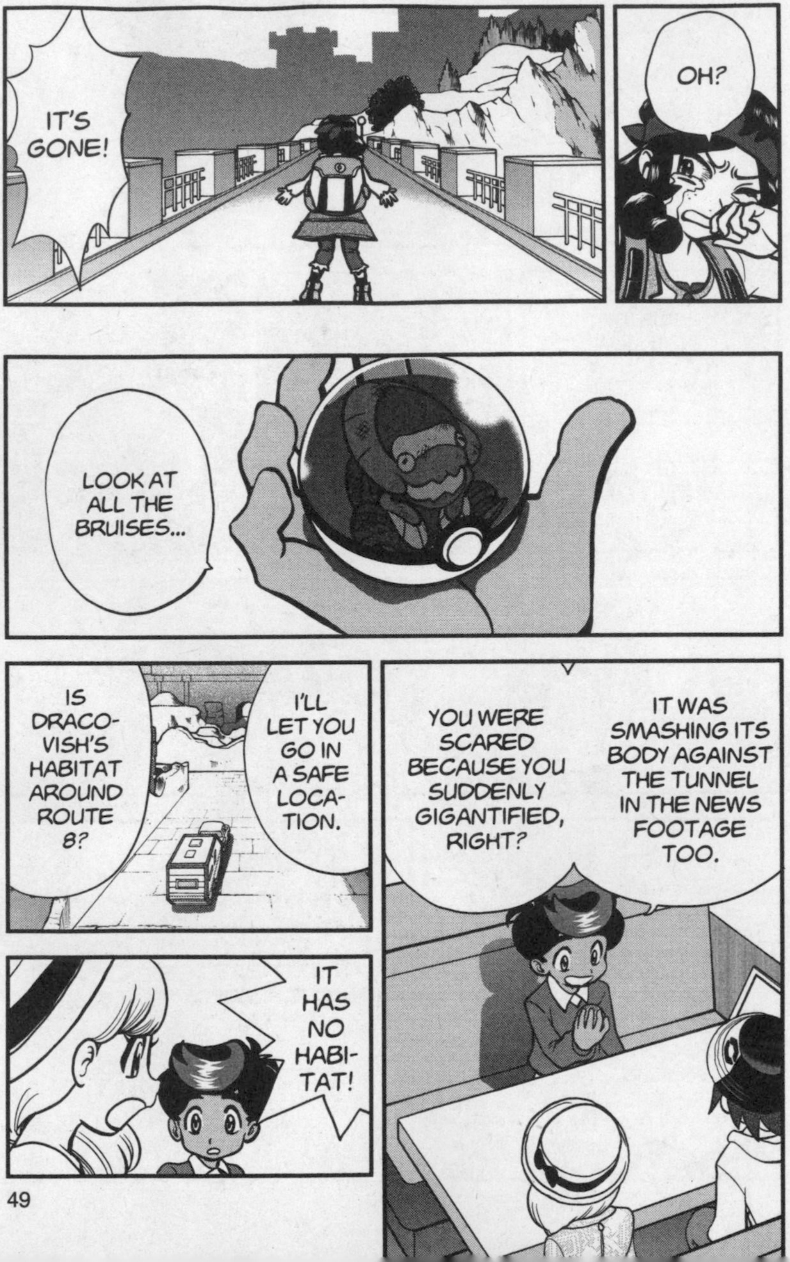
OH?
IT'S GONE!
LOOK AT ALL THE BRUISES...
IT WAS SMASHING ITS BODY AGAINST THE TUNNEL IN THE NEWS FOOTAGE TOO.
YOU WERE SCARED BECAUSE YOU SUDDENLY GIGANTIFIED, RIGHT?
I'LL LET YOU GO IN A SAFE LOCATION.
IS DRACOVISH'S HABITAT AROUND ROUTE 8?
IT HAS NO HABITAT!

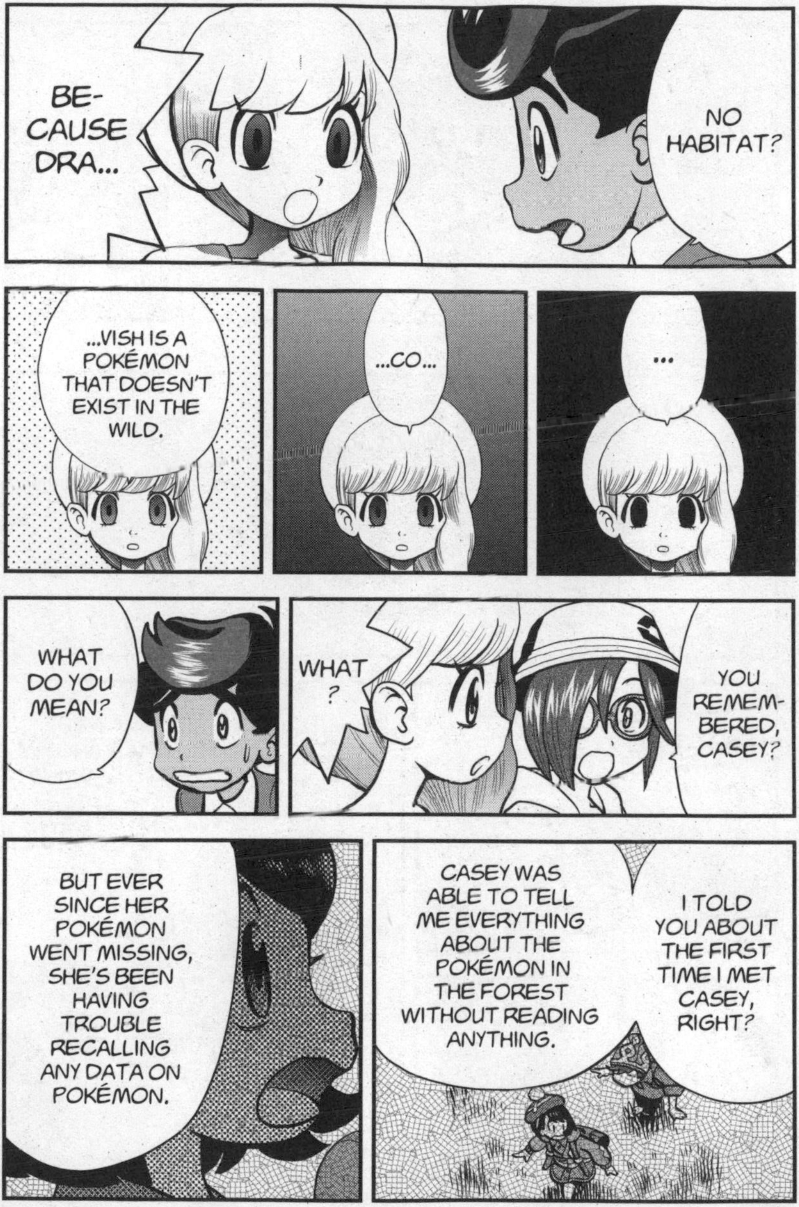
NO HABITAT?
BE-CAUSE DRA...
...
...CO...
...VISH IS A POKÉMON THAT DOESN'T EXIST IN THE WILD.
YOU REMEMBERED, CASEY?
WHAT?
WHAT DO YOU MEAN?
I TOLD YOU ABOUT THE FIRST TIME I MET CASEY, RIGHT?
CASEY WAS ABLE TO TELL ME EVERYTHING ABOUT THE POKÉMON IN THE FOREST WITHOUT READING ANYTHING.
BUT EVER SINCE HER POKÉMON WENT MISSING, SHE'S BEEN HAVING TROUBLE RECALLING ANY DATA ON POKÉMON.

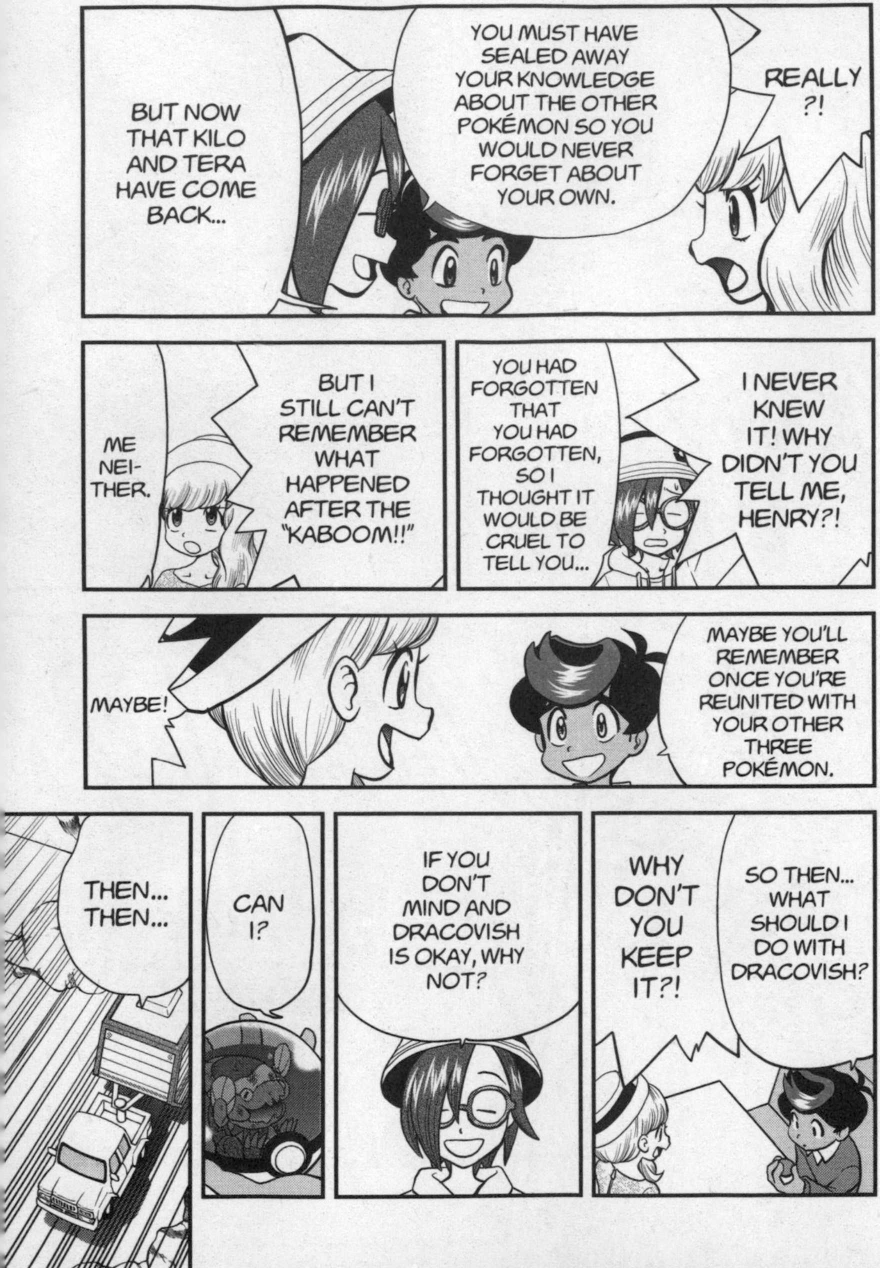
YOU MUST HAVE SEALED AWAY YOUR KNOWLEDGE ABOUT THE OTHER POKÉMON SO YOU WOULD NEVER FORGET ABOUT YOUR OWN.
REALLY ?!
BUT NOW THAT KILO AND TERA HAVE COME BACK...
I NEVER KNEW IT! WHY DIDN'T YOU TELL ME, HENRY?!
YOU HAD FORGOTTEN THAT YOU HAD FORGOTTEN, SO I THOUGHT IT WOULD BE CRUEL TO TELL YOU...
BUT I STILL CAN'T REMEMBER WHAT HAPPENED AFTER THE "KABOOM!!"
ME NEI-THER.
MAYBE YOU'LL REMEMBER ONCE YOU'RE REUNITED WITH YOUR OTHER THREE POKÉMON.
MAYBE!
SO THEN... WHAT SHOULD I DO WITH DRACOVISH?
WHY DON'T YOU KEEP IT?!
IF YOU DON'T MIND AND DRACOVISH IS OKAY, WHY NOT?
CAN I?
THEN... THEN...

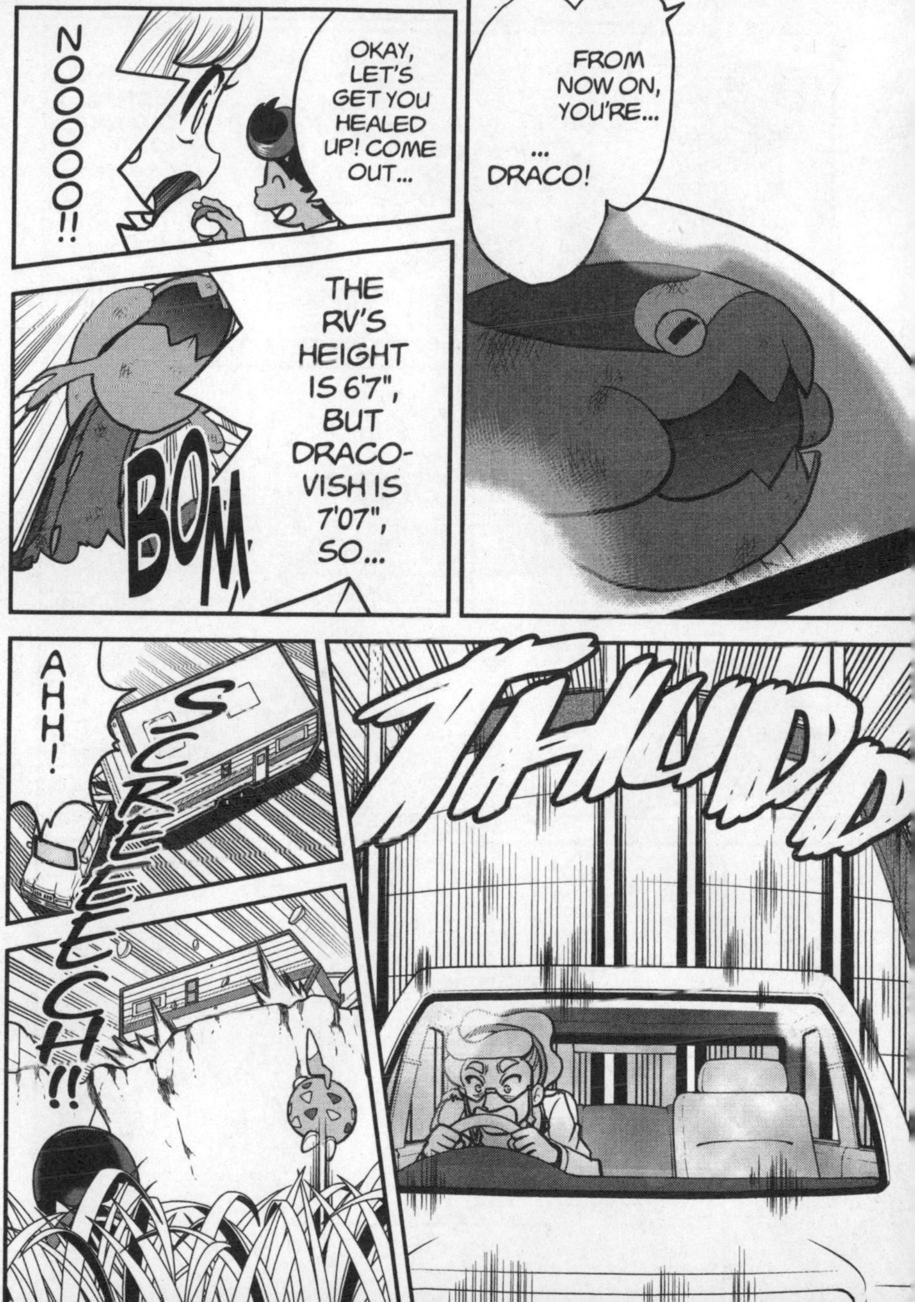
FROM NOW ON, YOU'RE...
... DRACO!
OKAY, LET'S GET YOU HEALED UP! COME OUT...
NOOOOOO!!
THE RV'S HEIGHT IS 6'7", BUT DRACOVISH IS 7'07", SO...
BOM
THUDD
AHH!
SCREEEECH!!

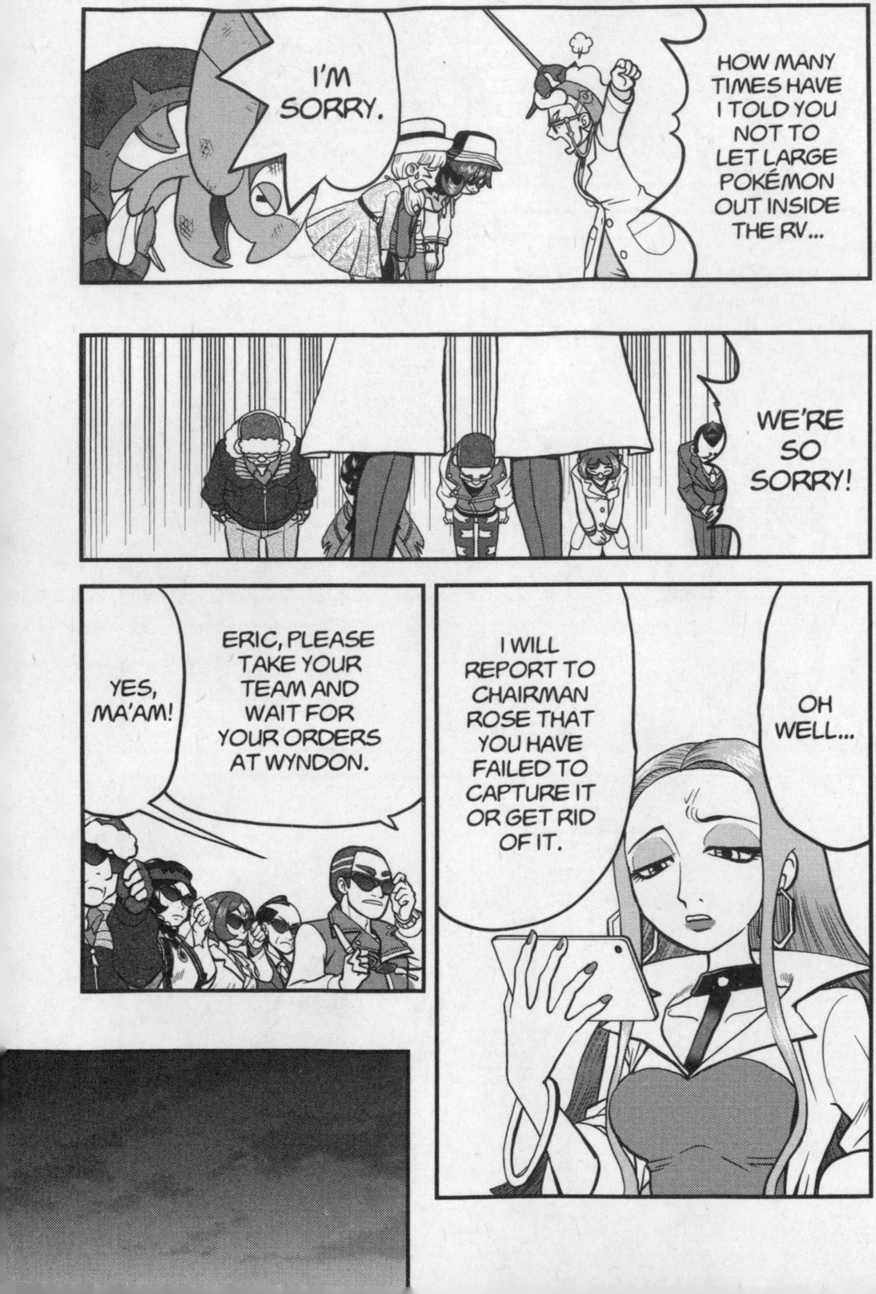
HOW MANY TIMES HAVE I TOLD YOU NOT TO LET LARGE POKÉMON OUT INSIDE THE RV...
I'M SORRY.
WE'RE SO SORRY!
OH WELL...
I WILL REPORT TO CHAIRMAN ROSE THAT YOU HAVE FAILED TO CAPTURE IT OR GET RID OF IT.
ERIC, PLEASE TAKE YOUR TEAM AND WAIT FOR YOUR ORDERS AT WYNDON.
YES, MA'AM!

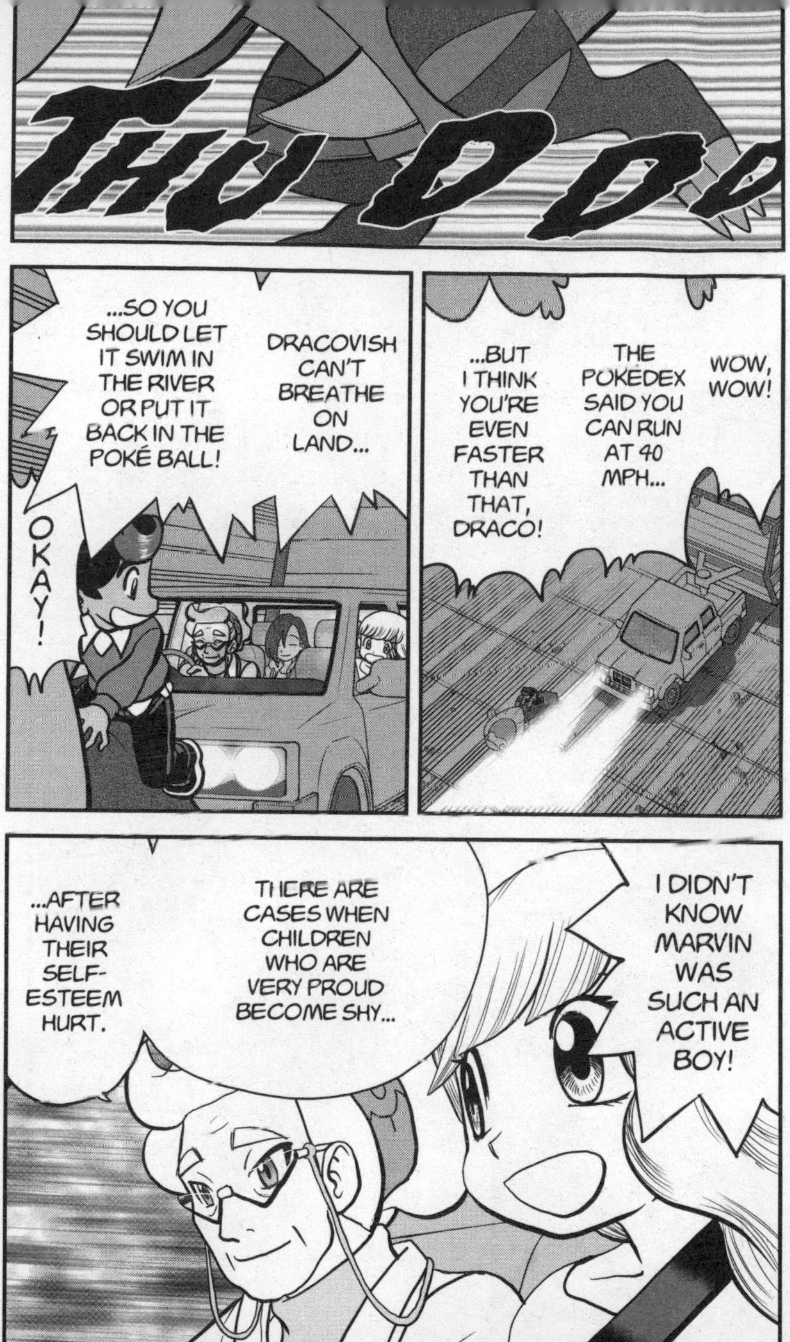
THUD DU
WOW, WOW!
THE POKEDEX SAID YOU CAN RUN AT 40 MPH...
...BUT I THINK YOU'RE EVEN FASTER THAN THAT, DRACO!
DRACOVISH CAN'T BREATHE ON LAND...
...SO YOU SHOULD LET IT SWIM IN THE RIVER OR PUT IT BACK IN THE POKÉ BALL!
OKAY!
I DIDN'T KNOW MARVIN WAS SUCH AN ACTIVE BOY!
THERE ARE CASES WHEN CHILDREN WHO ARE VERY PROUD BECOME SHY...
...AFTER HAVING THEIR SELF-ESTEEM HURT.

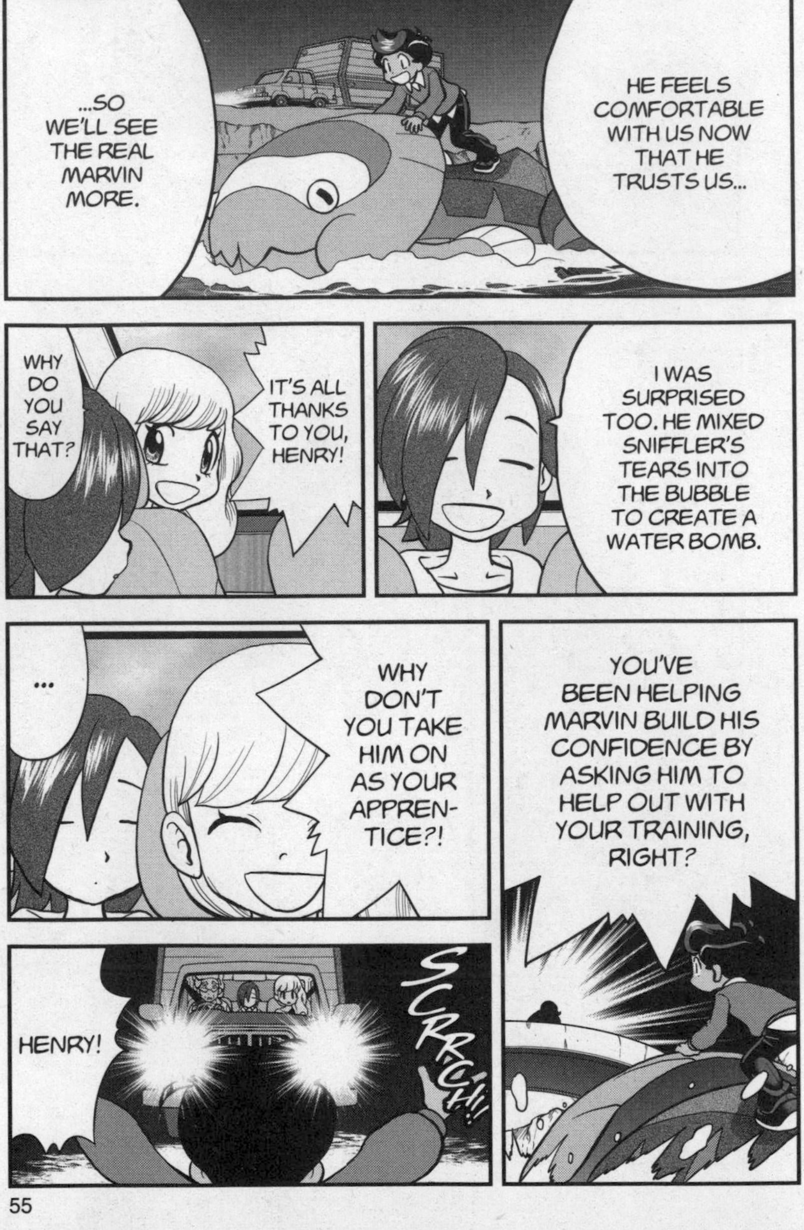
HE FEELS COMFORTABLE WITH US NOW THAT HE TRUSTS US...
...SO WE'LL SEE THE REAL MARVIN MORE.
I WAS SURPRISED TOO. HE MIXED SNIFFLER'S TEARS INTO THE BUBBLE TO CREATE A WATER BOMB.
IT'S ALL THANKS TO YOU, HENRY!
WHY DO YOU SAY THAT?
YOU'VE BEEN HELPING MARVIN BUILD HIS CONFIDENCE BY ASKING HIM TO HELP OUT WITH YOUR TRAINING, RIGHT?
WHY DON'T YOU TAKE HIM ON AS YOUR APPREN-TICE?!
...
SCRRCH!!
HENRY!

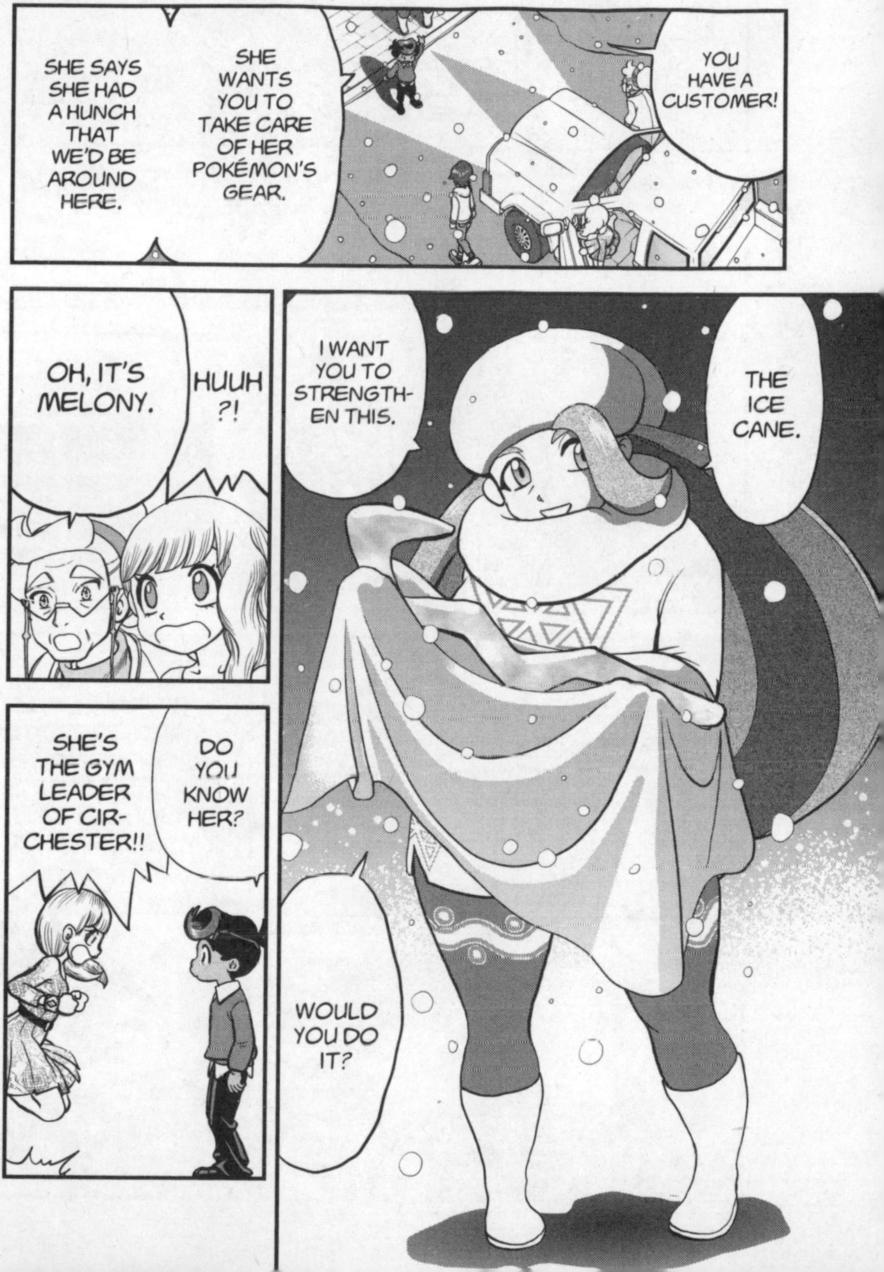
YOU HAVE A CUSTOMER!
SHE WANTS YOU TO TAKE CARE OF HER POKÉMON'S GEAR.
SHE SAYS SHE HAD A HUNCH THAT WE'D BE AROUND HERE.
THE ICE CANE.
I WANT YOU TO STRENGTH-EN THIS.
WOULD YOU DO IT?
HUUH ?!
OH, IT'S MELONY.
DO YOU KNOW HER?
SHE'S THE GYM LEADER OF CIR-CHESTER!!

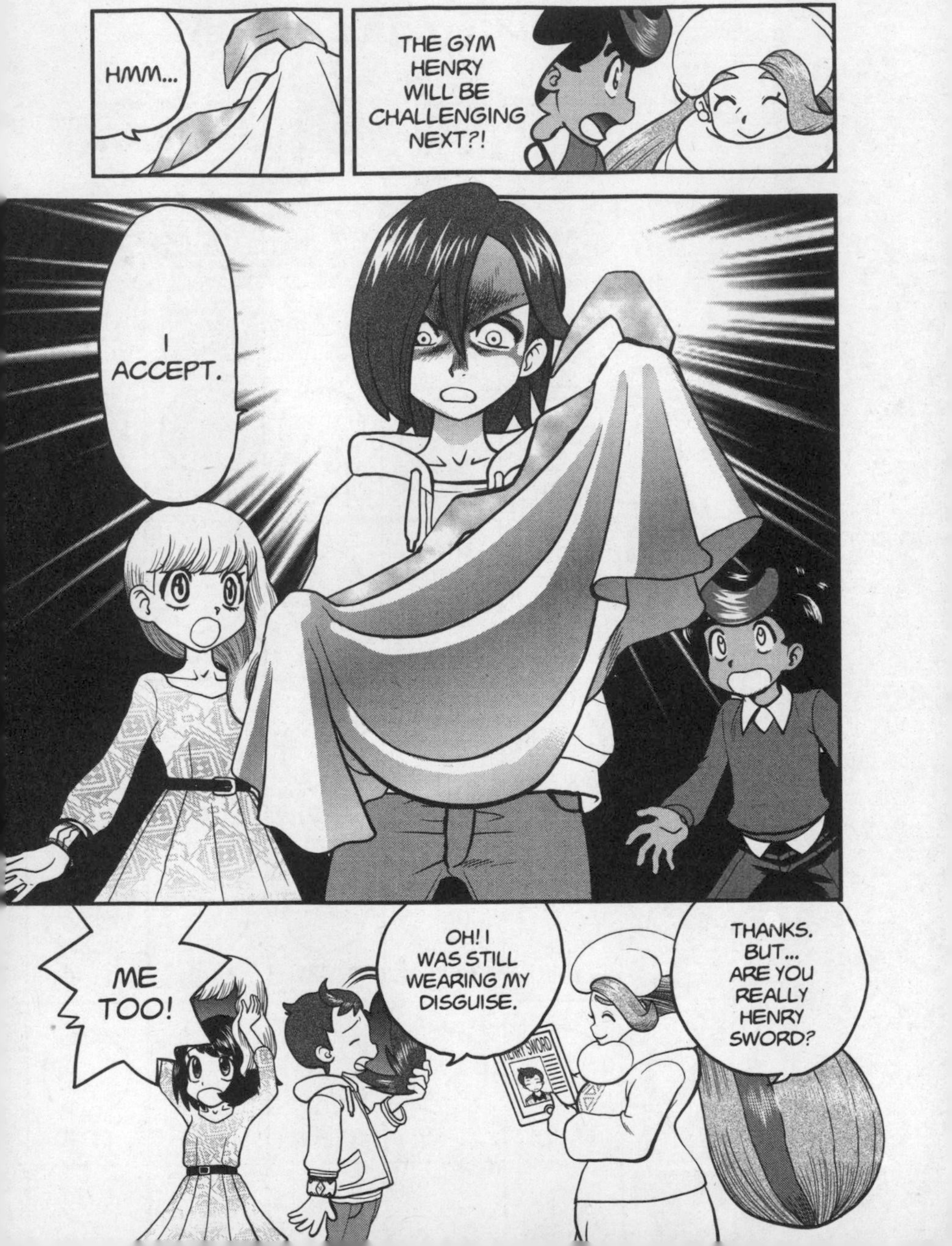
THE GYM HENRY WILL BE CHALLENGING NEXT?!
HMM...
I ACCEPT.
THANKS. BUT... ARE YOU REALLY HENRY SWORD?
HENRY SWORD
OH! I WAS STILL WEARING MY DISGUISE.
ME TOO!

(Pokémon League)

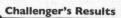

● Challenger's Results   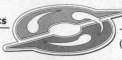   Gym Challenge ●

○:Victory
●: Defeat

(2–0): Remaining Pokémon

		TURFFIELD STADIUM **MILO**	HULBURY STADIUM **NESSA**	MOTOSTOKE STADIUM **KABU**	STOW-ON-SIDE STADIUM **BEA** ALLISTER	BALLONLEA STADIUM **OPAL**
ENDORSED BY THE CHAMPION	**HENRY**	○ (2–0)	○ (2–0)	○ (3–0)	○ (2–0)	○ (2–0)
	CASEY	○ (1–0)	○ (1–0)	○ (1–0)	○ (1–0)	● (0–3)
ENDORSED BY THE CHAIRMAN	**BEDE**	○ (2–0)	○ (1–0)	○ (2–0)	DISQUALIFIED	■ ■ ■
NORMAL CHALLENGERS	**HOP**	○ (1–0)	○ (2–0)	○ (1–0)	○ (1–0)	○ (1–0)
	MARNIE	○ (1–0)	○ (1–0)	○ (2–0)	○ (1–0)	○ (1–0)

Adventure 19 Crunch!! Snowy Battle

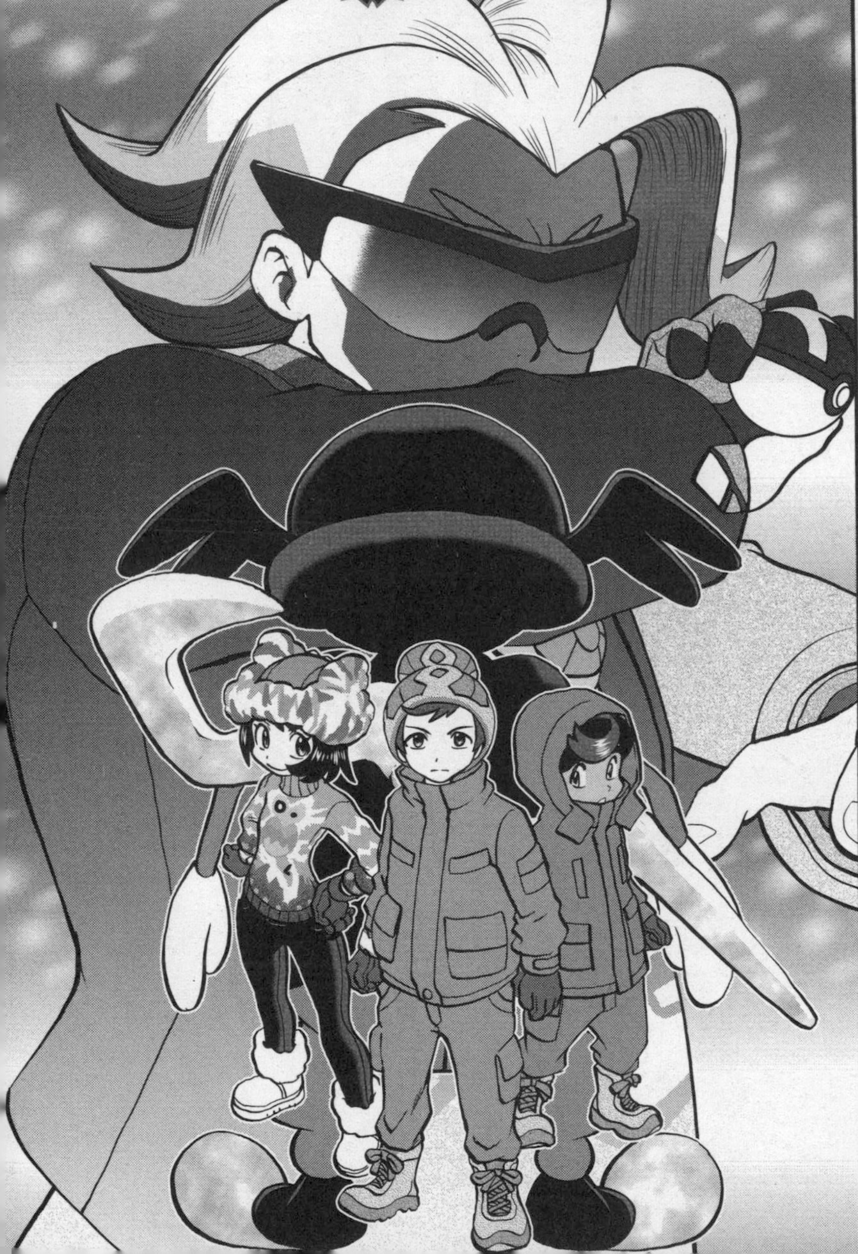

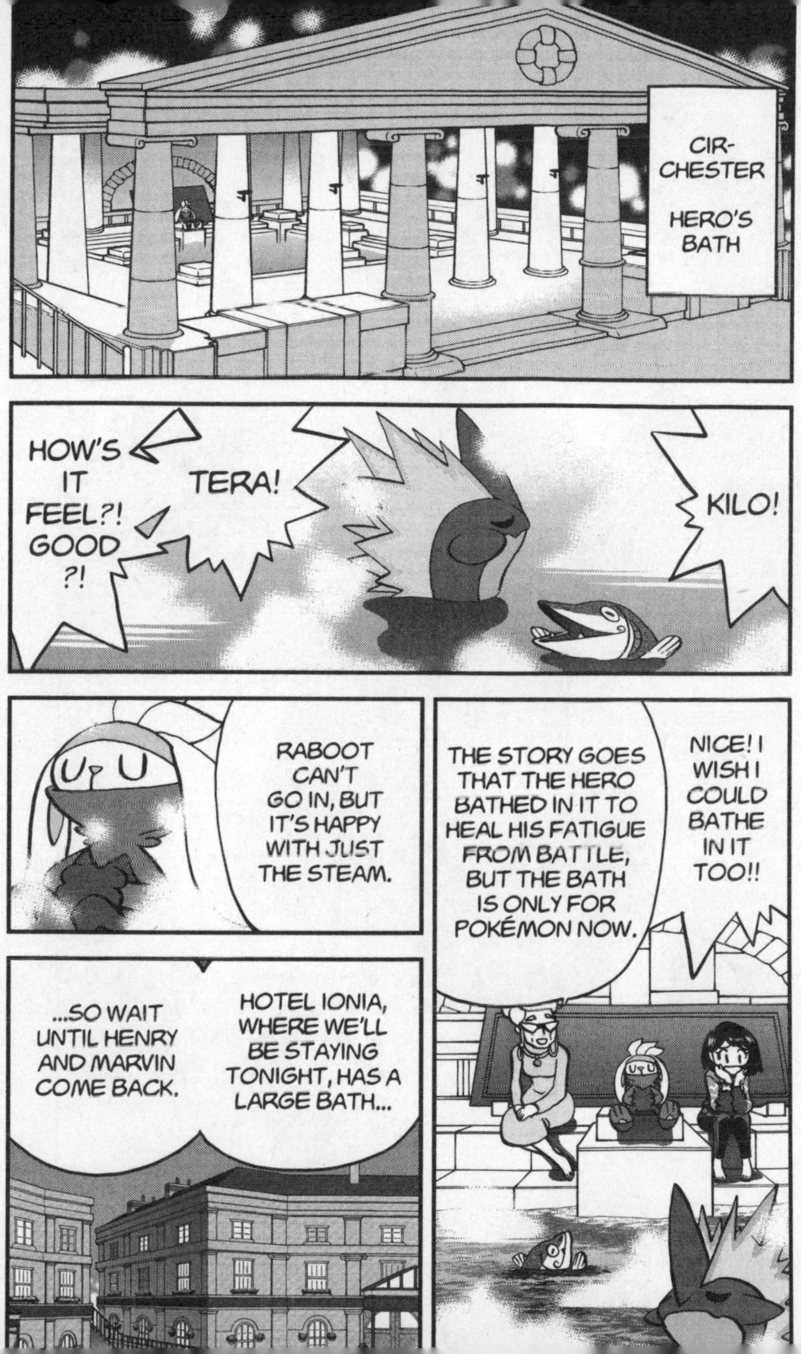
CIR-CHESTER
HERO'S BATH
KILO!
TERA!
HOW'S IT FEEL?! GOOD?!
NICE! I WISH I COULD BATHE IN IT TOO!!
THE STORY GOES THAT THE HERO BATHED IN IT TO HEAL HIS FATIGUE FROM BATTLE, BUT THE BATH IS ONLY FOR POKÉMON NOW.
RABOOT CAN'T GO IN, BUT IT'S HAPPY WITH JUST THE STEAM.
HOTEL IONIA, WHERE WE'LL BE STAYING TONIGHT, HAS A LARGE BATH...
...SO WAIT UNTIL HENRY AND MARVIN COME BACK.

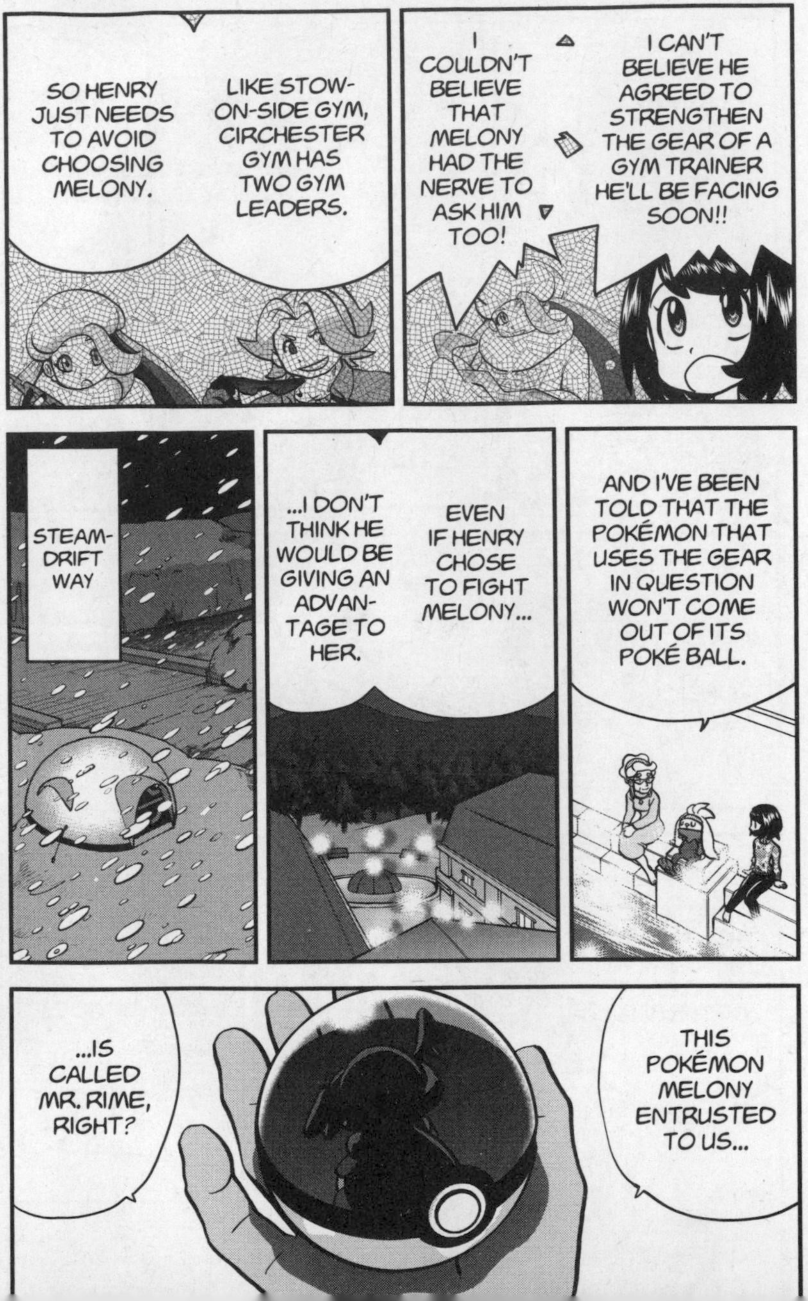
I CAN'T BELIEVE HE AGREED TO STRENGTHEN THE GEAR OF A GYM TRAINER HE'LL BE FACING SOON!!
I COULDN'T BELIEVE THAT MELONY HAD THE NERVE TO ASK HIM TOO!
LIKE STOW-ON-SIDE GYM, CIRCHESTER GYM HAS TWO GYM LEADERS.
SO HENRY JUST NEEDS TO AVOID CHOOSING MELONY.
AND I'VE BEEN TOLD THAT THE POKÉMON THAT USES THE GEAR IN QUESTION WON'T COME OUT OF ITS POKÉ BALL.
EVEN IF HENRY CHOSE TO FIGHT MELONY...
...I DON'T THINK HE WOULD BE GIVING AN ADVANTAGE TO HER.
STEAMDRIFT WAY
THIS POKÉMON MELONY ENTRUSTED TO US...
...IS CALLED MR. RIME, RIGHT?

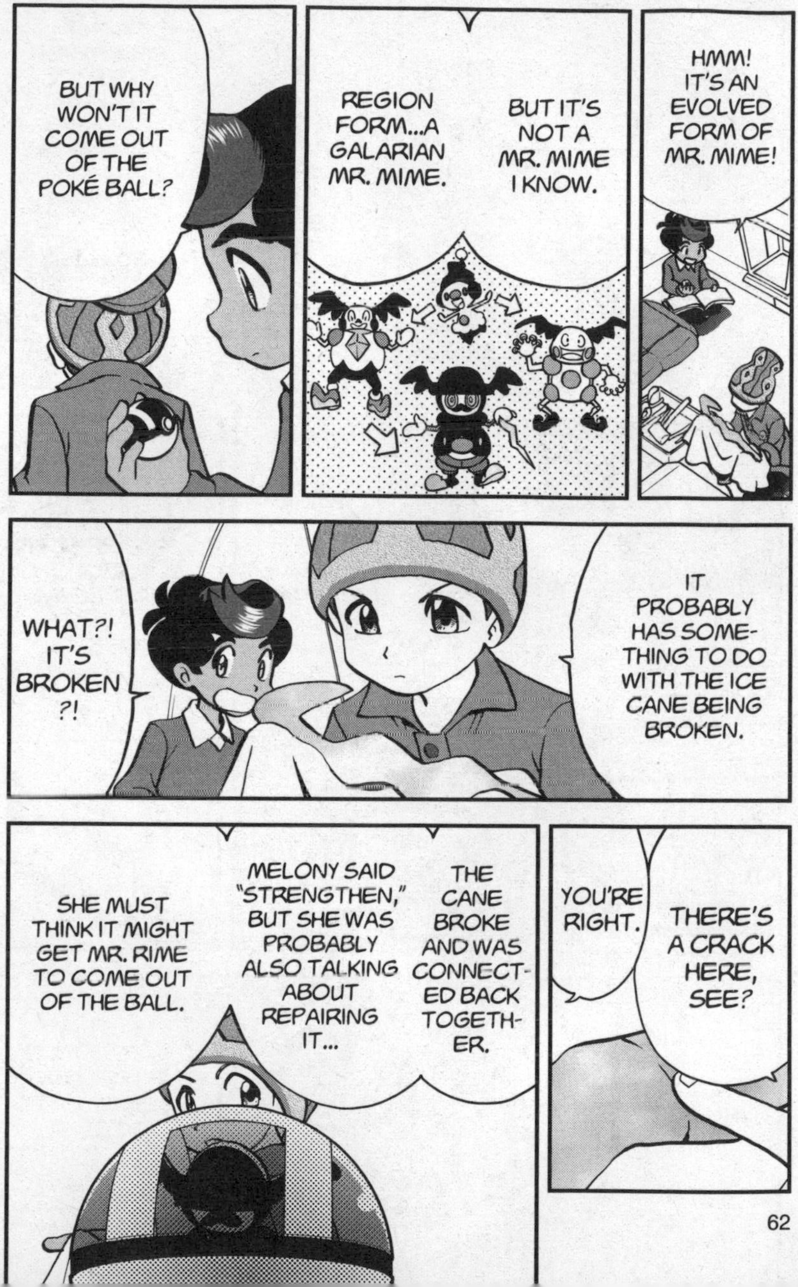
HMM! IT'S AN EVOLVED FORM OF MR. MIME!
BUT IT'S NOT A MR. MIME I KNOW.
REGION FORM...A GALARIAN MR. MIME.
BUT WHY WON'T IT COME OUT OF THE POKÉ BALL?
IT PROBABLY HAS SOME-THING TO DO WITH THE ICE CANE BEING BROKEN.
WHAT?! IT'S BROKEN?!
THERE'S A CRACK HERE, SEE?
YOU'RE RIGHT.
THE CANE BROKE AND WAS CONNECT-ED BACK TOGETH-ER.
MELONY SAID "STRENGTHEN," BUT SHE WAS PROBABLY ALSO TALKING ABOUT REPAIRING IT...
SHE MUST THINK IT MIGHT GET MR. RIME TO COME OUT OF THE BALL.

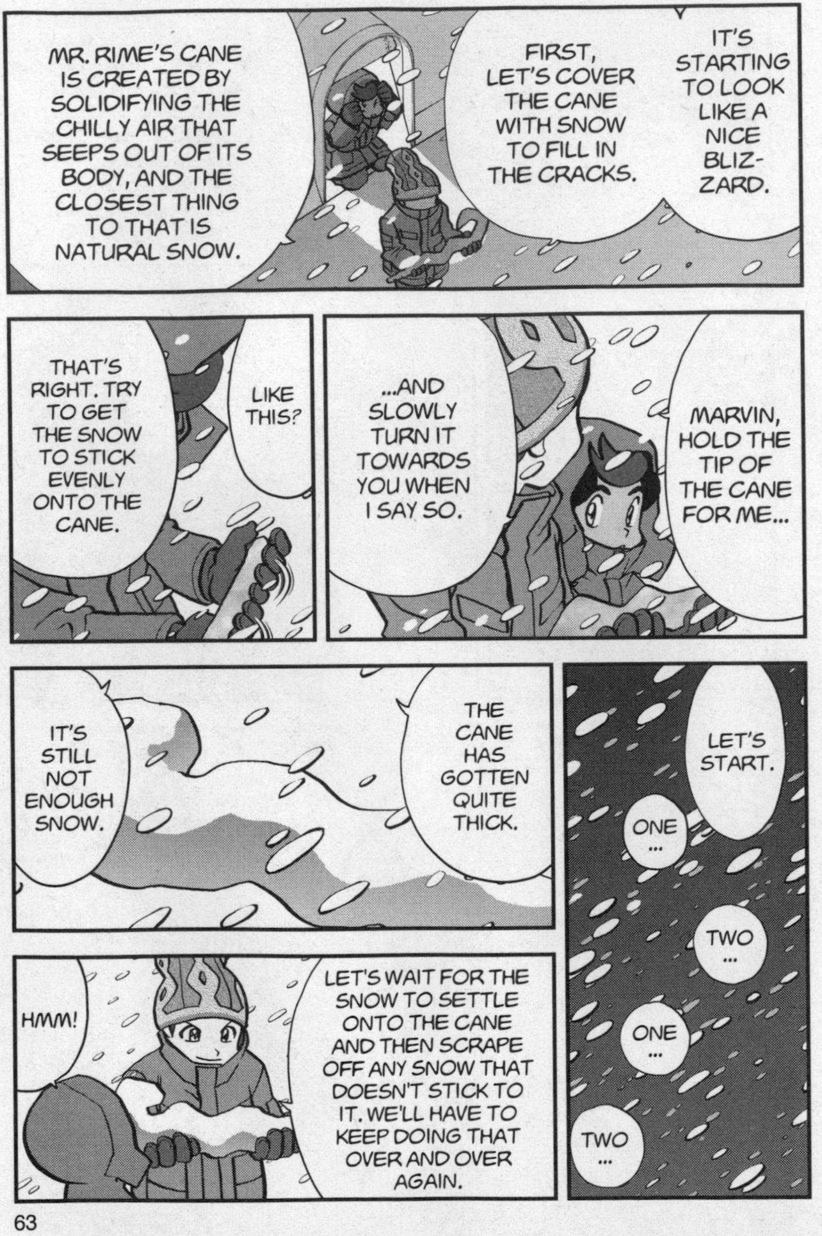
IT'S STARTING TO LOOK LIKE A NICE BLIZ- ZARD.
FIRST, LET'S COVER THE CANE WITH SNOW TO FILL IN THE CRACKS.
MR. RIME'S CANE IS CREATED BY SOLIDIFYING THE CHILLY AIR THAT SEEPS OUT OF ITS BODY, AND THE CLOSEST THING TO THAT IS NATURAL SNOW.
MARVIN, HOLD THE TIP OF THE CANE FOR ME...
...AND SLOWLY TURN IT TOWARDS YOU WHEN I SAY SO.
LIKE THIS?
THAT'S RIGHT. TRY TO GET THE SNOW TO STICK EVENLY ONTO THE CANE.
LET'S START.
ONE ...
TWO ...
ONE ...
TWO ...
THE CANE HAS GOTTEN QUITE THICK.
IT'S STILL NOT ENOUGH SNOW.
LET'S WAIT FOR THE SNOW TO SETTLE ONTO THE CANE AND THEN SCRAPE OFF ANY SNOW THAT DOESN'T STICK TO IT. WE'LL HAVE TO KEEP DOING THAT OVER AND OVER AGAIN.
HMM!

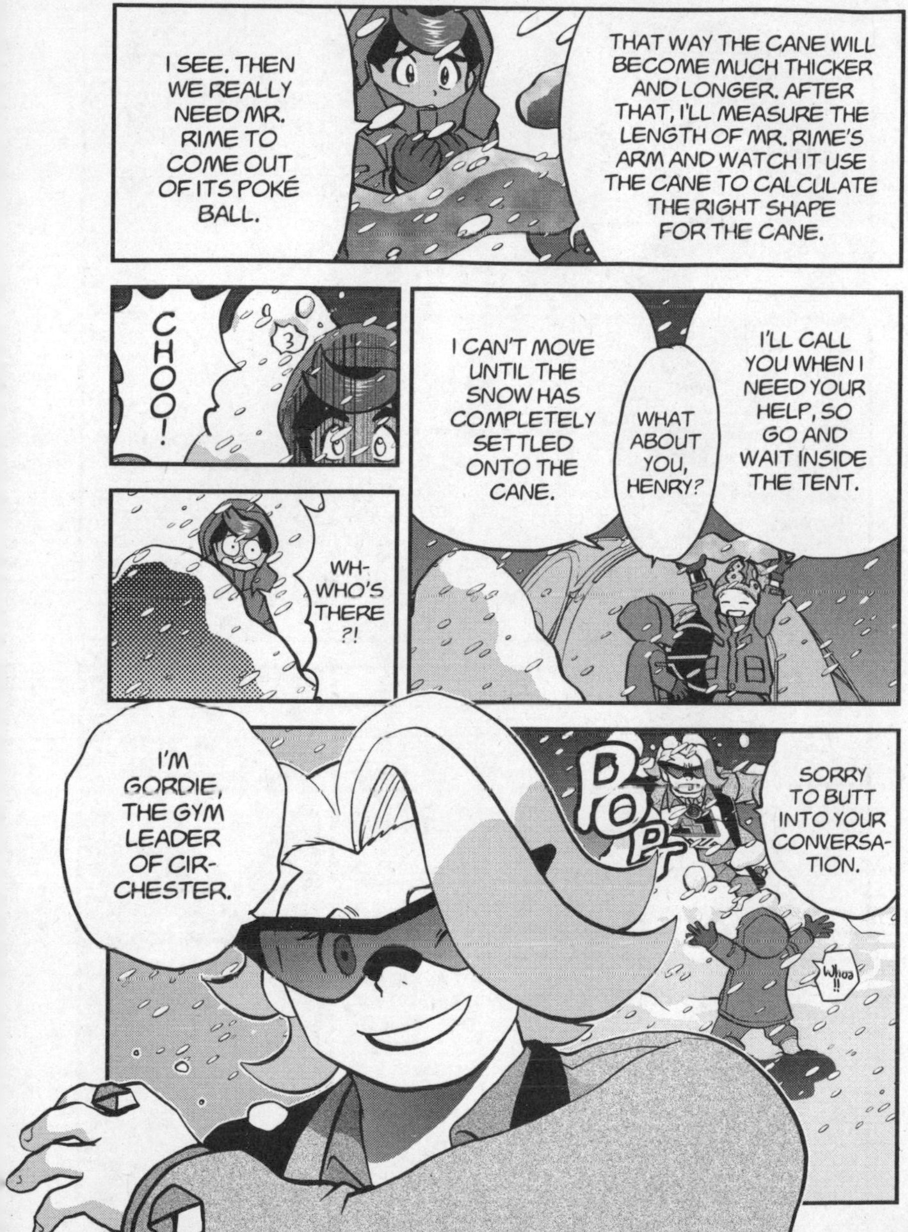
THAT WAY THE CANE WILL BECOME MUCH THICKER AND LONGER. AFTER THAT, I'LL MEASURE THE LENGTH OF MR. RIME'S ARM AND WATCH IT USE THE CANE TO CALCULATE THE RIGHT SHAPE FOR THE CANE.
I SEE. THEN WE REALLY NEED MR. RIME TO COME OUT OF ITS POKÉ BALL.
I'LL CALL YOU WHEN I NEED YOUR HELP, SO GO AND WAIT INSIDE THE TENT.
WHAT ABOUT YOU, HENRY?
I CAN'T MOVE UNTIL THE SNOW HAS COMPLETELY SETTLED ONTO THE CANE.
CHOO!
WH-WHO'S THERE ?!
SORRY TO BUTT INTO YOUR CONVERSATION.
POP
Whoa !!
I'M GORDIE, THE GYM LEADER OF CIRCHESTER.

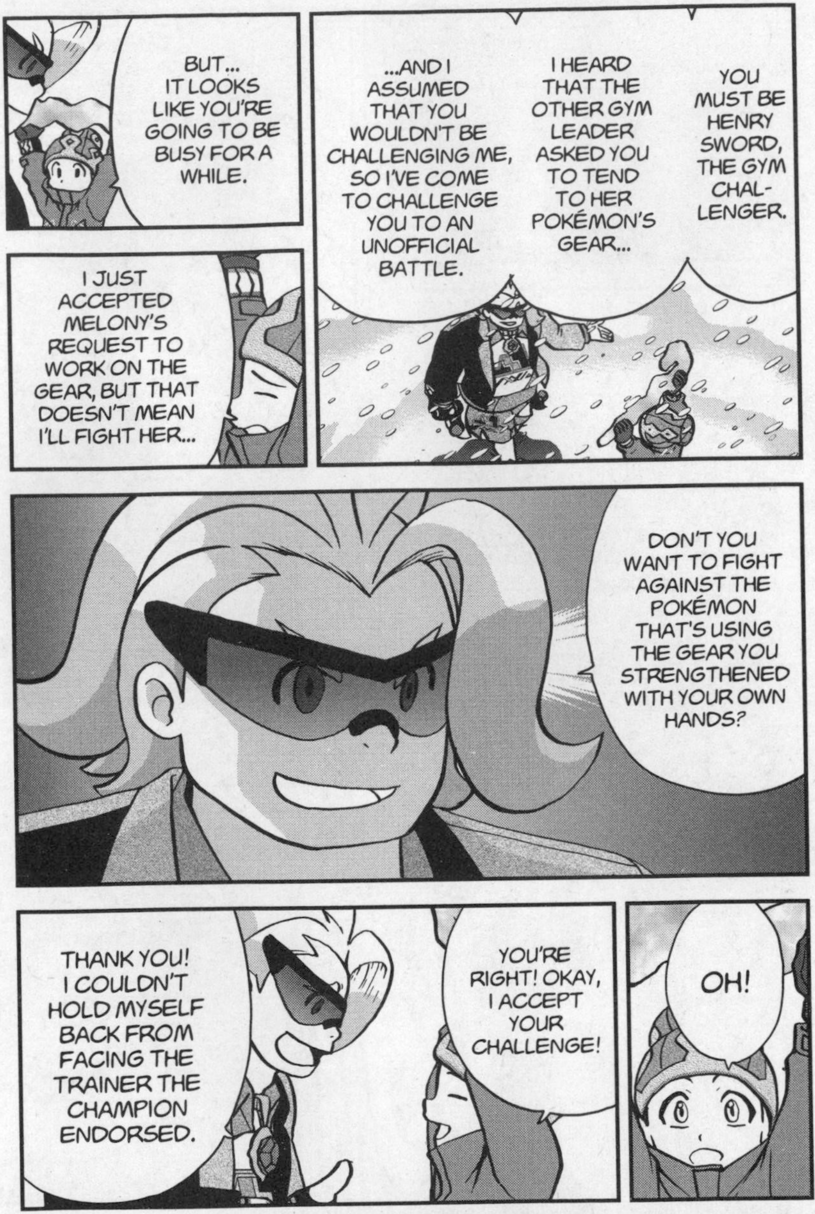
YOU MUST BE HENRY SWORD, THE GYM CHAL-LENGER.
I HEARD THAT THE OTHER GYM LEADER ASKED YOU TO TEND TO HER POKÉMON'S GEAR...
...AND I ASSUMED THAT YOU WOULDN'T BE CHALLENGING ME, SO I'VE COME TO CHALLENGE YOU TO AN UNOFFICIAL BATTLE.
BUT... IT LOOKS LIKE YOU'RE GOING TO BE BUSY FOR A WHILE.
I JUST ACCEPTED MELONY'S REQUEST TO WORK ON THE GEAR, BUT THAT DOESN'T MEAN I'LL FIGHT HER...
DON'T YOU WANT TO FIGHT AGAINST THE POKÉMON THAT'S USING THE GEAR YOU STRENGTHENED WITH YOUR OWN HANDS?
OH!
YOU'RE RIGHT! OKAY, I ACCEPT YOUR CHALLENGE!
THANK YOU! I COULDN'T HOLD MYSELF BACK FROM FACING THE TRAINER THE CHAMPION ENDORSED.

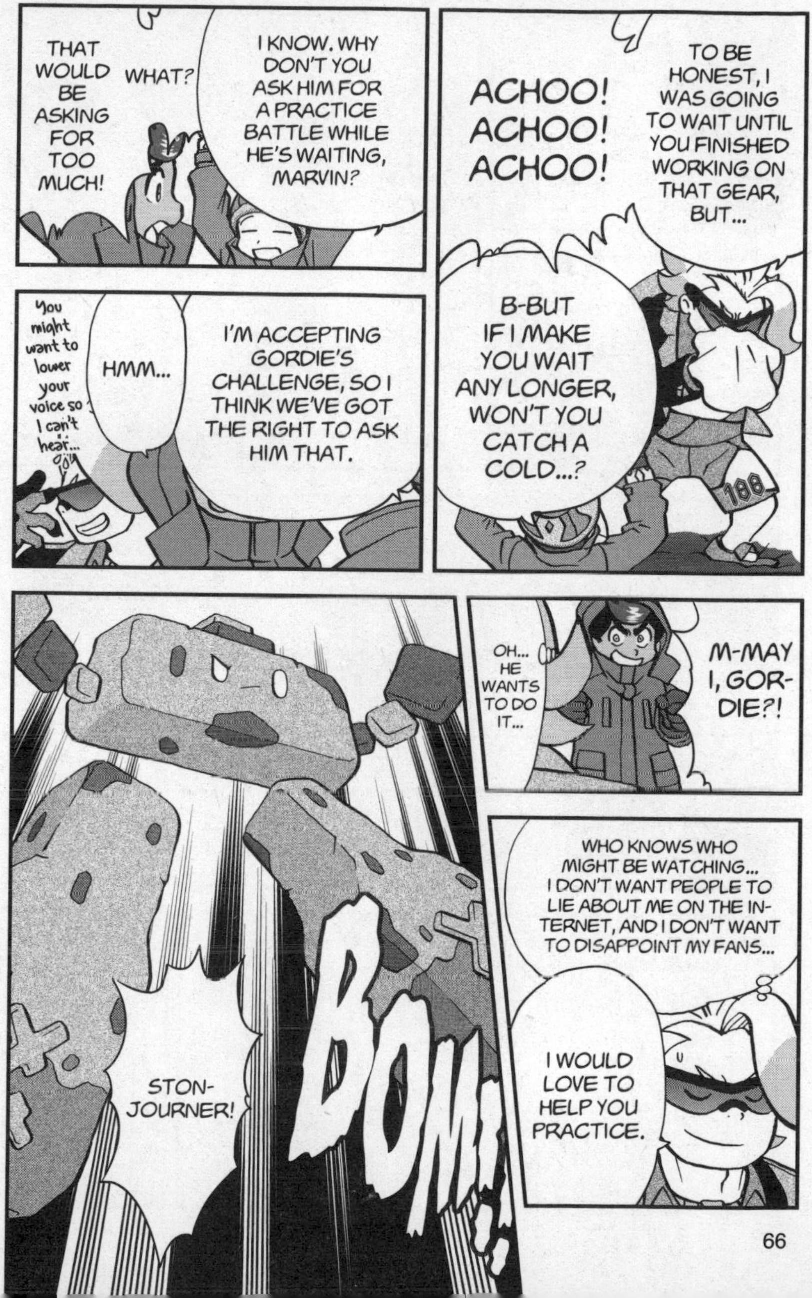

TO BE HONEST, I WAS GOING TO WAIT UNTIL YOU FINISHED WORKING ON THAT GEAR, BUT...
ACHOO! ACHOO! ACHOO!
I KNOW. WHY DON'T YOU ASK HIM FOR A PRACTICE BATTLE WHILE HE'S WAITING, MARVIN?
WHAT?
THAT WOULD BE ASKING FOR TOO MUCH!
B-BUT IF I MAKE YOU WAIT ANY LONGER, WON'T YOU CATCH A COLD...?
I'M ACCEPTING GORDIE'S CHALLENGE, SO I THINK WE'VE GOT THE RIGHT TO ASK HIM THAT.
HMM...
You might want to lower your voice so I can't hear...
M-MAY I, GOR-DIE?!
OH... HE WANTS TO DO IT...
WHO KNOWS WHO MIGHT BE WATCHING... I DON'T WANT PEOPLE TO LIE ABOUT ME ON THE IN-TERNET, AND I DON'T WANT TO DISAPPOINT MY FANS...
I WOULD LOVE TO HELP YOU PRACTICE.
BOM
STON-JOURNER!

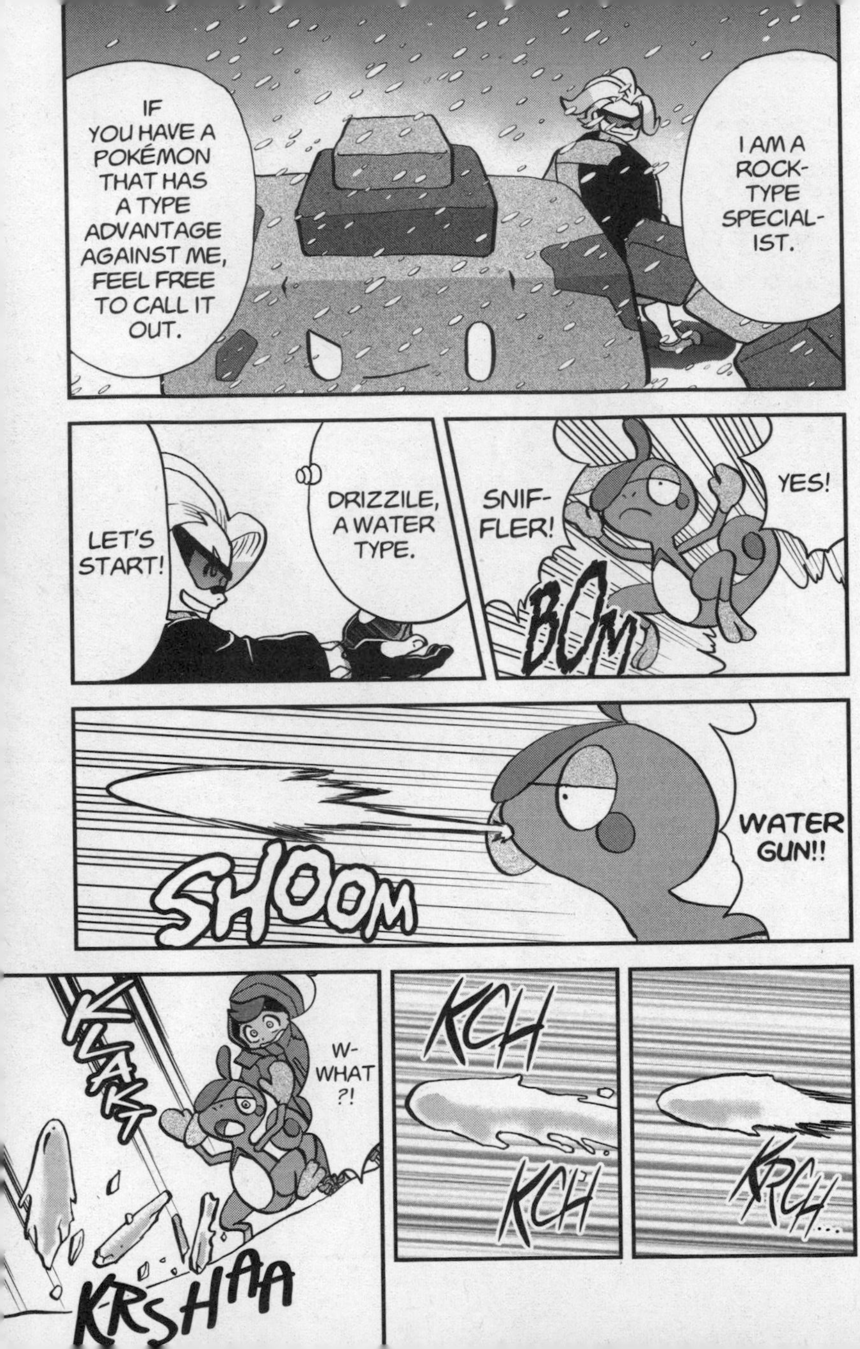
I AM A ROCK-TYPE SPECIAL-IST.
IF YOU HAVE A POKÉMON THAT HAS A TYPE ADVANTAGE AGAINST ME, FEEL FREE TO CALL IT OUT.
YES!
SNIF-FLER!
BOM
DRIZZILE, A WATER TYPE.
LET'S START!
WATER GUN!!
SHOOM
KRCH...
KCH
KCH
W-WHAT?!
KLAK
KRSHAA

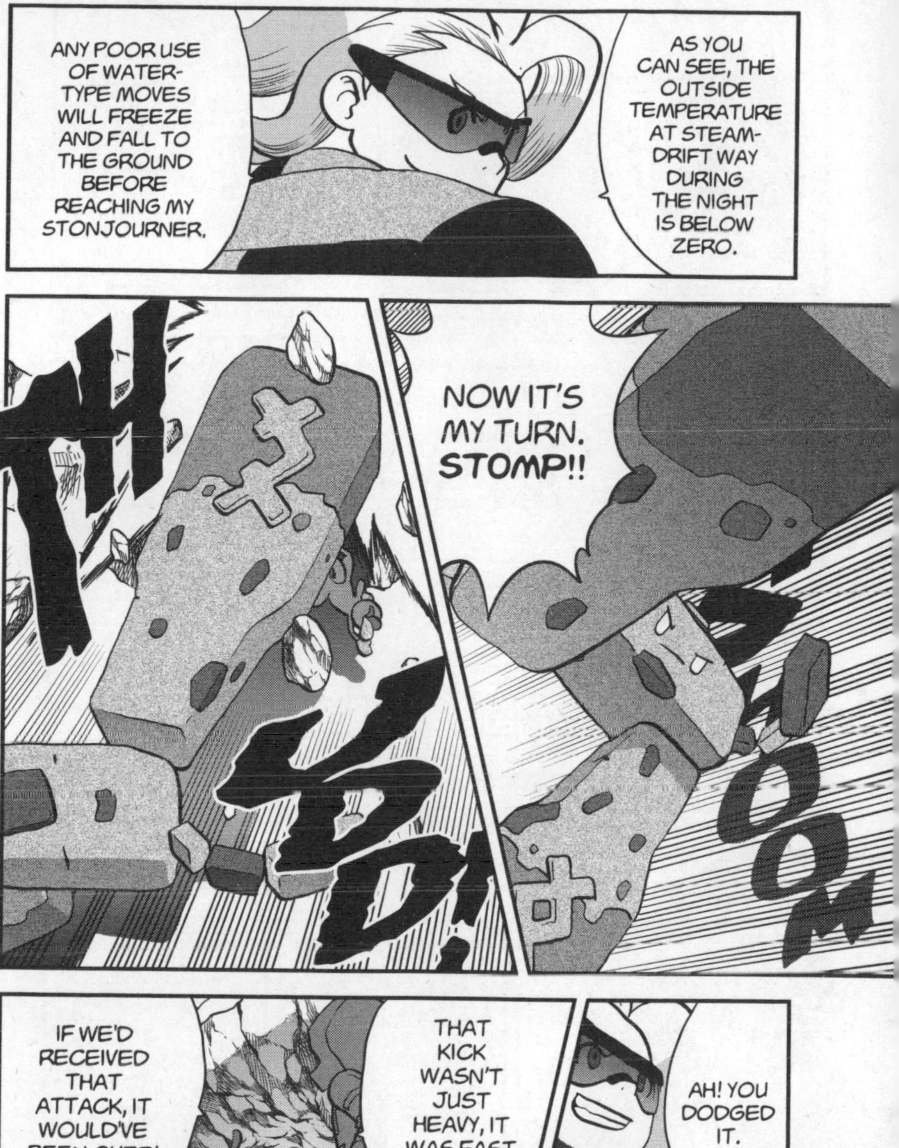
AS YOU CAN SEE, THE OUTSIDE TEMPERATURE AT STEAM-DRIFT WAY DURING THE NIGHT IS BELOW ZERO.
ANY POOR USE OF WATER-TYPE MOVES WILL FREEZE AND FALL TO THE GROUND BEFORE REACHING MY STONJOURNER.
NOW IT'S MY TURN. **STOMP!!**
AH! YOU DODGED IT.
THAT KICK WASN'T JUST HEAVY, IT WAS FAST TOO!
IF WE'D RECEIVED THAT ATTACK, IT WOULD'VE BEEN OVER!

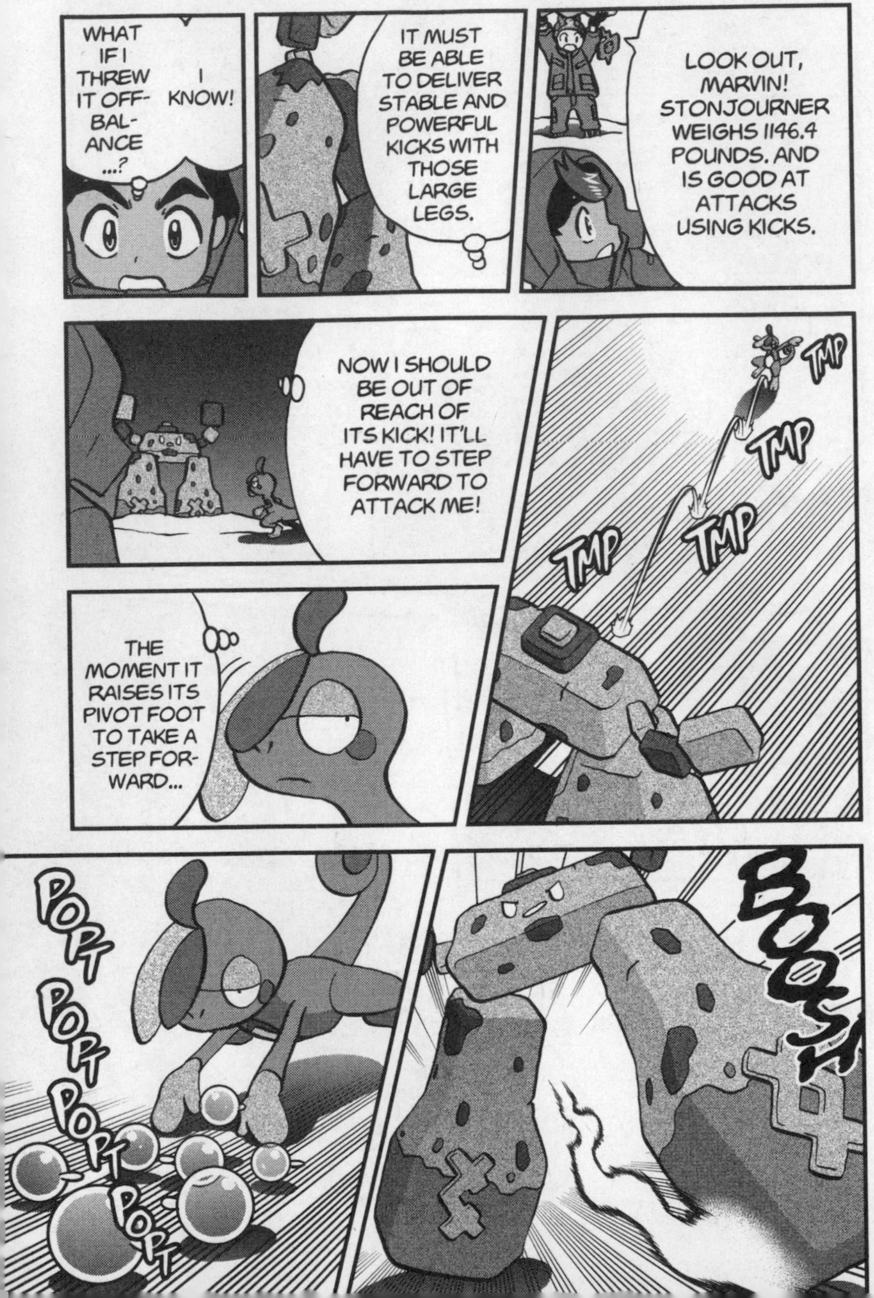
LOOK OUT, MARVIN! STONJOURNER WEIGHS 1146.4 POUNDS. AND IS GOOD AT ATTACKS USING KICKS.
IT MUST BE ABLE TO DELIVER STABLE AND POWERFUL KICKS WITH THOSE LARGE LEGS.
I KNOW!
WHAT IF I THREW IT OFF-BALANCE ...?
TMP
TMP
TMP
TMP
NOW I SHOULD BE OUT OF REACH OF ITS KICK! IT'LL HAVE TO STEP FORWARD TO ATTACK ME!
THE MOMENT IT RAISES ITS PIVOT FOOT TO TAKE A STEP FORWARD...
BOOSH
POPT POPT POPT POPT POPT

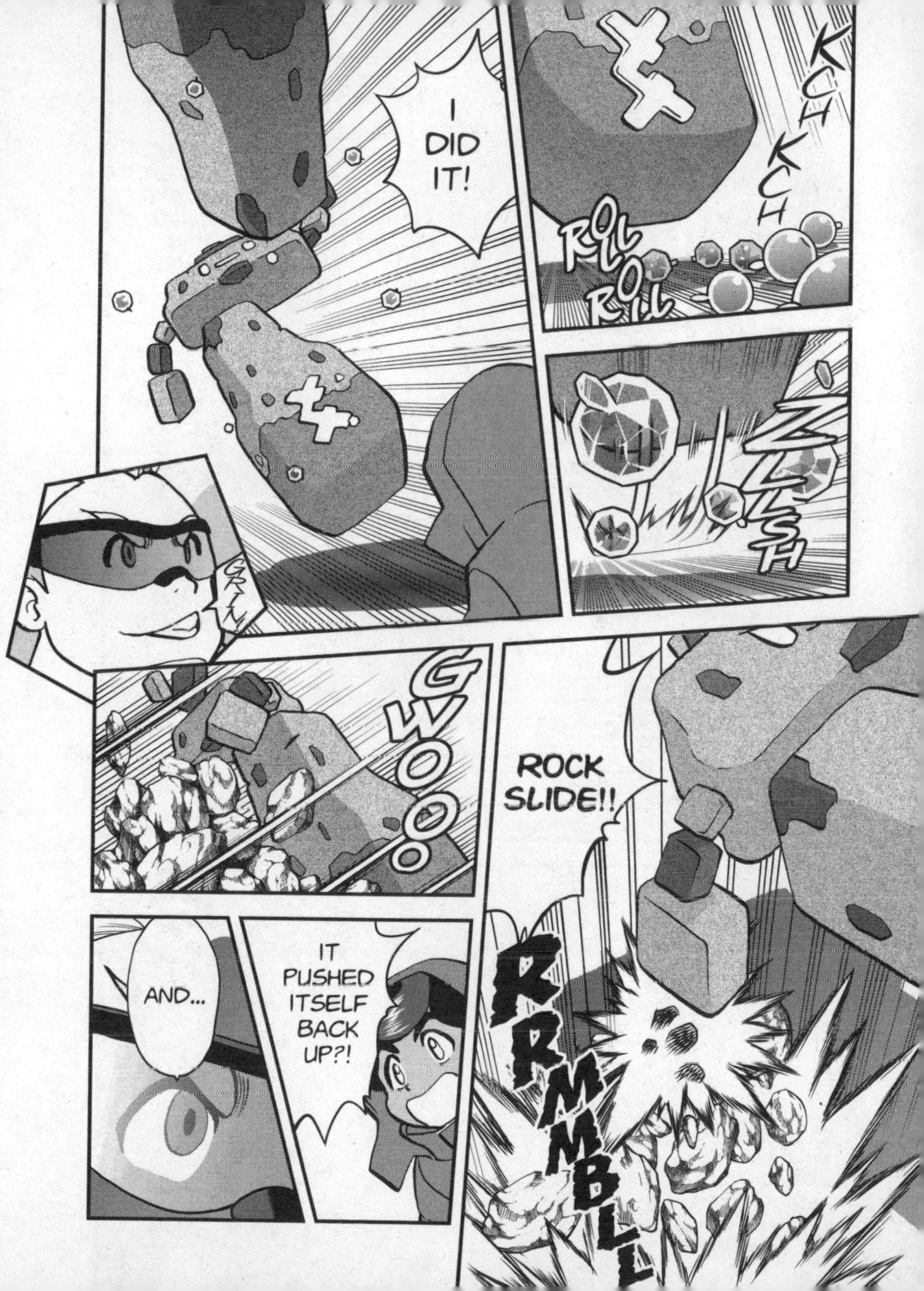
KCH KCH KCH
ROLL ROLL
ZZLLSH
I DID IT!
GRIN
ROCK SLIDE!!
RRMMBLL
GWOOOO
IT PUSHED ITSELF BACK UP?!
AND...

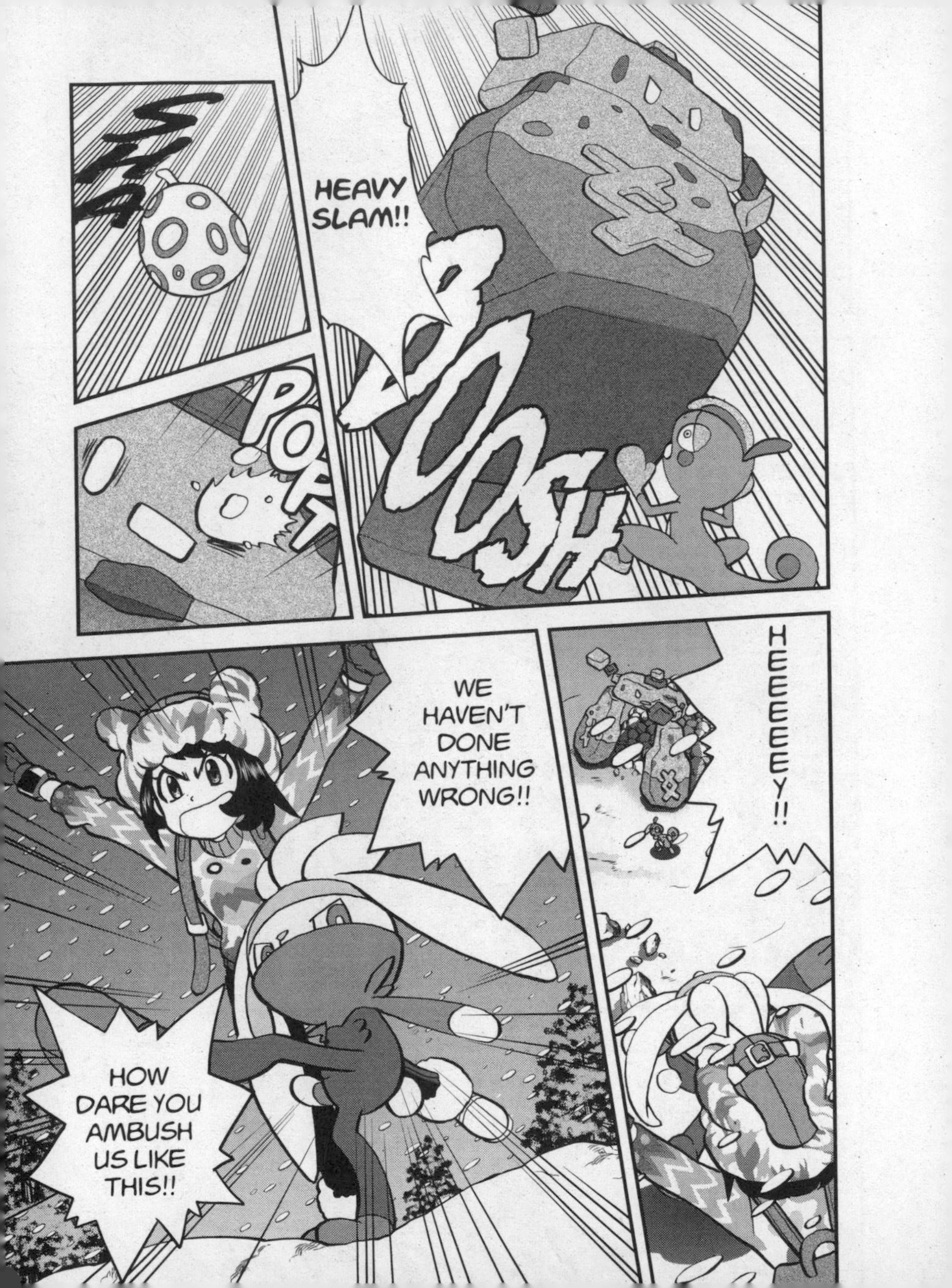
HEAVY SLAM!!
VOOSH
SHA
POP
HEEEEEY!!
WE HAVEN'T DONE ANYTHING WRONG!!
HOW DARE YOU AMBUSH US LIKE THIS!!

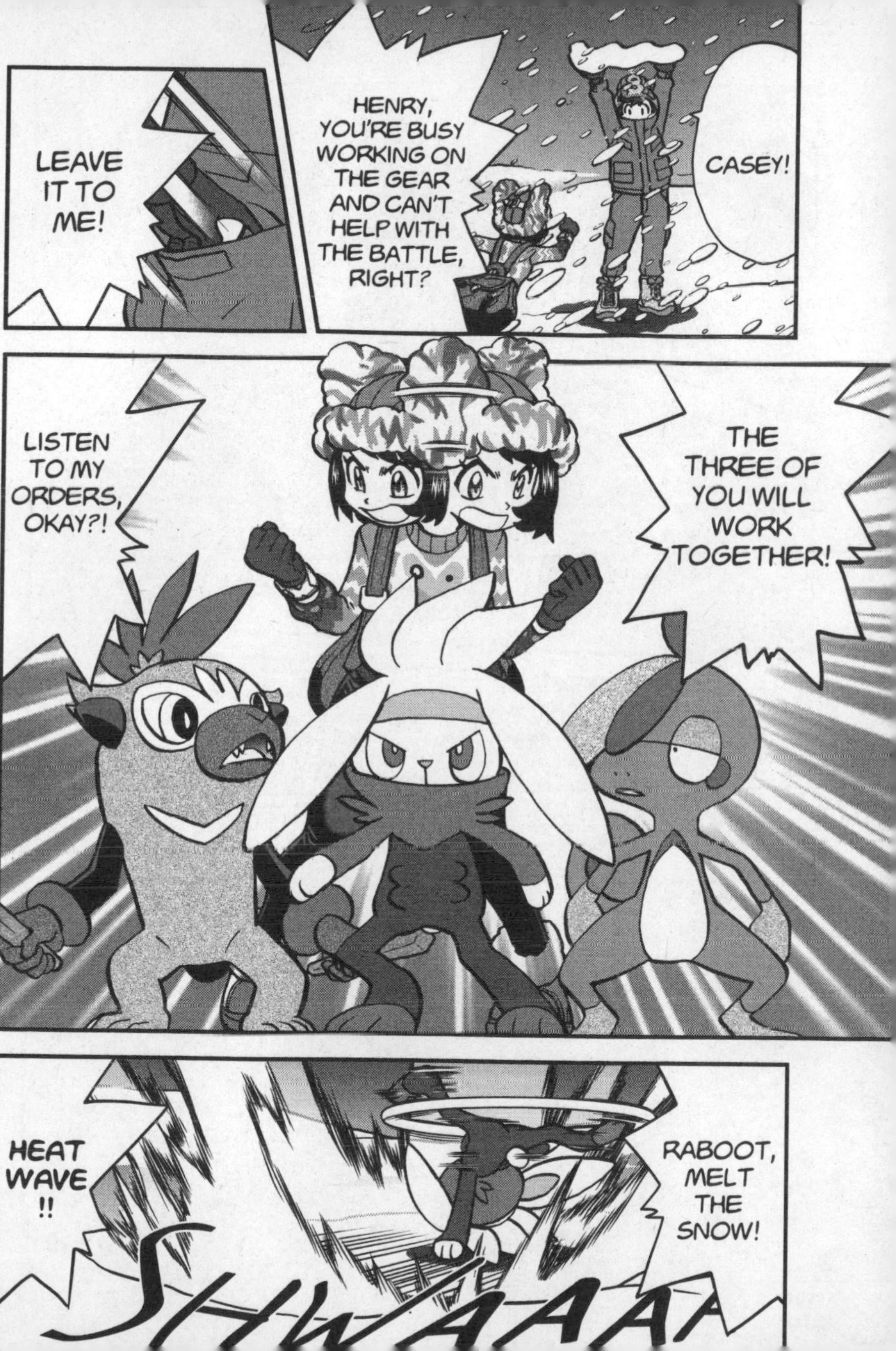
CASEY!
HENRY, YOU'RE BUSY WORKING ON THE GEAR AND CAN'T HELP WITH THE BATTLE, RIGHT?
LEAVE IT TO ME!
THE THREE OF YOU WILL WORK TOGETHER!
LISTEN TO MY ORDERS, OKAY?!
RABOOT, MELT THE SNOW!
HEAT WAVE !!
SHWAAAA

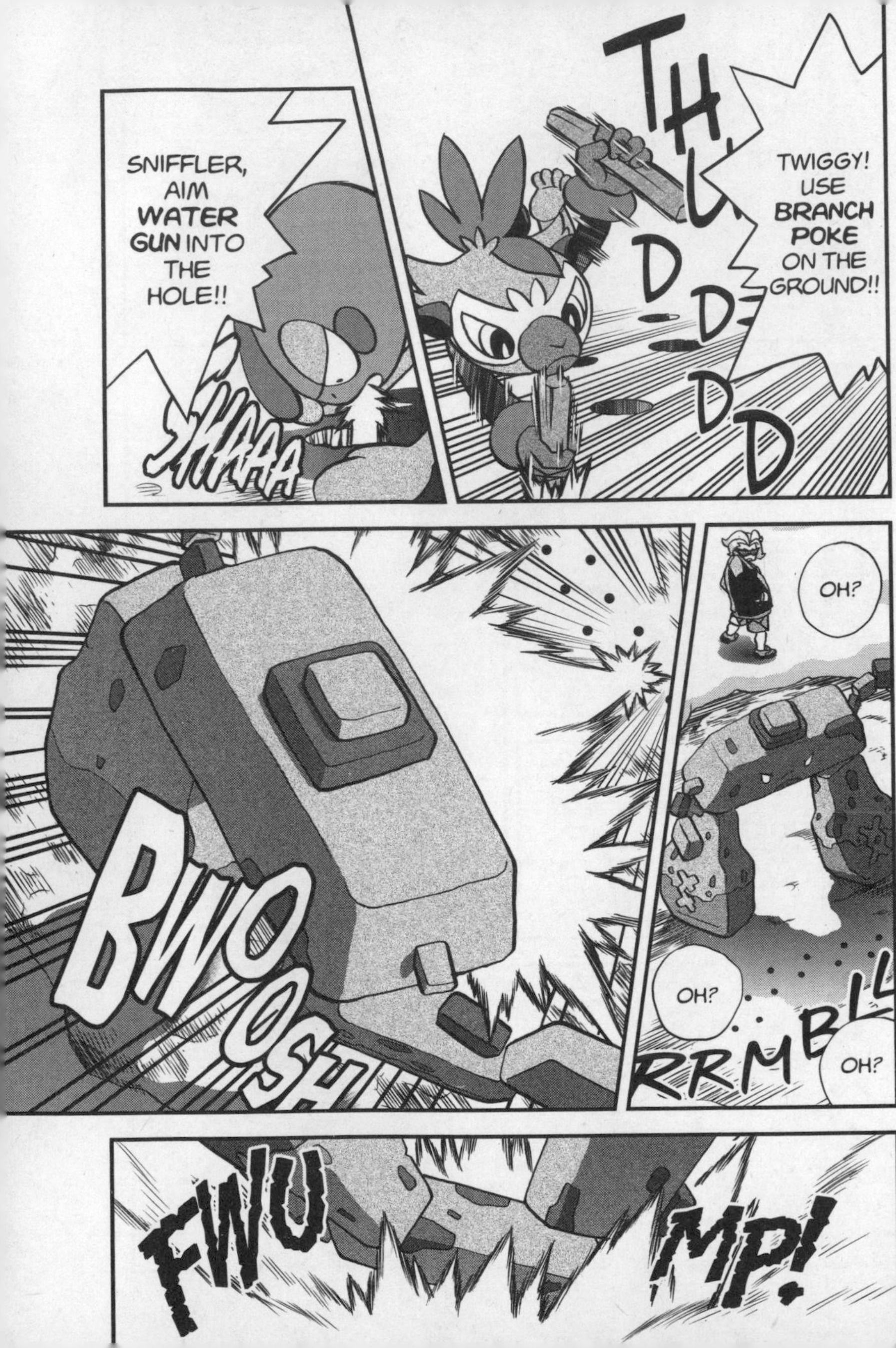
TWIGGY! USE BRANCH POKE ON THE GROUND!!
THUDDDDD
SNIFFLER, AIM WATER GUN INTO THE HOLE!!
WHAAA
OH?
OH?
RRMBLL
OH?
BWOOSH
FWUMP!

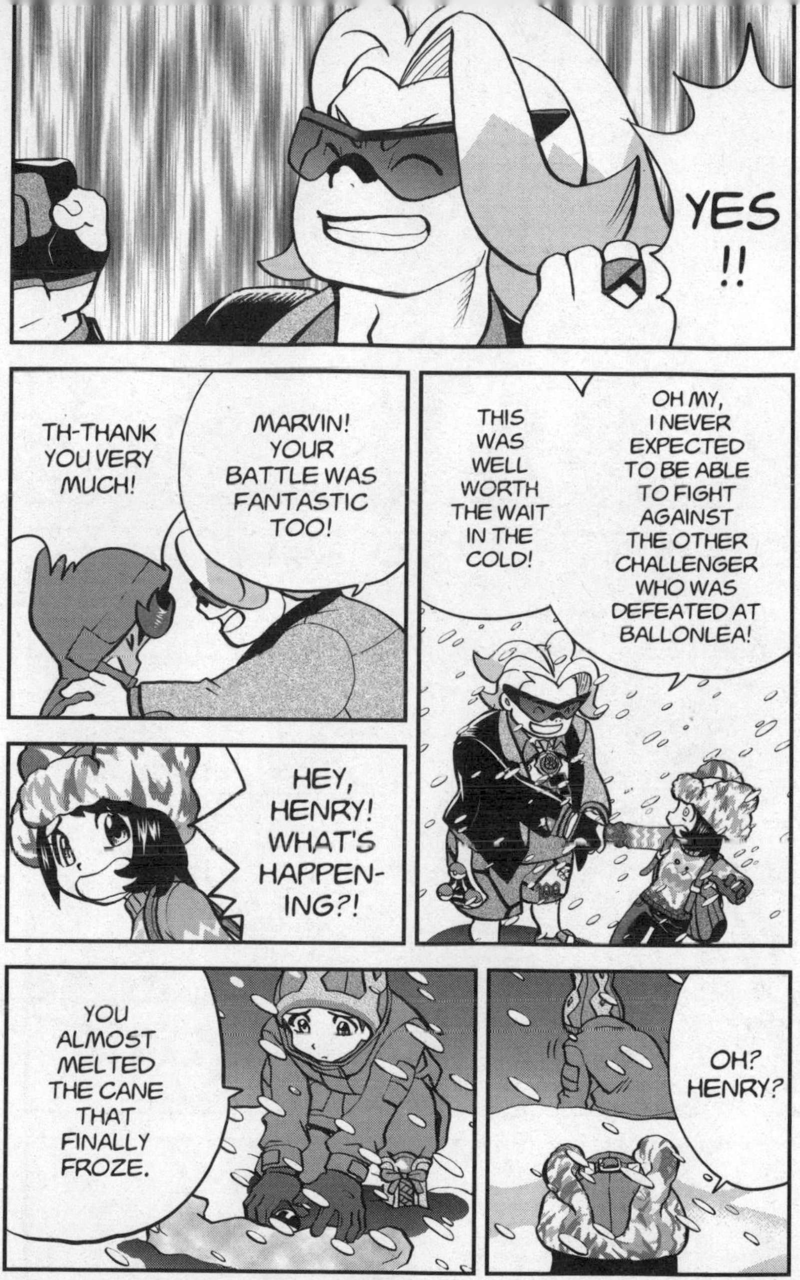
YES !!
OH MY, I NEVER EXPECTED TO BE ABLE TO FIGHT AGAINST THE OTHER CHALLENGER WHO WAS DEFEATED AT BALLONLEA!
THIS WAS WELL WORTH THE WAIT IN THE COLD!
MARVIN! YOUR BATTLE WAS FANTASTIC TOO!
TH-THANK YOU VERY MUCH!
HEY, HENRY! WHAT'S HAPPEN-ING?!
OH? HENRY?
YOU ALMOST MELTED THE CANE THAT FINALLY FROZE.

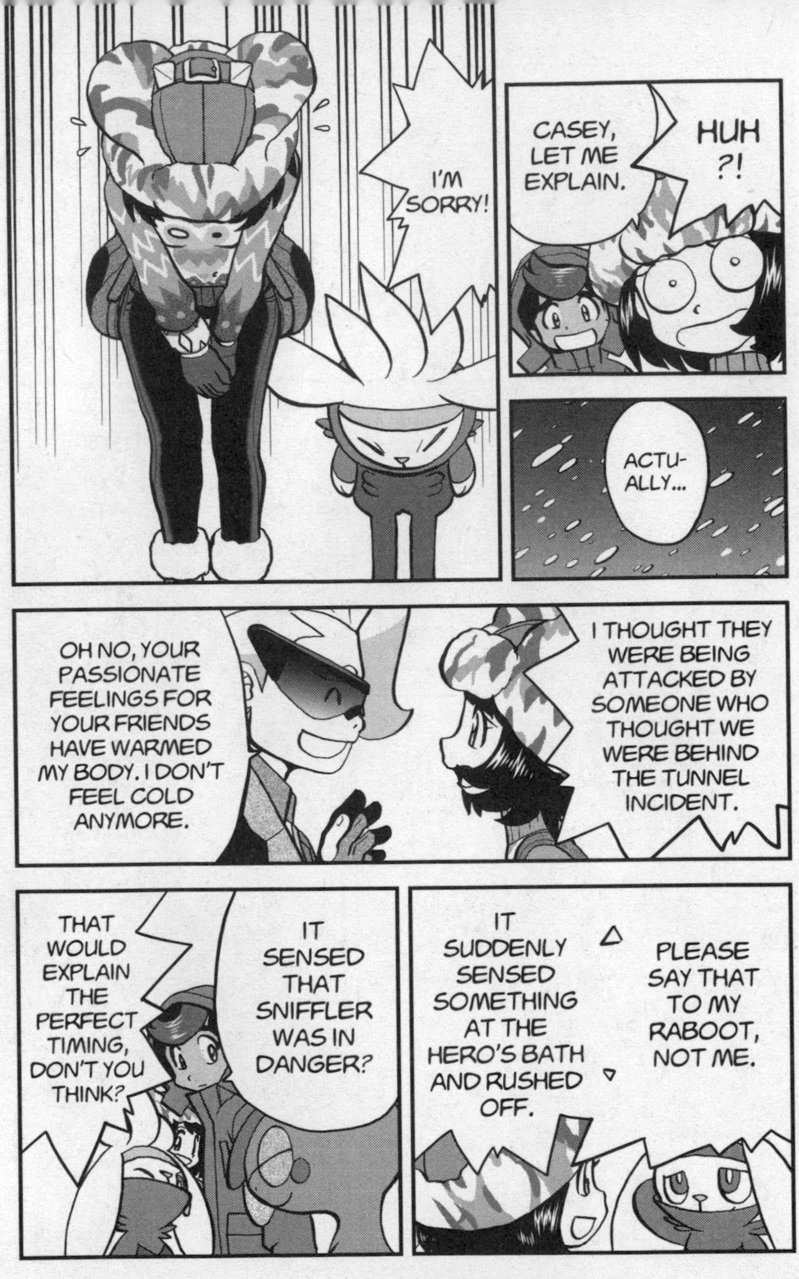
HUH ?!
CASEY, LET ME EXPLAIN.
ACTU-ALLY...
I'M SORRY!
I THOUGHT THEY WERE BEING ATTACKED BY SOMEONE WHO THOUGHT WE WERE BEHIND THE TUNNEL INCIDENT.
OH NO, YOUR PASSIONATE FEELINGS FOR YOUR FRIENDS HAVE WARMED MY BODY. I DON'T FEEL COLD ANYMORE.
PLEASE SAY THAT TO MY RABOOT, NOT ME.
IT SUDDENLY SENSED SOMETHING AT THE HERO'S BATH AND RUSHED OFF.
IT SENSED THAT SNIFFLER WAS IN DANGER?
THAT WOULD EXPLAIN THE PERFECT TIMING, DON'T YOU THINK?

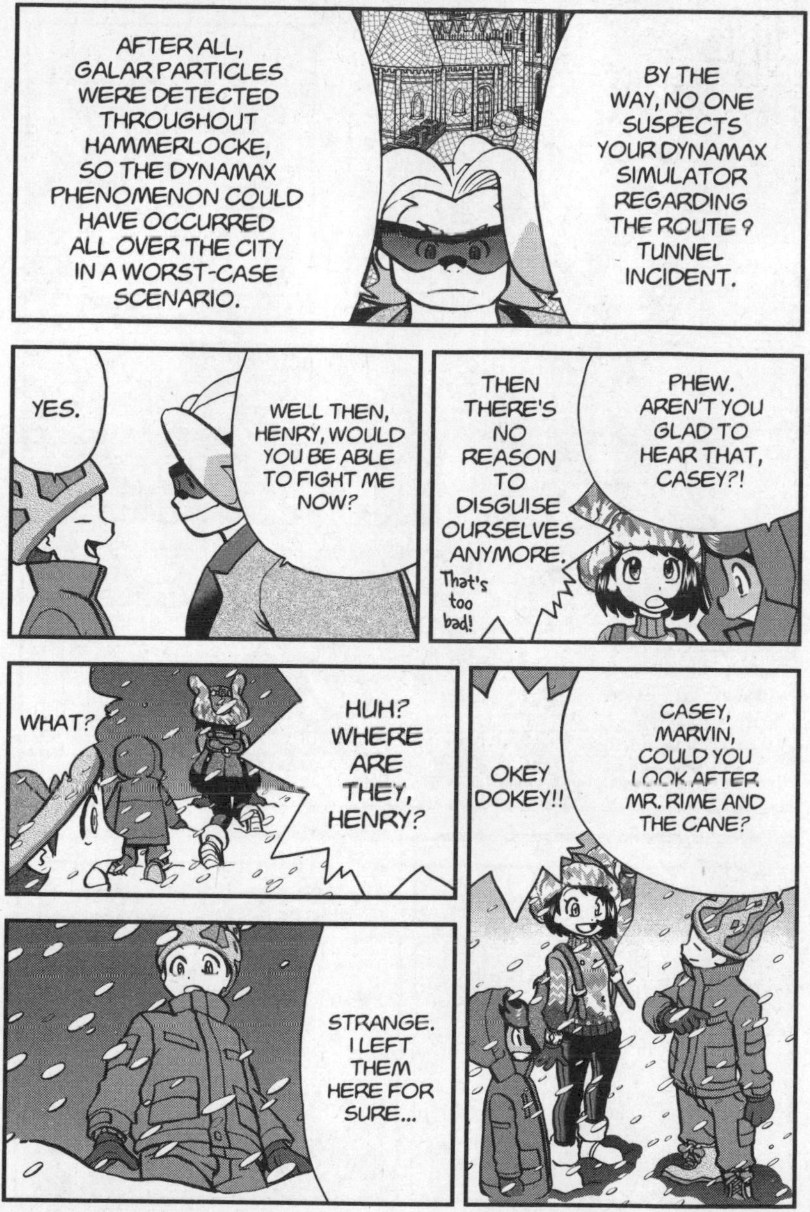
BY THE WAY, NO ONE SUSPECTS YOUR DYNAMAX SIMULATOR REGARDING THE ROUTE 9 TUNNEL INCIDENT.
AFTER ALL, GALAR PARTICLES WERE DETECTED THROUGHOUT HAMMERLOCKE, SO THE DYNAMAX PHENOMENON COULD HAVE OCCURRED ALL OVER THE CITY IN A WORST-CASE SCENARIO.
PHEW. AREN'T YOU GLAD TO HEAR THAT, CASEY?!
THEN THERE'S NO REASON TO DISGUISE OURSELVES ANYMORE.
That's too bad!
WELL THEN, HENRY, WOULD YOU BE ABLE TO FIGHT ME NOW?
YES.
CASEY, MARVIN, COULD YOU LOOK AFTER MR. RIME AND THE CANE?
OKEY DOKEY!!
HUH? WHERE ARE THEY, HENRY?
WHAT?
STRANGE. I LEFT THEM HERE FOR SURE...

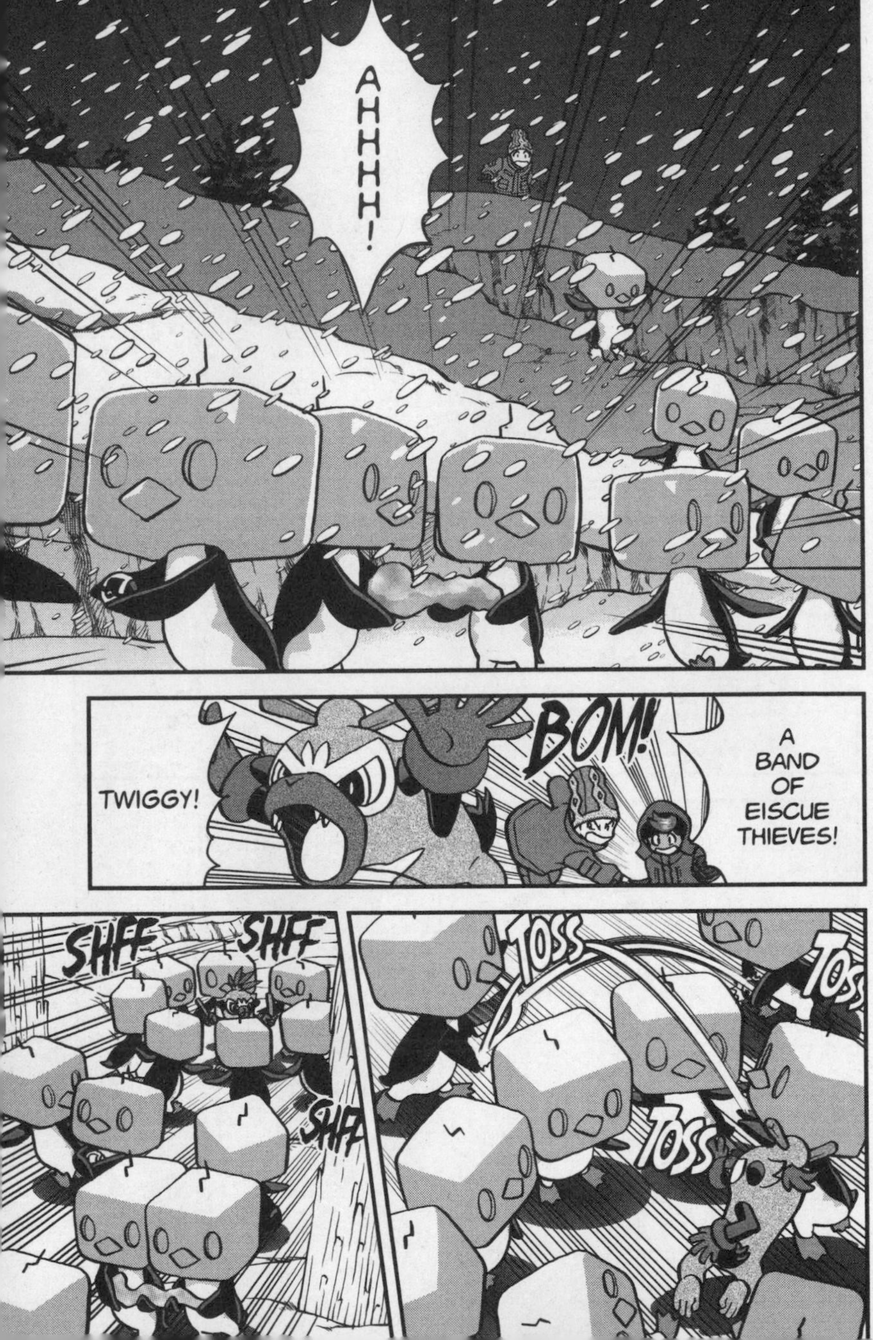
AHHHH!
A BAND OF EISCUE THIEVES!
BOM!
TWIGGY!
TOSS
TOSS
TOSS
SHFF
SHFF
SHFF

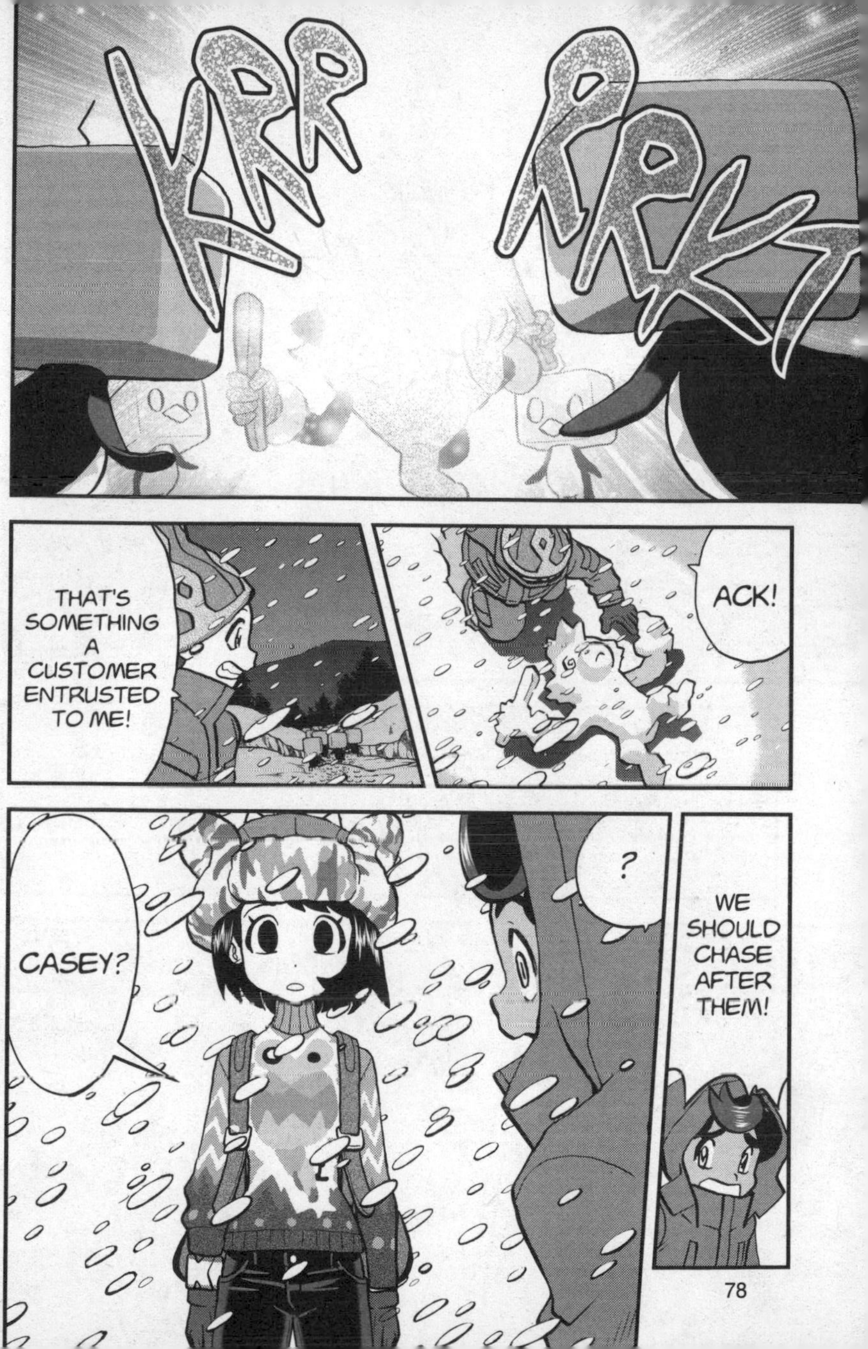
KRR
RRKT
ACK!
THAT'S SOMETHING A CUSTOMER ENTRUSTED TO ME!
WE SHOULD CHASE AFTER THEM!
?
CASEY?

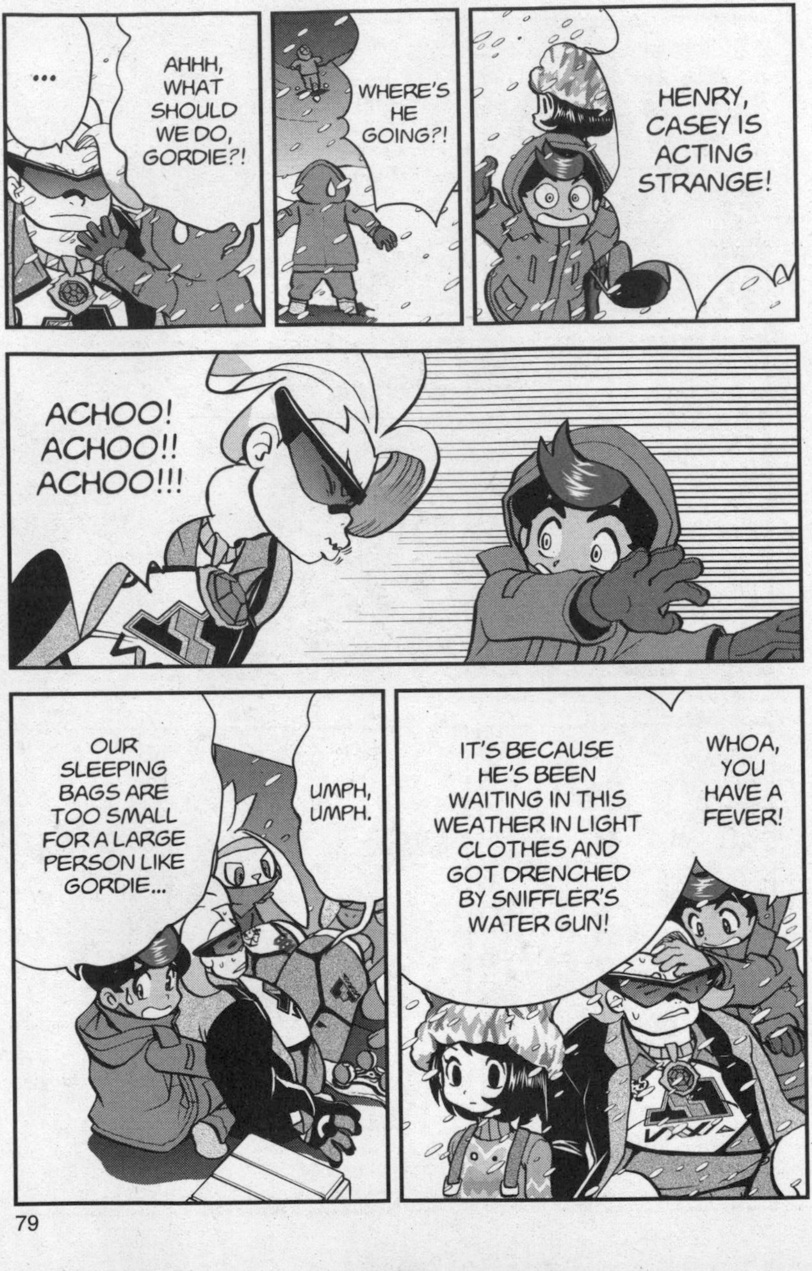
HENRY, CASEY IS ACTING STRANGE!
WHERE'S HE GOING?!
AHHH, WHAT SHOULD WE DO, GORDIE?!
...
ACHOO! ACHOO!! ACHOO!!!
WHOA, YOU HAVE A FEVER!
IT'S BECAUSE HE'S BEEN WAITING IN THIS WEATHER IN LIGHT CLOTHES AND GOT DRENCHED BY SNIFFLER'S WATER GUN!
UMPH, UMPH.
OUR SLEEPING BAGS ARE TOO SMALL FOR A LARGE PERSON LIKE GORDIE...

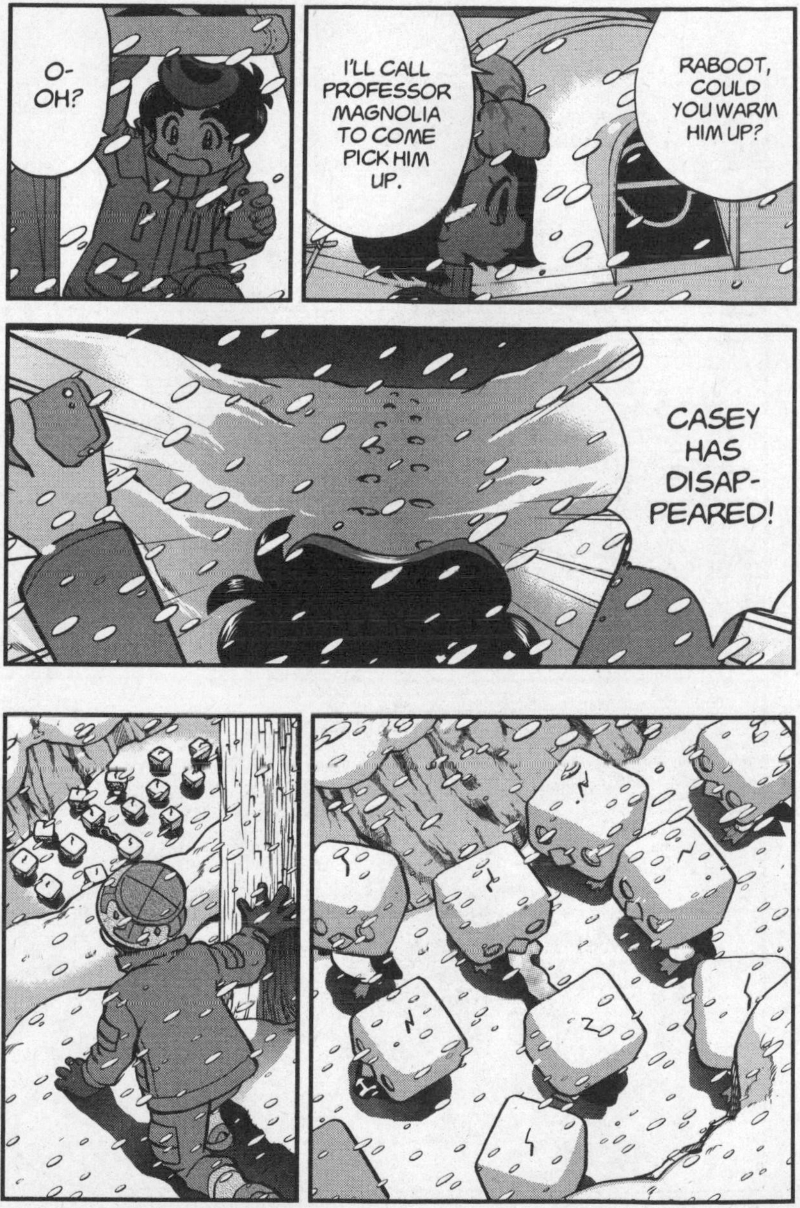
RABOOT, COULD YOU WARM HIM UP?
I'LL CALL PROFESSOR MAGNOLIA TO COME PICK HIM UP.
O-OH?
CASEY HAS DISAP-PEARED!

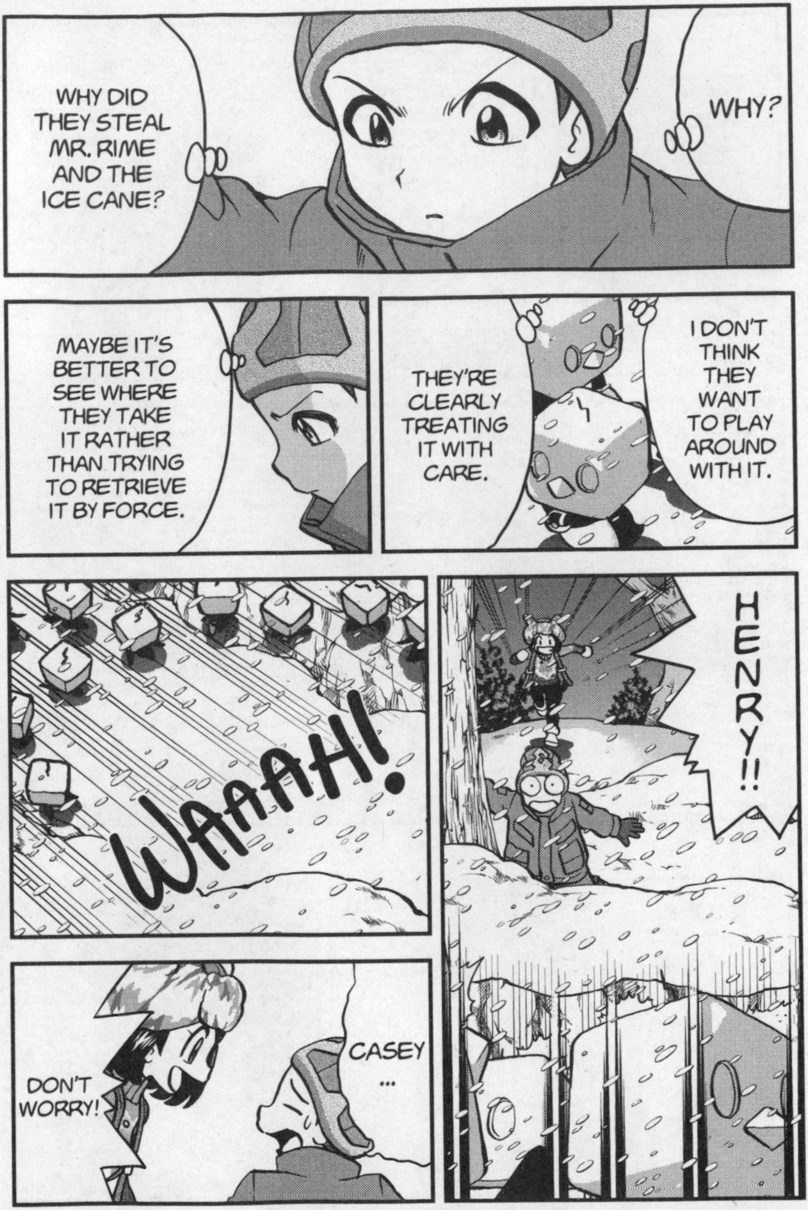
WHY?
WHY DID THEY STEAL MR. RIME AND THE ICE CANE?
I DON'T THINK THEY WANT TO PLAY AROUND WITH IT.
THEY'RE CLEARLY TREATING IT WITH CARE.
MAYBE IT'S BETTER TO SEE WHERE THEY TAKE IT RATHER THAN TRYING TO RETRIEVE IT BY FORCE.
HENRY!!
WAAAH!
CASEY ...
DON'T WORRY!

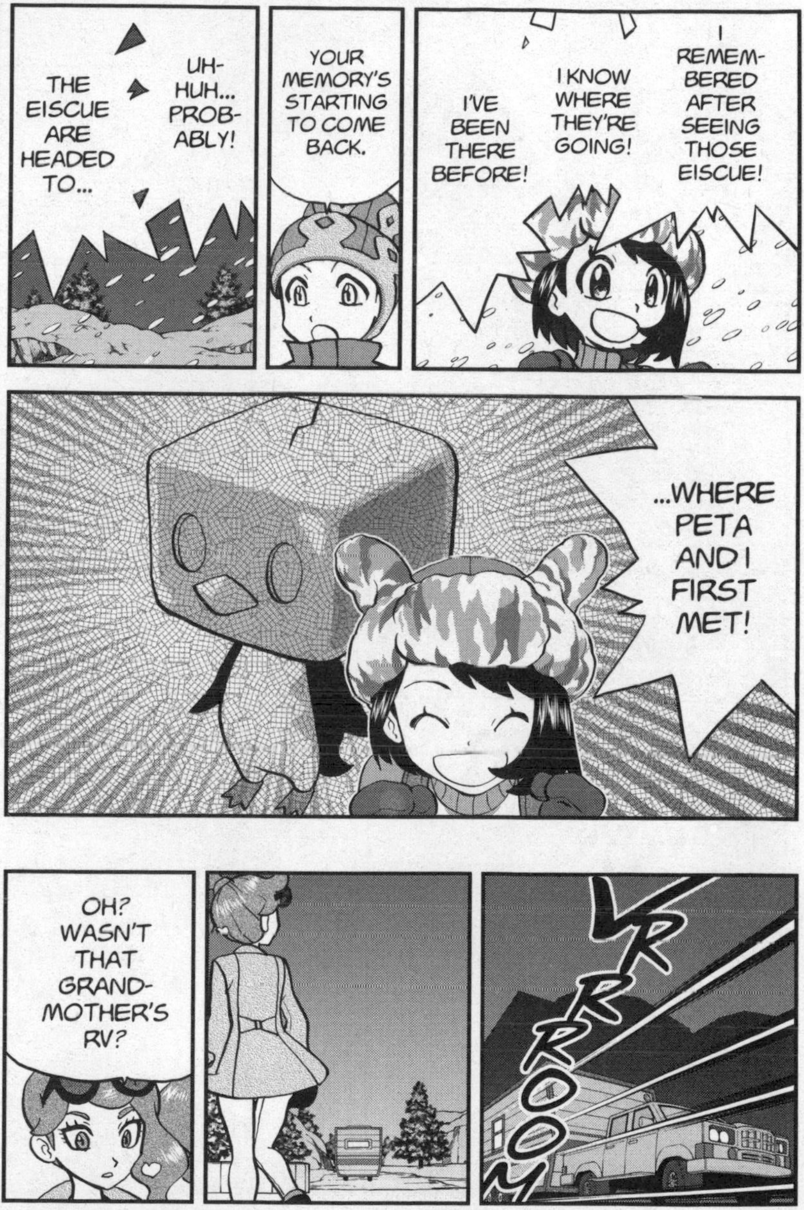
I REMEMBERED AFTER SEEING THOSE EISCUE!
I KNOW WHERE THEY'RE GOING!
I'VE BEEN THERE BEFORE!
YOUR MEMORY'S STARTING TO COME BACK.
UH-HUH... PROBABLY!
THE EISCUE ARE HEADED TO...
...WHERE PETA AND I FIRST MET!
VRRROOM
OH? WASN'T THAT GRANDMOTHER'S RV?

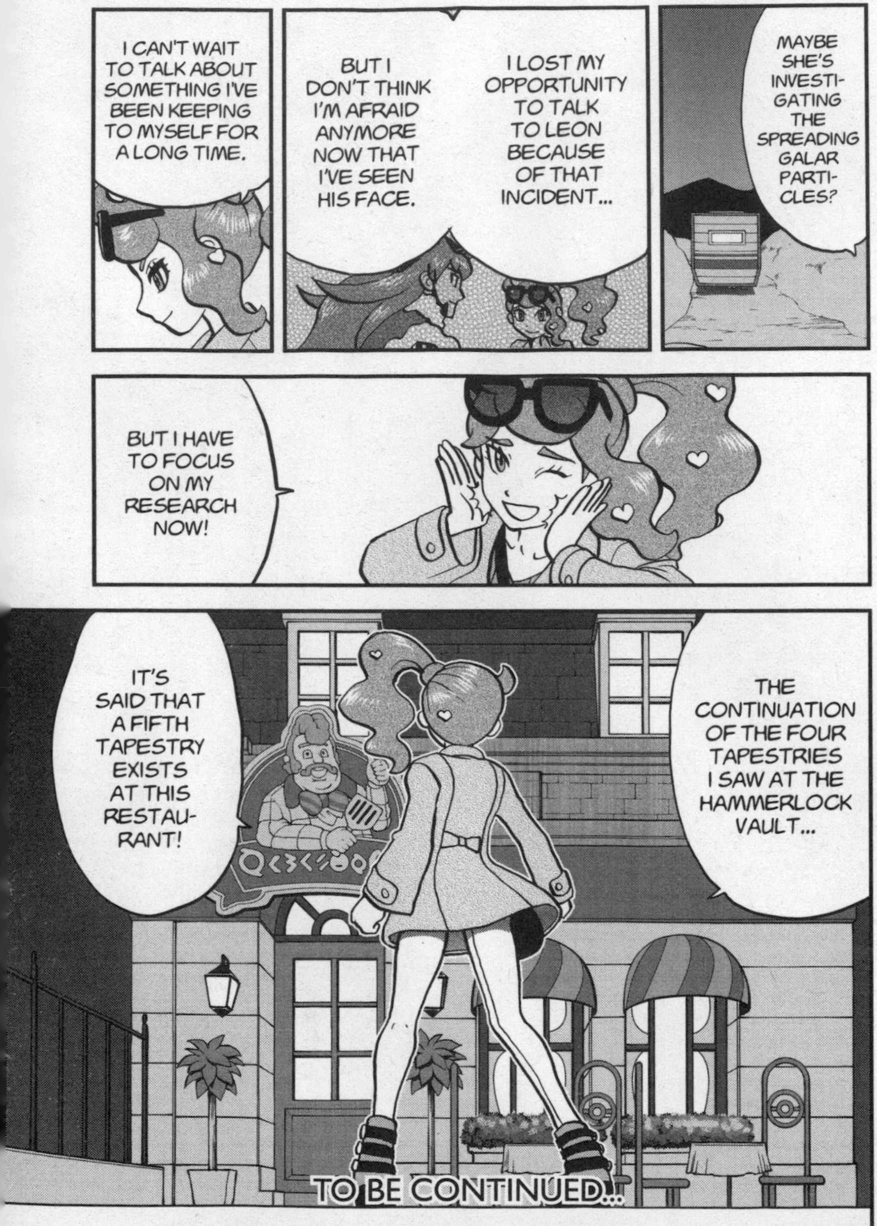
MAYBE SHE'S INVESTI-GATING THE SPREADING GALAR PARTI-CLES?
I LOST MY OPPORTUNITY TO TALK TO LEON BECAUSE OF THAT INCIDENT...
BUT I DON'T THINK I'M AFRAID ANYMORE NOW THAT I'VE SEEN HIS FACE.
I CAN'T WAIT TO TALK ABOUT SOMETHING I'VE BEEN KEEPING TO MYSELF FOR A LONG TIME.
BUT I HAVE TO FOCUS ON MY RESEARCH NOW!
THE CONTINUATION OF THE FOUR TAPESTRIES I SAW AT THE HAMMERLOCK VAULT...
IT'S SAID THAT A FIFTH TAPESTRY EXISTS AT THIS RESTAU-RANT!
TO BE CONTINUED...

POKÉMON™

SWORD & SHIELD

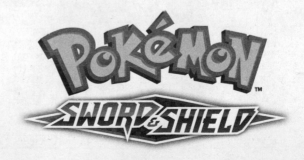

HENRY SWORD – POKÉMON DATA

LANCELOT (SIRFETCH'D ♂) LV. 32

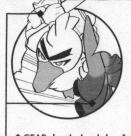

GEAR: Leek, Leek Leaf

IT GREW STRONGER AS HENRY'S JOURNEY PROGRESSED. IT HAS BECOME THE ACE OF THE TEAM DURING THE GYM CHALLENGES. THE LEEK AND LEAF THAT SWORD WORKED ON ARE POWERFUL AND STRONG ENOUGH TO DRIVE THE ENEMIES AWAY!

TWIGGY (THWACKEY ♂) LV. 21

GEAR: Stick

IT STARTED OUT AS A GROOKEY AND EVOLVED INTO A THWACKEY LATER ON. IT NOW HOLDS TWO STICKS IN ITS HANDS AND IS CAPABLE OF DRUMMING RHYTHMICALLY WITH THEM. THE SOUND WAVES FROM THEM CHEER EVERYONE UP!

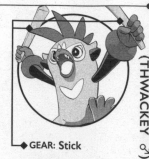

STEELER (GURDURR ♂) LV. 28

GEAR: Steel Beam

A POWERFUL FIGHTER CAPABLE OF SWING-ING AROUND A HEAVY STEEL BEAM. THE MOVES DELIVERED FROM ITS MUSCULAR BODY ARE VERY POWERFUL. THERE IS NO DOUBT THAT IT WILL BE A GREAT HELP IN THE FUTURE GYM BATTLES.

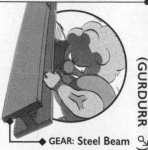

FANGURU (ORANGURU ♂) LV. 31

GEAR: Fan

THE LATEST ADDITION TO THE TEAM. IT HOLDS A SPECIAL FAN CAPABLE OF CONTROLLING THE POKÉMON AROUND IT AND IS SAID TO BE EXTREMELY INTELLIGENT. IT FIGHTS BRILLIANTLY WITH ITS PSYCHIC-TYPE MOVES!

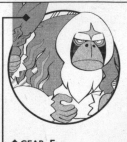

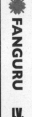

DYNAMAX

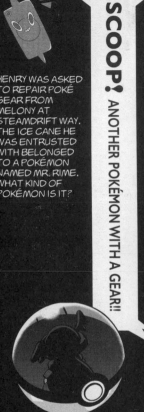

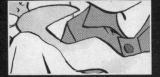

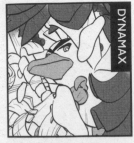

▶ LANCELOT DYNAMAXED AT BALLONLEA STADIUM. EVEN OPAL WAS IMPRESSED AT HOW IT MANAGED TO DODGE AND REPEL ALL OF THE CREAM PELLETS SHOT OUT AT IT BY THE POWERFUL ALCREMIE.

DYNAMAX
THOK

▲ A POWERFUL STRIKE WITH ITS STICK! THE STICKS WERE USED TO HIT THE OPPONENT DURING THE BATTLE AGAINST NESSA AT HULBURY STADIUM. THE BRILLIANT STRATEGY USED TO DEFEAT THE TOUGH-SHELLED POKÉMON WAS SO MEMORABLE...

DYNAMAX

▶ THE STEEL BEAM IS ITS PRIDE AND JOY. HOWEVER, SINCE IT IS METAL, IT CAN BE EASILY HEATED UP, MAKING IT HARD TO HOLD ON TO. STEELER SHOULD TRY TO DEFEAT THE OPPONENT BEFORE IT CAN USE ANY SPECIAL MOVES.

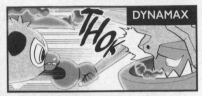

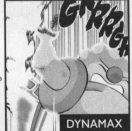

DYNAMAX
I'LL END THIS BATTLE WITH FANGURU.

▶ FANGURU MADE THE DECISIVE VICTORY DURING THE BATTLE AGAINST ALLISTER AT STOW-ON-SIDE STADIUM. FAN-GURU HAD JUST JOINED HENRY'S TEAM, BUT THEIR TEAMWORK WAS ALREADY PERFECT!

SCOOP! ANOTHER POKÉMON WITH A GEAR!!

HENRY WAS ASKED TO REPAIR POKÉ GEAR FROM MELONY AT STEAMDRIFT WAY. THE ICE CANE HE WAS ENTRUSTED WITH BELONGED TO A POKÉMON NAMED MR. RIME. WHAT KIND OF POKÉMON IS IT?

(MR. RIME ♂)

◆ GEAR: Cane

▲ HENRY REPAIRED THE CRACK IN THE CANE AND STRENGTHENED IT. HE COATED THE CANE WITH REAL SNOW AND HAILSTONES BEFORE SCRAPING THE CANE INTO SHAPE.

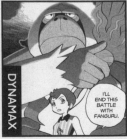

EMERGENCY INVESTIGATION

Follow the GALAR LEGEND MYSTERY!!!

SONIA

THE VAST GALAR REGION HAS A LONG HISTORY BEHIND IT. NUMEROUS LEGENDS HAVE BEEN PASSED DOWN ALL OVER GALAR, AND THEY ALL ULTIMATELY SEEM TO CONNECT TO ONE LEGEND. LET'S TAKE A LOOK BACK AT THE INFORMATION SONIA HAS GATHERED!

1 BUDEW DROP INN HERO STATUE

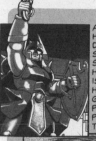

A STATUE HOLDING A DISTINCTIVE SWORD AND SHIELD. THE HERO WHO IS SAID TO HAVE SAVED GALAR FROM PERIL STANDS PROUDLY IN THE INN!

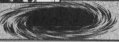

▲ THE HERO WARDED OFF THIS DARK WHIRLPOOL IN THE SKY, WHICH WAS SAID TO BE A SOURCE OF DISASTER.

2 TURFFIELD GEOGLYPH

A CREATURE THAT HAS GIGANTIFIED AFTER BEING SHOWERED WITH SOME SORT OF ENERGY. THE EERIE IMAGE OF THAT CREATURE WAS WRITTEN ON THE MOUNTAINSIDE!

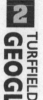

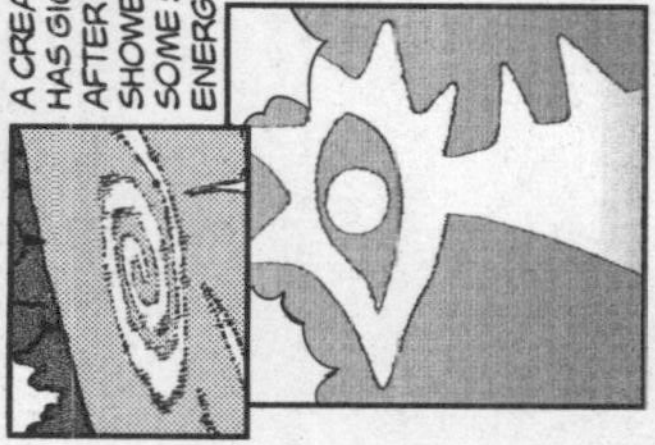

▲ THE WHIRLPOOL IN THE SKY CAN BE SEEN HERE TOO. IT MUST HAVE STRUCK FEAR IN THE HEARTS OF THE ANCIENT PEOPLE.

3 HAMMERLOCKE VAULT TAPESTRY

THE YOUNG MEN WHO ACTUALLY FACED THE DARKEST DAY. DETAILED ILLUSTRATIONS WERE DRAWN ON A SERIES OF TAPESTRIES!

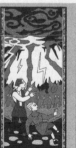

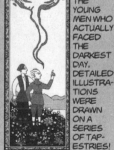

▲ WATCHING THE WISHING STAR. THIS IS AN IMPORTANT CLUE.

▲ THE DISASTER. GALAR WAS FACED WITH DESTRUCTION!

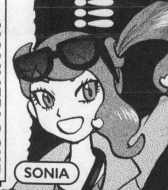

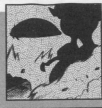

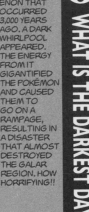

WHAT IS THE DARKEST DAY?

A SUPER-NATURAL PHENOMENON THAT OCCURRED 3,000 YEARS AGO. A DARK WHIRLPOOL APPEARED. THE ENERGY FROM IT GIGANTIFIED THE POKÉMON AND CAUSED THEM TO GO ON A RAMPAGE, RESULTING IN A DISASTER THAT ALMOST DESTROYED THE GALAR REGION. HOW HORRIFYING!!

▲ A HUGE MASS OF ENERGY EMERGED. WHAT DOES THAT MEAN ABOUT THE ORIGIN OF THE DYNAMAX PHENOMENON?

GALAR'S ENERGY WILL BE DEPLETED IN A THOUSAND YEARS.
CHAIRMAN ROSE

▲ THE DARKEST DAY IS A MASS OF NEGATIVE ENERGY, AS STATED ABOVE. BUT CHAIRMAN ROSE SEEMS TO HAVE A PLAN.

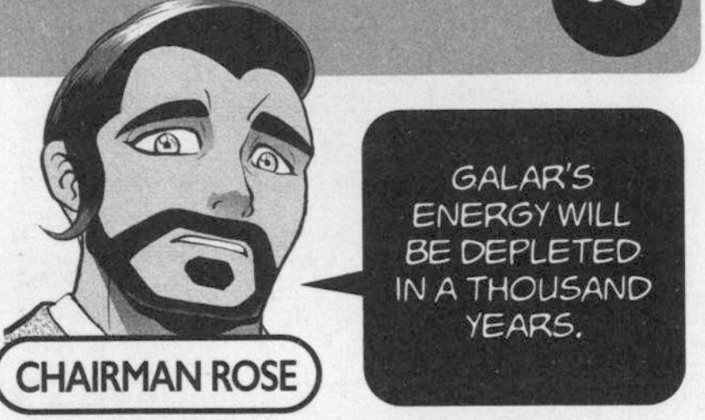

4 AN EXPLOSION AT THE ENERGY PLANT AND A DYNAMAX PHENOMENON OUTSIDE THE POWER SPOTS

ACCORDING TO THE TAPESTRIES, WE CAN ASSUME THAT THE WISHING STAR SOMEHOW TRIGGERED THE DARKEST DAY. THERE IS SOMETHING A LITTLE DUBIOUS ABOUT THE ACTIONS OF THE CHAIRMAN, WHO USED BEDE TO GATHER THE WISHING STARS. HE SEEMED TO BE FEEDING THE WISHING STARS TO SOMETHING, AND THE STRANGE SOUND AT HAMMERLOCKE SEEMS SUSPICIOUS TOO.

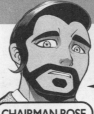

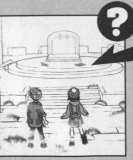

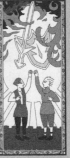

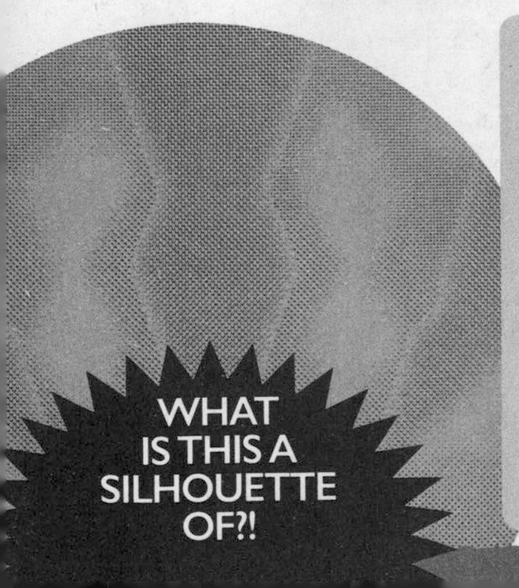

▲ THE LEGENDARY SWORD AND SHIELD DRIVE THE EVIL AWAY. DO THEY SEEM FAMILIAR?

▲ HENRY SAW THE SWORD AND SHIELD SLUMBERING WEALD SOME TIME AGO. THEY LOOKED SIMILAR TO WHAT WAS DEPICTED IN THE TAPESTRIES!

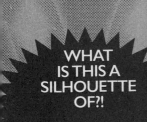

WHAT IS THIS A SILHOUETTE OF?!

Hidenori Kusaka is the writer for *Pokémon Adventures*. Running continuously for over 20 years, *Pokémon Adventures* is the only manga series to completely cover all the *Pokémon* games and has become one of the most popular series of all time. In addition to writing manga, he also edits children's books and plans mixed-media projects for Shogakukan's children's magazines. He uses the Pokémon Electrode as his author portrait.

Satoshi Yamamoto is the artist for *Pokémon Adventures*, which he began working on in 2001, starting with volume 10. Yamamoto launched his manga career in 1993 with the horror-action title *Kimen Senshi*, which ran in Shogakukan's *Weekly Shonen Sunday* magazine, followed by the series *Kaze no Denshosha*. Yamamoto's favorite manga creators/artists include FUJIKO F FUJIO (*Doraemon*), Yukinobu Hoshino (*2001 Nights*), and Katsuhiro Otomo (*Akira*). He loves films, monsters, detective novels, and punk rock music. He uses the Pokémon Swalot as his artist portrait.

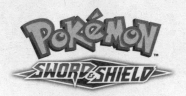

Pokémon: Sword & Shield
Volume 6
VIZ Media Edition

Story by HIDENORI KUSAKA
Art by SATOSHI YAMAMOTO

©2023 Pokémon.
©1995–2021 Nintendo / Creatures Inc. / GAME FREAK inc.
TM, ®, and character names are trademarks of Nintendo.
POCKET MONSTERS SPECIAL SWORD SHIELD Vol. 3
by Hidenori KUSAKA, Satoshi YAMAMOTO
© 2020 Hidenori KUSAKA, Satoshi YAMAMOTO
All rights reserved.
Original Japanese edition published by SHOGAKUKAN.
English translation rights in the United States of America, Canada, the United Kingdom,
Ireland, Australia and New Zealand arranged with SHOGAKUKAN.

Original Cover Design—Hiroyuki KAWASOME (grafio)

Translation—Tetsuichiro Miyaki
English Adaptation—Molly Tanzer
Touch-Up & Lettering—Annaliese "Ace" Christman
Cover Color—Philana Chen
Design—Alice Lewis
Editor—Joel Enos

Special thanks to Trish Ledoux and Misao Oki at The Pokémon Company International.

The stories, characters, and incidents mentioned
in this publication are entirely fictional.

No portion of this book may be reproduced or transmitted
in any form or by any means without written permission
from the copyright holders.

Printed in the U.S.A.

Published by VIZ Media, LLC
P.O. Box 77010
San Francisco, CA 94107

10 9 8 7 6 5 4 3 2 1
First printing, April 2023

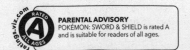
PARENTAL ADVISORY
POKÉMON: SWORD & SHIELD is rated A
and is suitable for readers of all ages.

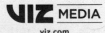
viz.com

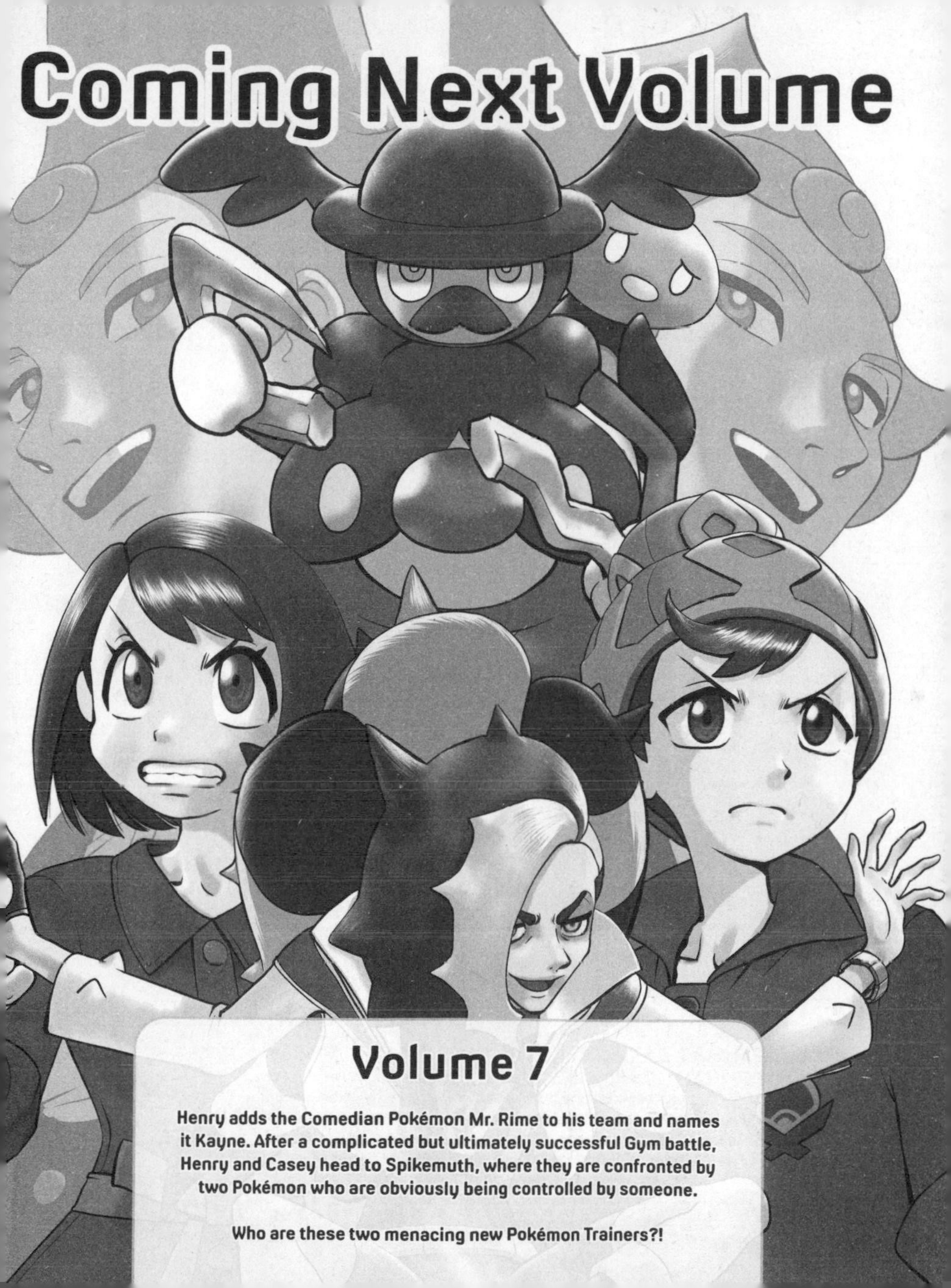
Coming Next Volume
Volume 7
Henry adds the Comedian Pokémon Mr. Rime to his team and names it Kayne. After a complicated but ultimately successful Gym battle, Henry and Casey head to Spikemuth, where they are confronted by two Pokémon who are obviously being controlled by someone.
Who are these two menacing new Pokémon Trainers?!

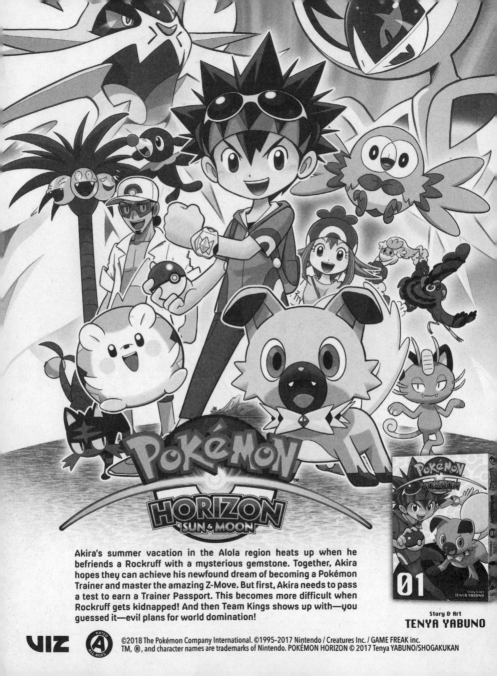

Akira's summer vacation in the Alola region heats up when he befriends a Rockruff with a mysterious gemstone. Together, Akira hopes they can achieve his newfound dream of becoming a Pokémon Trainer and master the amazing Z-Move. But first, Akira needs to pass a test to earn a Trainer Passport. This becomes more difficult when Rockruff gets kidnapped! And then Team Kings shows up with—you guessed it—evil plans for world domination!

Story & Art
TENYA YABUNO

©2018 The Pokémon Company International. ©1995–2017 Nintendo / Creatures Inc. / GAME FREAK inc. TM, ®, and character names are trademarks of Nintendo. POKÉMON HORIZON © 2017 Tenya YABUNO/SHOGAKUKAN.

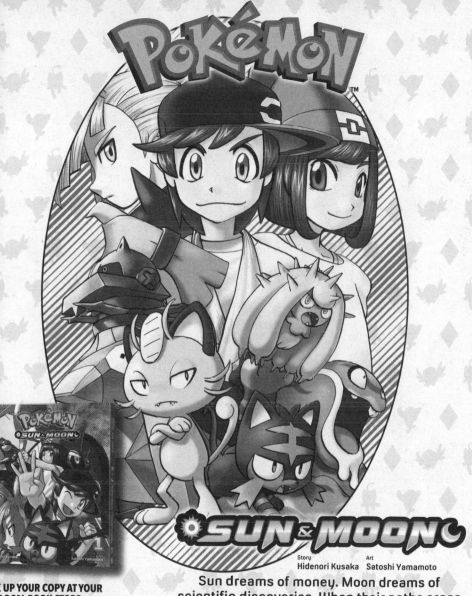

POKÉMON

SUN & MOON

Story
Hidenori Kusaka

Art
Satoshi Yamamoto

Sun dreams of money. Moon dreams of
scientific discoveries. When their paths cross
with Team Skull, both their plans go awry...

K UP YOUR COPY AT YOUR
LOCAL BOOK STORE.

©2018 The Pokémon Company International. ©1995-2017 Nintendo / Creatures Inc. / GAME FREAK inc.
TM, ®, and character names are trademarks of Nintendo.
POCKET MONSTERS SPECIAL SUN • MOON © 2017 Hidenori KUSAKA, Satoshi YAMAMOTO/SHOGAKUKAN

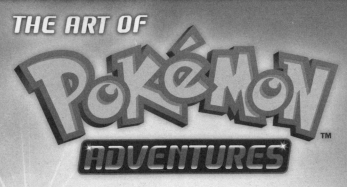

POKÉMON ADVENTURES 20TH ANNIVERSARY ILLUSTRATION BOOK

THE ART OF Pokémon ADVENTURES ™

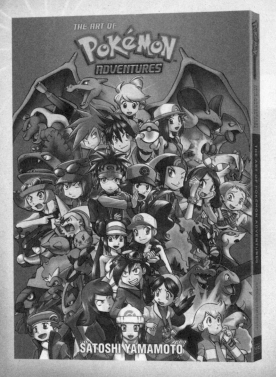

STORY AND ART BY
Satoshi Yamamoto

A collection of beautiful full-color art from the artist of the Pokémon Adventures graphic novel series! In addition to illustrations of your favorite Pokémon, this vibrant volume includes exclusive sketches and storyboards, four pull-out posters, and an exclusive manga side story!

©2018 The Pokémon Company International. ©1995-2016 Nintendo / Creatures Inc. / GAME FREAK inc.
TM, ®, and character names are trademarks of Nintendo. POCKET MONSTERS SPECIAL YAMAMOTO SATOSHI GASHU THE ART OF POCKET MONSTERS SPECIAL© 2016 Hidenori KUSAKA, Satoshi YAMAMOTO/SHOGAKUKAN

viz.com

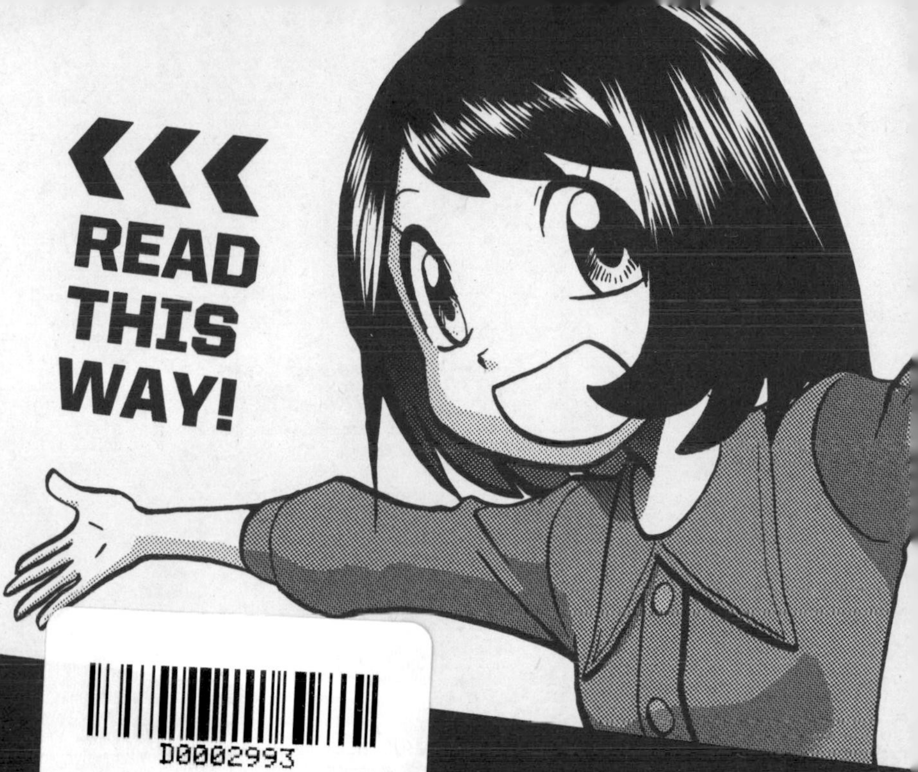
READ
THIS
WAY!

THIS IS THE END OF THIS GRAPHIC NOVEL!

To properly enjoy this VIZ Media graphic novel, please turn it around and begin reading from right to left.

This book has been printed in the original Japanese format in order to preserve the orientation of the original artwork. Have fun with it!

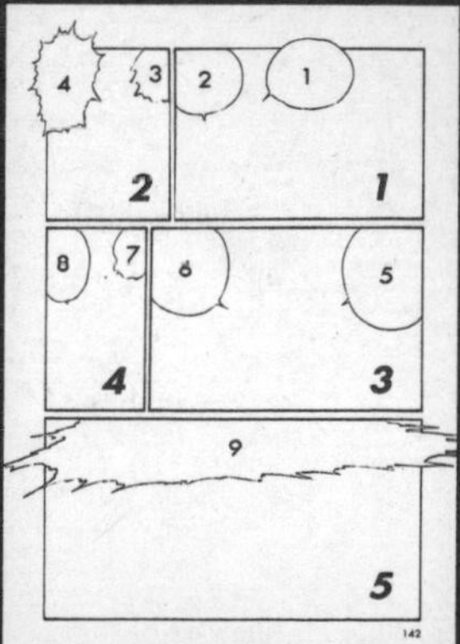

Follow the action this way.